PRACE FOR Up From the River

"ONE INSTANT OF HAZARD IN THE GOOD LIFE OF AN honest warehouseman can indeed web out and reverberate with alarm on the quiet, tree-lined streets of the best neighborhoods in town. Matt's entirely believable, richly detailed 'case' makes a dramatic novel no American can fail to see himself living out at any instant when things may change unexpectedly for the worse. Aren't so many of us—not just Matt—two or three paychecks from poverty? And altruism can also become a deadly hazard when brotherly love, leadership, and the political will to help—to 'promote the general Welfare'—are kicked into the gutter of any street in this broad nation, sea to sea."

Linda Whitney Hobson, author of *Understanding Walker Percy*
(University of South Carolina Press, 1988)

Up From the River

A novel based on a true story

Linda Hardister Rodriguez

LYSTRA BOOKS
& Literary Services

UP FROM THE RIVER
A Novel by Linda Hardister Rodriguez
© 2013 by Linda Hardister Rodriguez

Published in the United States
ISBN print book 978-0-9884164-7-5
ISBN ebook 978-0-9884172-8-2
Library of Congress Control Number 2013953835

"The characters of Matthew and Lillie Bradfurd—not their true names—are inspired by real persons. The story follows events that occurred in their lives. All other characters—their thoughts, feelings, motivations, and actions—are products of the author's imagination."

Linda Hardister Rodriguez, author

Print books may be ordered online and through bookstores.

Ebooks are available online for all devices and software.

Author's photograph by EA Photography, used with permission.
Cover photograph by Nora Gaskin Esthimer, used with permission.
Book design by Kelly Prelipp Lojk

Publication managed by Lystra Books & Literary Services, LLC
www.lystrabooks.com

For my husband, Hector

Prologue

MATT BRADFURD'S APPOINTMENT WITH THE DISABILITY attorney was for eleven. At ten fifteen, he stood half a block off Main Street at a door that looked like a storefront. A hardware store was to its left, a Hallmark shop to its right. Flower pots with red geraniums brightened those doors. Brown paint peeled from the frame of this one. Instead of opening the door, he peeked through the open blinds. The small reception room held two chairs and a table piled high with magazines. A vase of yellow chrysanthemums as large as grapefruits nearly covered the desk in the far corner. That made him grin and reach for the door knob. Then he pulled back. Something's wrong. *A good lawyer would have a better place than this. And Dr. Latham did say he had never met him.*

Deciding to take a few minutes to think, Matt swung his crutches around and headed for the town square. Shivering, he stopped to zip up his jacket. October had brought unusually cold air. They would need more heating oil soon. Where would he get two hundred fifty dollars for that? Lillie's five hundred a month was keeping them alive, but if the house was cold, the children she babysat couldn't be there. He had to take some action. If only he knew what and with whom.

Matt brushed red and yellow leaves off the closest bench and sat down by the statue of the Confederate soldier. The rifle he held reminded Matt of his desire to turn his own gun against himself. But something—someone, he believed—had stopped him. No one knew about his visions except Lillie, and she only knew about the first one. He was afraid people would laugh and try to convince him that he had imagined them. That's what he would have said. *Grandad found a way to reach me.* Although he couldn't say how, Matt was certain of it. And that meant he had to keep going. Matt stood. He would just have to trust Dr. Latham and the lawyer.

Looking up at the clock tower, Matt, momentarily, confused the minute and hour hands, seeing ten minutes to five instead of twenty-five after ten. Similar incidents had occurred during the past three months: he lost his train of thought, and familiar words sometimes made no sense. Although he had tried to pass it off as feeling goofy, he knew it was another reason to reach for help.

The woman behind the desk smiled broadly when Matt stepped into the reception room. "I bet you're Mr. Bradfurd. Go on and have a seat. I'll close that door for you and let my husband know you're here."

Robert Grimes nodded and extended his hand. He wore a white shirt, frayed at the collar, and a tie loosened at the neck. White socks and running shoes showed below his khaki pants. He looked like he was about 30. *Uh-oh.* Matt said to himself.

Hesitating before the chair Mr. Grimes pulled out for him, Matt said, "I don't have a dime to pay you."

The lawyer sat down behind a battered desk and placed a yellow legal pad in front of him. He mouthed, "Go ahead." and motioned for him to come on.

Matt leaned forward, bracing himself against the desk. He wanted to be honest with this man, but didn't want to share his visions, the mandolin, and his desire to end his life. He hoped they didn't slip out. "Can I start at the very beginning? You gotta know something: I wasn't always like I am now."

Four and a half years earlier in September...

A LIGHT FALL BREEZE UNBURDENED BY ITS WEIGHT OF summer moisture slipped through the kitchen window, carrying the squawk of a woodpecker. Matt Bradfurd laid the Cross Hill *Dispatch* on the slick white table cover and turned an ear toward the hickory tree at the window. Each time he heard a woodpecker, he listened for the coo of a dove. Like him and Lillie: he with his aggressive racket and she with her gentle flutter. Their physical appearances matched their voices—he tall with an unruly black crest of hair and she short, fat, and soft.

An article at the bottom of the front page stole Matt's attention from the birds. He shoved the newspaper across the table toward Lillie, knocking over the salt and pepper. "Look at that, girl! They sent the President of the United States barbeque from our little joint! You see what a high falutin place I take you to Friday nights? You're going to have to buy new clothes before we can go back."

Lillie chuckled as she rose and picked up his breakfast plate, stopping to kiss her husband on his crown. "Well, Mr. Big Shot, you better get going and earn the money. And I've got to wake Beth. She'll be late for school."

But Matt didn't need to look at his watch to know he had plenty of time to get to the shampoo factory by six-fifty-five. His routine was the same every morning. "Hope they sent the President lean-brown-chopped."

When Matt arrived outside the employee entrance, two friends from shipping were waiting. They grinned and winked at each other as they asked him who was going to win the World Series. Confessing his ignorance about *this one thing*, he told them instead who to vote for in the November election and why.

The shipping supervisor greeted Matt with a slap on the shoulder. "He's my right-hand man," he said to the new trainee who was standing beside him.

Matt felt his cheeks redden and reminded himself to tell Lillie.

It was quarter past three—his shift would end in fifteen minutes—when Matt noticed the supervisor leave the warehouse floor. Feeling the weight of his new title, he looked around. The trainee was practicing on the fork lift.

At that moment, the lift lurched forward and bumped an eight-foot-high column of boxes packed with shampoo. Matt yelled, "Don't!" and ran toward it, just as the top carton tilted. His two friends were coming fast from the other direction. Envisioning men and machine crashing into each other on slippery liquid, he dove, ending up on his knees beside the column. When the falling box landed in his arms in one piece, Matt groaned and laid his cheek against it. Thank God!

With a look on his face that shifted from fear to relief, the young trainee gave Matt a hesitant thumbs-up and spun the machine around.

A sharp pain grabbed Matt's lower back and held it. He wanted to jump up but found he couldn't move. As his two buddies lifted him to a standing position, he gave a strained shout. "I'm gonna try out for the Falcons!"

1

Two years later...

MATT LAY IN THE VALLEY ON HIS SIDE OF THE MATTRESS
with arms pressed to his sticky, sweaty sides trying not to turn too much and awaken Lillie. But
his thoughts swirled and bounced like bumper cars
trapped in a small rink. He wanted to scream out to
anyone who would listen but knew he'd sound like
a raving lunatic if he did. *Pain is a monster. Grabs
me around my waist. Walks on my back and down
my legs. Can't afford Lillie's seizure medicine. Need
to find food—Beth's hungry.*

He turned the glowing face of the square plastic
clock toward him—1:27 a. m. Grasping the edge of
the mattress, he whispered to the pain, "Go to hell,"
then limped to the kitchen. The eerie, cold light of
the full moon added to his feeling of being someplace
else. He jerked open the refrigerator door—eggs,
margarine, half gallon of milk, a cut-up chicken,
and the strawberry jam Lillie made last summer. He
turned to the pantry—Wonder Bread, peanut butter,

pinto beans, potatoes, cornmeal, and Cheerios. He sighed. At least there was food for a few days. Outside the kitchen window, the undersides of the peach tree leaves shone in the moonlight, causing him to lean over the sink for a closer look. The green fruit was the size of walnuts and wouldn't be ready for a couple of months. Mumbling, "Need money, need money," he staggered back to the bedroom.

The edge of the mattress dipped to the wooden frame when Matt sat on it. Reaching into the drawer of the bedside table, he took out the small bottle of blue pain pills and shook them into his hand. *One, two, three—eleven. Why not swallow them all?* The pills rolled around in his palm. *If they killed me, so what? At least I'd get some sleep.* Shuddering in disgust, he threw them in the drawer and fell back on his pillow.

It had been two years since his accident. Why hadn't the surgery taken away the pain? How was a man supposed to support himself and his family when he couldn't work? What had he done wrong?

Matt rolled over to face Lillie and eased his hand onto her hip. Memories of the day in his orthopedist's office three months after his surgery when he feared life was out of his control—possibly forever—rushed forward.

Matt sat on an examination table staring at the half-page of notebook paper he held in his hand. He mouthed the questions he had scribbled there at three o'clock that morning and hoped he could understand the doctor's answers. As he struggled to keep the blue paper gown pulled down over his knees, he wondered whether his shivering was from sitting half-naked in a cold room or his sense of dread.

The door swung open, hitting the metal cabinet behind it. Doctor Ramsey rushed into the examination room, bringing with him a jumble of words that Matt couldn't make sense of. Not wanting to interrupt what he hoped were solutions to his problems, he stayed silent. The orthopedist checked his watch, then pressed hard around the three-inch incision down the middle of Matt's lower back. Matt instinctively jerked away from the cold fingers.

"Hmm, okay," the doctor said, as if talking to himself. Glancing at his watch again, he moved quickly around the examination table. With practiced smooth motions, he lifted Matt's knee, tapped it with a rubber hammer, and dragged the steel end across the bottom of his foot. Dr. Ramsey leaned on the counter, rested his head in one hand, and jotted notes on the chart. "You're doing fine here. Everything looks good. See you in a month."

Matt grasped the edge of the table and slipped off, wincing from the stabbing pain it caused. He raised his six-foot frame as straight as the pain would allow and called, "Wait a minute!" just before the doctor closed the door. Surprised at the force behind his words, Matt stepped backward. Rising within was a childhood admonition from his mother—*Don't act ugly. Watch that temper.*

Doctor Ramsey snapped his head around. Eyes the color of a cold winter sky held Matt's gaze for the first time that morning.

"Yes?"

Stunned at the harsh look on the doctor's face, Matt clasped his hands together to stop them from shaking. When able to speak he tried to keep his voice even and not show what he felt. "My left leg—it folds up on me. Why? And why all the pain?"

As he stepped close to Matt, the doctor's white coat filled with air, making him look like a circus man on stilts. An additional four inches of height allowed him to lean over his patient. "You're having pain because you're in the recovery phase of a lumbar laminectomy." Dr. Ramsey answered in a flat voice. "It's part of the healing process."

Matt held to the table with both hands and shook his head. "But this is February twentieth. Tomorrow will be three months. You said I'd be ready for work. And," searching the doctor's eyes for support, he found none, so he looked down. "I've used all my savings. There's no money left." He cleared his throat in an attempt to sound strong, more substantial. "I'm barely forty-two years old. Why so long to get well?"

The orthopedist swung his arm up, fingers open, and sighed. "Three months was just a ballpark figure. There's no way to predict."

The men stared at each other without moving. A furnace fan came on, making a whirring sound, as if trying to warm the space between them. Matt smelled dust and felt his gown flapping against his bare thighs. The words he had written on the scrap of paper during the night slipped from his mouth. "Are you *sure* this was what I needed?"

Dr. Ramsey smacked the tan Formica counter with Matt's chart. "Mr. Bradfurd, two discs slipped out of place in the lower part of your spine and pressed on your cord. They could have paralyzed you." Throwing his arms wide, he sounded like the frustrated parent of a teenage boy. "I explained all that."

Matt was suddenly conscious of his appearance. He noticed dirt under two of his long ragged fingernails and wondered why it was there, since he had done nothing the past three months except lie in bed, sit in his La-Z-Boy, and whine. Moving his right hand over his head, he smoothed down hair that hadn't been cut during that time, silently asked for help from anybody up there, and allowed that, "I'm afraid I'll lose my job."

Matt searched the doctor's face, so still that it looked like it had been cut from wood. Then Matt saw something different—maybe, the beginning of a smile—before the doctor spoke.

"Well, now, that's very interesting, because I heard from your employer last week." He pointed to the chart on the counter. "Note's right there. He wonders whether you *want* to work again." The smile turned into a smirk. "He thinks you might not be all that *motivated*. Said he hoped I wouldn't have as much trouble with you as he's had."

Hands slippery with sweat, Matt held more tightly to the edge of the table. The pain in his back had shot down his left leg, numbing it. He needed to sit but couldn't move. "Mr. Hartman called you?" His voice was shrill.

The doctor reached for the doorknob. "Look, Matthew, I have people waiting," he said with some gentleness. "You *will* get well. I've seen this before. See you in a month."

"Be patient," Dr. Ramsey added as he stepped from the room and closed the door behind him.

His mind on what the doctor had said about his employer, Matt ignored the signals from his leg and fell to the floor, landing on his hands and knees. The harsh jarring of his body caused pain to explode throughout his back and hips. The strong smell of disinfectant caused him to gag. A sudden fear that he might be paralyzed flashed through his mind.

Afraid he would be seen in that position, he crawled to a straight metal chair. If he had been a child, he would have just lain there and cried. "How did I end up here?" he whispered before slamming his fist on the seat and growling, "Dumb redneck."

MATT FELT LIKE A RAG DOLL THAT CHILDREN HAD dragged around by the neck as he eased into the passenger seat beside his cousin's wife. Myra neatly folded her newspaper as she turned toward him, auburn curls swaying at her neck. Her voice was cheerful. "Doctor have good news?"

Matt looked out the side window. "Says I have to give it time." He kept his gaze on the pavement to his right to avoid seeing her reaction as he asked, "You in a hurry to get home? Something I'd like to do."

Myra laid her hand on his shoulder. Her gentle voice reminded Matt of the way Lillie's had sounded since his surgery. "Just name it."

"Will you take me to see my boss?"

Halfway out of the parking space, Myra braked the Saturn hard, causing the curls to bounce. Her smile disappeared and her eyes widened. "Right now? You're awful pale."

Matt had jumped into deep water, uncertain he could swim, but intended to stay. "Got to—have to ask him something."

Out of the corner of his eye, he saw Myra glance at him several times, but he looked straight ahead, pretending not to notice. He knew she wanted to say more, but he was grateful she didn't. The drive to the factory would take fifteen minutes, and he needed every second to figure out what to say to his boss.

Matt had worked at Organic Botanicals five and a half years—from the day it had opened in Cross Hill. Although he wondered why a Northerner without people in the area would move his shampoo manufacturing company to a small town in the South, he was grateful that he had. It was his best job—far better than the last one unpacking vegetables at the grocery store—and he planned to work there until the day he retired.

His pay from the factory hadn't made him rich, but with Lillie's income, he felt satisfied. At the end of every month, he paid his bills in full and bought food and clothes for her, their daughter, and himself. Most of the time, there had been enough left to go out for barbeque on Friday nights. And, for the first time in his life, he was proud to say he had a real savings account.

What Dr. Ramsey had told him Mr. Hartman said puzzled Matt. He thought the doctor must have misunderstood since he had never had any problems with anyone at work. He had started in shipping and worked his way up to the supervisor's right-hand man. His only personal contacts with Mr. Hartman—two or three times—were related to his surgery. And his boss had handled that like a real stand-up guy.

When the car hit a pothole, Myra shouted, "Oh, no! That must have hurt."

Pain from the fall in the doctor's exam room filled Matt's lower back, so he hardly felt the bounce from the pothole. But it did remind him of the day he was driving home from work and realized he had a problem that wasn't going away. For months after the accident he had tried to deny his back pain. But like water rising from saturated soil, it had become more and more obvious. When he arrived home from work, in spite of his intention to go to the kitchen where Lillie was cooking supper, his body turned toward the bedroom where he reached for the heating pad. Most evenings, he ate in bed, staying there—unable to sleep—until light around the edge of the window shade told him it was time to get ready for work.

After seven months, he had given in to his wife's pleas and gone to his internist, who sent him to Dr. Ramsey. The orthopedist said he needed surgery immediately, but Matt had refused until he met with his boss. He told Mr. Hartman that the most important thing, next to his family, was his job, and he wouldn't take a chance of losing it. If necessary, he would live with the pain.

As Myra swung the car into the factory driveway, Matt's attention returned to the present. Excited, he felt a surge of warmth. *Beautiful!* The sight of the two-story yellow cement-block building where he made a living for his family almost brought tears to his eyes.

Surrounded on three sides by longleaf pines, the factory was connected to a parking lot by a twenty-foot cement walk bordered by patches of grass and weeds. Myra drove across the grass and the walk, stopping the car three feet from the front door. She shrugged her shoulders and smiled. "Hope nobody minds. I didn't want you to have to walk far."

Taking a moment to catch his breath after getting out of the car, Matt leaned his head and arms against the front door, allowing the warmth of the February sun to soothe him. As he listened to the swish of pines in the wind, he reviewed his last meeting with Mr. Hartman.

After giving him the surgery date, Matt said that he would return in three months—February twenty-first. He had memorized his boss' response. "The important thing is for you to be healthy. The job will be here when you're ready." But when they shook hands, Mr. Hartman asked, "Now, you're not blaming me for your problem, are you?"

2

JIM HARTMAN CURSED WHEN HE BUMPED HIS ANKLE against his daughter's skateboard. He hadn't cared that the garage was jammed with toys before he bought the BMW, but now he cringed at the thought of one of the girls scraping a bicycle handle against it. When his wife, Melanie, had asked him to set up a shed for the lawn mower and garbage cans to make more room, he had said he would but hadn't. He thought it was a waste of money.

He shivered in the morning cold—aware of a mild feeling of disappointment—as he dusted the two-week-old car. It was silver though he had wanted black. But after the salesman had hinted that his sophisticated and successful customers chose silver, Jim had felt stuck because that was the image he wanted to convey to the world—especially to his father and younger brother.

As he tossed the long-handled duster on the floor and slid into the driver's seat, he chuckled. *My silver bullet.* Slamming the door harder than necessary, he thought of what the sound represented:

it was the life he was striving for—solid, rich, and free.

Light hadn't yet arrived in these streets of middle-class brick houses. Amid some fog, Jim eased out of the driveway, grasped the black leather-covered steering wheel with both hands, and smiled without having to force it. *Okay, baby, we've got thirty minutes. Let's rip!*

The tachometer needle of the M5 was thrown to the right as if blown by a strong wind. When he reached the middle of a long curve on the way to the main highway, he pushed the accelerator closer to the floor. As he pulled out of the curve, an orange triangle appeared in his headlight beam. Reacting with the instincts of a fighter pilot, Jim swung the car around the plodding tractor with inches to spare. As his gleeful eyes met the frightened ones of the gray-headed driver, he let out a "Boo-yah!" and—wishing this drive could last forever—danced his torso back and forth before reluctantly pressing on the brake.

Jim glided into his reserved parking space, then tossed the cover over his car and struggled to fit it in place. *If I was taller. Had longer arms. Damn!* His resemblance to his mother—five-eight with curly brown hair—instead of his father and brother—six-one and smoothly blond—was something he had resented since his teens. It was unfair, like so many other things had been in his family.

Jim unlocked the back door of the two-story building and reached in the darkness for the alarm pad. For a second, each time he entered, though it had been five and a half years now, he felt like he was doing something wrong. He still had trouble believing that half the building and everything in it belonged to him. That he of all people was a manufacturer of shampoos and conditioners, creator and half-owner of Organic Botanicals Company. Forty-five employee cards lined up beside the time clock. *Fucking amazing.*

The elevator made an unusual grinding noise as it lifted Jim to his second floor office. He would have to have it checked, he guessed. The first contractor he interviewed had bragged about building with quality to last, but Jim searched until he had found one who got the message: he wanted ten years out of the structure, no more. By that time, his products would be established and a big company would buy him out. For all he cared, the building could collapse after that. He'd be back in Ann Arbor.

When Jim stepped into the hallway, the scents of rosemary and mint struck him. But this time, his thoughts of Ann Arbor made it harder to push back his memories of Starshine, and he allowed himself to enjoy the warmth flowing through him as he envisioned the twenty-one-year-old who had made his career possible. It made him uncomfortable to miss her. Pushing the puzzling feelings away, he chuckled. *That girl. Had to have it all natural. Even organic pot.* Jim shook his head and sighed. *No idea what she was handing me when she gave me those formulas.*

After Jim flipped on the light, he considered his office—little more than a square with empty white walls, a metal desk and three straight chairs. Pictures of Melanie and their daughters were the only personal items in the room. He groaned. Melanie was meeting him here later in the morning, and she didn't approve of the way it looked.

She had tried to convince him to make it more comfortable and attractive, arguing that it was important to show his desire to treat people, including himself, well. "Seeing that you value them," Melanie said, "will encourage them to trust you." But Jim had rejected all that. He wasn't there to coddle people, just to make big money and to do it fast. Not a penny would be spent for anything beyond bare necessities.

Matt opened the reception room door and paused to catch his breath. Every time he stepped into this room, he asked himself the same questions. *How can she work in such a small place? Without a window?*

Mr. Hartman's secretary, Tibby, raised her head from her work and smiled when she saw him.

Matt's hips and back had weakened to the point that he couldn't lift his feet to walk well, so he shuffled over and dropped down hard into one of the molded plastic chairs along the wall. The pain it caused made him want to cry out, but he bit his lower lip and waited until able to speak.

"You don't know how much I've missed this place." Then he hesitated, tilting his head to the right, as he did when uncertain, and tried to decide what was bothering him. Tibby's warm hello was as expected, but her eyes showed something else. Maybe she didn't feel well. "You all right?"

She nodded.

"Look at me," Matt said, spreading his arms. "I'm down to a hundred eighty-two. Lost nineteen pounds. Lillie says she's jealous. Boy, am I ready to get back to work."

The secretary raised her eyebrows. "I hope so. I'll tell Mr. Hartman you're here." Her smile gave way to a worried look. Gently placing the phone back on the receiver, she leaned forward and whispered, "Be careful."

About what? Distracted by Tibby's words, Matt left the door open when he entered his boss's office. He wasn't invited to sit, so he remained standing, holding onto the back of a straight chair in front of the desk.

Mr. Hartman looked relaxed but his voice sounded strained, as if he was having trouble getting the words out. "Matthew, this is a surprise. What can I do for you?"

Matt felt himself leaning on the light chair and hoped it would support him. His plan was to remain positive, giving his boss the benefit of the doubt.

"Well, sir, it's been three months, and I'm ready to go to work."

Mr. Hartman's voice held genuine surprise. "You are?" He leaned forward in his desk chair and raised his voice. "You're able to stand and move around without any trouble? You can lift boxes again?"

As he shifted his weight from one leg to the other, Matt dipped on his weak leg before restoring his balance. Although the room was cool, sweat trickled down his back. His arms trembled. "Not sure I could lift right yet. Or stand a long time. Is there something else I could do here until my strength comes back?" he asked, his voice almost carrying a begging sound.

Mr. Hartman's tone was flat, and his eyes were focused on Matt's hands. "I'm sorry, Matthew, there isn't."

Matt lowered his head in an unsuccessful attempt to meet his boss's eyes. "Could you train me to do anything else—just until I'm on my feet? Then I'll go back to shipping, anywhere. Help me out a little while?" Matt had tried to tamp down the pleading in his voice the last time he spoke but these new words slapped him in the face. Realizing that Tibby could also hear them made him feel ashamed. In pain, he forced his back to straighten. "I'll be healthy again—always been."

"Your job's in shipping—whenever you're able." Continuing to stare at the chair, Mr. Hartman picked up a pen and a manila folder. "Now, I'd better get back to work."

Matt's left leg was acting like a rubber hose. He had to hurry. Repeating the fall he had taken in the doctor's office might doom his job. His attention shifted to the reason he had come. "What did you say to Dr. Ramsey about me?" After he asked, he wondered why he had said what he did.

Mr. Hartman laid down the folder and met Matt's eyes. His face brightened. "Oh, Dr. Ramsey, have you seen him lately?"

"This morning. He said you told him I might not *want* to work." Matt waited a few minutes, expecting a reaction that didn't come. "Why would you say that?"

"No, no." His boss got up, walked around the desk, and laid his hand on Matt's shoulder. "He must have misunderstood. I said I *wanted* you back at work. You're a valuable employee." He smiled and patted Matt on the back. "But you don't look too good right now. You should go on home and call me when you're ready."

Matt tilted his head and stared at his boss. He wanted to smile, shake the man's hand, and say thank you, sir, but something felt wrong. His voice sounded rougher than he intended. "I'm glad to hear that, because you made me a promise, and I *am* coming back."

Jim placed the sole of his foot against his office door and kicked. Then he faced the closed door with hands on his hips and his feet apart. He felt his body grow almost square when anger puffed it out.

It created a wall that he had mastered at his father's dinner table. No one could tell him what to do. *So you say, Matthew Bradfurd. Your body's a wreck. You'll never work here again.*

He walked stiffed-legged back to his desk and dropped down in his uncomfortable chair. *Don't even think about workers' comp. Another person tried it before you. And more will if they hear you collected. My premiums would skyrocket and ruin a company this size. I'll hold you off until the time to file is over. I've done it before!*

Imagining what his wife would say if she could hear him, Jim pounded the desk with his fist. *But why should I subsidize him? Hell, I already do. Health care costs go up and up. Why didn't he save to take care of himself? What about extra shifts, overtime work? Matthew Bradfurd always went home at 3:30, the minute the buzzer sounded.*

Jim jerked the bottom desk drawer open and grabbed a cigar from the box of Macanudos his partner had smuggled in from Cuba. Thinking of the high-grade marijuana he had enjoyed daily in college, he drew the smoke deeply into his lungs and wished he had a joint. *The guy should have gone to college, like I did!*

He paced around his desk, puffing hard on the cigar. Then Jim clenched it between his teeth, stopped in front of the two-way mirror, and looked down into the lab where the chemist and his team were testing a new product. Knowing he could watch them but not be seen or heard gave him a special pleasure. "Hey, you people," he growled. "I built this company, and, goddamn it, I don't owe you anything. You won't take me down with your claims."

Startled by a heavy knock on the door, Jim spun around to see his wife pushing it open. Melanie halted in the doorway, wrinkled her nose, and waved her hand back and forth in front of her face.

Seeing her slender, beautiful body made Jim forget everything else. A feeling of pride surged in him when he realized this goddess belonged to him. Her long golden hair shone through the smoky haze. Knowing his own would be a mess, he ran his fingers through it. Then Jim remembered what he was holding. Hurriedly stumbling toward his desk, he stuffed the cigar in the ashtray and shouted, "Tibby, turn on the air conditioning. Mel! It couldn't be eleven."

Melanie closed the door and picked up a yellow pad from his desk to use as a more effective fan. Leaning forward, she whispered, "Couldn't you walk over and ask her? Did you have to yell?" She turned to her right, and then to her left, hair swinging about her shoulders. "Who were you talking to in here? Who's trying to take you down?"

Jim cleared his throat and shook his head. "Hon, I yelled because I was in a hurry to get rid of the smoke."

She sighed heavily and sat down. "You told me you had quit."

Jim spoke in a singsong. "All I said was I wouldn't smoke at home. I didn't mention the office."

Melanie rolled her eyes. "Jim, do I know you?"

He dropped down in the chair beside her and gestured vaguely. "Didn't you come here to talk about the children?"

Leaning across the space between them, Melanie linked fingers with her husband's. A sadness had come over her face, but her words returned to their usual gentleness. "Let's start over. I love you, Jim."

He pulled his chair close enough to touch her leg with his. The soft voice made him feel like he was being caressed.

She squeezed his hand. "Jim, are you listening? I have something important to say."

Staring at her blue eyes made it hard for him to hold his own during a discussion. He released her hand, hunched over, and looked away. "Yeah. Go ahead."

"Now don't rush me." Melanie's voice trembled. "I want to start at the beginning." Surprised to hear her sounding nervous, Jim turned toward her. "Okay," she continued, "you know my family was never close. And I guess I thought that was normal—just the way things were for everybody." She straightened in her chair. "But since we've lived here, I've learned it isn't. I see families spending *time* with each other." She reached for her husband's hand. "The girls are six and nine. This is the perfect time to do things with them as a family—the four of us together, not just three."

Jim's eyes narrowed, and he jerked his hand away, "You telling me I'm not a good father?"

Melanie's voice remained even. "No. I'm saying you're an *absent* father."

Flushing, Jim felt a surge of embarrassment as well as something else he couldn't identify. Fear? "I have a company to run." Convinced, now, that it was anger, he raised his voice. "And you like what you get from my company, don't you? *You're* not out there making money to support yourself and the kids. *I'm* the one doing it," he concluded, stabbing his breastbone with his index finger.

Melanie propped her elbows on her knees, looked down at the floor, and sighed. "You're right," she said somberly. "You're *absolutely* right." As she swept her arm in the air, her voice rose. "But why can't you come home for dinner? Why do you have to be in this office thirteen hours a day? That makes no sense."

Jim leapt from his chair and planted his feet apart. His voice was harsh. "You don't understand what it takes to grow a business. I do. You know *damn* well I want to sell it five years from now. Why are you breaking my balls?" Seeing the stunned look on his wife's face, Jim sat down and lowered his voice. "Come on, hon. I thought we were in this together. Wanted the same things. Have you forgotten about the houses—our plans?"

Melanie's eyes glistened with tears. "Okay, okay. I hear you." Sniffing, she wiped her face with her palms and stood. "But let's think. What's *really* important here—impressing people or eating dinner with your family? How about watching your girls play softball? You're only thirty-six years old! You think they'll know their father after five more years? What's with you?"

3

LILLIE SQUEALED WHEN THE URINE HIT HER, AND THEN laughed, as she dabbed her apron and shirt sleeves with a baby wipe. Quickly fastening the diaper, she chided the four-month-old boy, "Why, you little rascal!" Lifting him to her face and nuzzling his cheek, she continued humming the Neil Diamond song—"You Don't Bring Me Flowers Anymore"—she had heard on Oldies But Goodies radio that morning.

People told Lillie she didn't look forty-three. Her skin was too smooth. "That's one good thing about being fat as a hippopotamus," she'd laugh and say. "It fills in the wrinkles." The rubber band holding her ponytail had slipped, and long strands of gray and brown hair hung around her ears. Her face remained bright, in contrast to the faded pants, shirt, and the threadbare red and blue checkered apron she wore when the children were with her.

As Lillie laid the baby in the Pack and Play, he fussed and reached for her. Leaning over the portable crib, she held out a finger for him to grasp. "Well, little darling, would you like to dance with me?" she gently teased. "But my man will be jealous. You know we used to turn on the radio and dance after supper?" The baby kicked his legs while Lillie stroked his head and smoothed his hair. "Be sure to dance with your wife." Sadness came into her voice. "And buy flowers on her birthday. I loved that."

Lillie and the children were in the playroom— the room she created from the dining room when she started her daycare business. Although she had little choice about which room to convert, since the house had only five, this one was ideally located. It could be seen from any place in the house except her bedroom. There was enough space for two portable cribs, a changing table, a bookshelf, and a child-sized round table with three small chairs. And since it was near the heating and air conditioning units, she could keep the temperature comfortable.

Hearing the front door open, Lillie turned to see Matt stumbling across the threshold. The paleness of his face exaggerated the dark circles under his eyes, and sweat shone on his forehead. Myra followed close behind, arms poised to catch him if he fell.

Matt was staring at the living room wall ahead of him and speaking in a voice so soft that Lillie had to pick up the baby and move closer to hear. "Doctor said there was nothing he could do. Told me to be patient. I'm going to lay down."

Lillie's heart sank. She wished she could ignore Myra and the children and wrap her arms around him with a magic touch that would make him well. But she nodded and turned to Myra. "How about some tea?" Giving the baby his pacifier, she laid him in the Pack and Play and touched the tops of the girls' heads. "Come on, sweet things, time for juice."

The four-and-a-half-year-old gathered a doll in her arms. The three-year-old picked up the doll's bottle and grabbed the corner of a blanket, dragging it behind her to the kitchen.

After handing each girl a small plastic cup of apple juice, Lillie poured the sweet tea she had brewed early that morning over ice and sat down beside Myra at the table.

Myra lowered her head and whispered, "Is Matt getting any better?"

Caught off guard by sadness, Lillie's smile faded. "Well, you can see what his body's like." She hesitated. "But what bothers me more is his spirit's leaving him. You know how he was before surgery—went on and on about what he read in the paper, told people what to think, argued about politics. Even made fun of himself for doing it! And when people hurt—dear God—he hurt with them." Lillie pointed to the window over the sink. "I saw birds flying in the shape of a V the other morning. That was him—head jutted forward, moving, mind lifted like the wings of those birds." Her eyes filled with tears. "What if he never comes back?"

Myra shook her head. "What about the pain pills?"

Lillie wiped her eyes with her shirt sleeve. "They're worthless! He takes them every four hours, just like the doctor told him. How long do they help? Maybe thirty minutes, no more than an hour. But, good grief, every four hours for three months! He's going to get hooked. You hear about it all the time."

"Can't you make him stop?"

Propping her elbow on the table, Lillie rested her forehead in her hand and waited a minute or two. "I hate to admit this, but his pain makes those big brown eyes look like a wild animal's. The pills take that wildness away long enough so it doesn't scare me as much."

Myra laid her hand on Lillie's. "You know, Bobby thinks he should go to another doctor. What if Ramsey's not doing something right?"

Lillie lifted both hands toward the ceiling and raised her voice. "Who? Even if we found somebody else, how could we afford it? What if the insurance company decided not to pay? We're just barely living on what I make from keeping these four children."

"Wait, Lillie, wait." Myra swung her head from side to side. "People go for second opinions all the time."

The three-year-old pulled at Lillie's apron and raised her arms. Lillie lifted the girl to her lap. "Well, there's another part. He doesn't want to make anybody mad. What if he went to somebody else and that doctor wasn't any good, and Ramsey wouldn't take him back? Then what?" She shrugged, "Oh, I don't know, Myra, maybe Dr. Ramsey's right, and all Matt needs is time." The older girl tugged at Lillie's arm. "All right, honey, you can come up, too."

Myra stood and put the glasses in the sink. "Just try not to worry." She nodded toward the girls. "Must be hard for you having a houseful."

Lillie's smile returned. "My goodness, if this was all I had to do, I'd feel like a lady of leisure. Taking care of these little darlings is as easy as breathing."

AS HE ENTERED THE BEDROOM, MATT GLANCED OVER his shoulder at Lillie and Myra. Myra was good to him, but he imagined she was getting tired of hauling him around, and he didn't blame her. He had become a weakling, pure and simple. If he had been tough enough, he would have marched right down to the loading dock at the factory. That's what he should have done—stood up straight and shown Mr. Hartman what he was made of—used to be, anyway.

The clack of the girls' shoes when they struck the kitchen linoleum reminded Matt of his grandfather's friend, old man Early. When the eighty-year-old lost his leg, he strapped a piece of wood onto his stump and went right on walking. A metal disk hammered into the bottom made a sound like a tap dancer's shoe. Matt could still hear it, every other step clicking, as the man's body rose and dipped, switching back and forth from a leg of flesh to one of wood. Matt shook his head. *Tough as an old pine knot. Wish I was like him.*

Matt took the small bottle of blue pills from the drawer of his bedside table and shook one out, then another, swallowing them without water. He thought he deserved the bitter taste for being weak and thanked God that his grandfather couldn't see him. Reaching for the damp gray handkerchief on the table, he wiped the sweat from his neck and begged for sleep.

Peering at the face of the clock on the bedside table, Matt searched through the fog in his head to distinguish between the short and the long hands, trying to figure out what time it was. *Uh—an hour!* He picked up the small black plastic clock and shook it. *You're killing me. Move forward or back— stop dragging.* He believed he had slept but wasn't certain. He had heard Myra say goodbye. Once he smelled grilled cheese sandwiches and heard the girls chattering at their little table. A baby cried. He heard Lillie say something about warming a bottle and there was a sound of the back door slamming.

Raising himself on his elbow, Matt lifted the cor- ner of the window curtain. The morning sun had disappeared, leaving clouds hovering so low that it looked like the sky wanted to lie down and rest, too.

The house was quiet; Lillie and the children must be outside. This would be a good time to get to his chair and show Lillie that he was getting well. He wanted her face to look relaxed again. And he wanted to see pride on her face when she looked at him. It had been hard living without those two things for the last months.

His chair was in a corner of the small living room. As Matt lowered into the La-Z-Boy and pushed on the back and arms to raise the footrest, pressure from the weight of his body shifted off his lower back and gave him momentary relief from pain. Looking over at the flattened-out couch and Lillie's wooden rocker, he felt both gratitude and shame that the only piece of furniture they'd purchased in the last ten years had been for him.

He heard Lillie call to the girls. "Five more minutes, then we go in. It's cold today." Matt thought of his wife and the children she cared for as a team of horses hooked together, every movement coordinated. She was a stubborn woman when it came to them. No compromises or shortcuts were possible. Her schedule included taking them outside twice a day, even in winter, wanting them to breathe fresh air and get exercise. And she believed it made them smarter to watch birds, insects, clouds, and anything else that came along. Exploring, she called it—and collecting.

The flat surfaces in the living room and playroom were covered with things they had found—pine cones, a bird's nest, small colored stones, leaves—once green, now brown and cracked. All of it too important to throw away.

Then there was Lillie's belief about children's need for love; she said it was equal in importance to food and water. Matt remembered the one time she hadn't liked a child who was brought to her. She had given him back because she said she probably wouldn't learn to love him.

Matt's eyes teared. He sniffed and cleared his throat, trying to rid himself of the question that briefly passed through his mind—how long will she love a worthless husband?

Picking up the remote from the table beside his chair, he pointed it at the television. Click. A divorce court. A woman yelled, "My husband has been screwing around with somebody, and I'm finished with him!" The audience cheered and clapped, while the judge smiled. Click. A talk program. A psychic told a woman, "You have brought something evil into your house and that is causing your troubles." Click. A talking lizard. Another click, and the television screen turned black. Matt tossed the remote control over to the couch.

"Dear God." His voice rose with a sorrow that ended in anger. "Why are You letting this happen to me? I should be at work." He put his head in his hands. "Or, maybe they're right—I'm too lazy and no good."

4

MATT RAN HIS FINGERS THROUGH HIS THICK BLACK HAIR, pulling some of it across his face; it had grown to be a shaggy, wild-looking mess. He knew people thought he was a bum when they saw him on the street. Settling into his chair as deeply as it would allow, he wondered what his father and grandfather would think of him now.

When Matt closed his eyes, he saw his grandfather lying in the casket in his living room. Twelve-year-old Matt stood beside it, placing his ear close to Grandad's face and whispered to his mother. "I hear a breath. His chest is moving. Maybe he's not dead."

"Yes, son, he is," she said. "And it's time for you to go to bed." Matt shook his head. "I need to stay. What if he opens his eyes and nobody sees?"

Waiting had been the right decision for young Matt. In a short while, Grandad took a deep breath, sat up, and smiled. He got out of the casket and motioned for Matt to follow him to the shed, where each picked up a hoe. They had to get busy. Weeds were taking over the garden, and the dirt around the corn needed breaking up. When they finished, they would eat supper, and everything would be all right again. Matt could go back to being a boy.

Three days later, Matt's mother took him by the hand and climbed the gently sloped road to Grandad's house. Without speaking, she and Matt made their way through the garden, beside rows of corn, tomatoes, and squash. They walked through the toolshed and the smokehouse. Opening the door to the coop, they heard chickens squawk and watched them flap their wings. They walked through the orchard, the back porch and the side porch.

As they entered the house, Matt stumbled. He saw Granny lying on Grandad's side of the bed. A wet washcloth covered her eyes and forehead. Matt leaned forward; his head felt too heavy to carry. His mother put her arm around his waist and led him down the hill, where his father waited with the car.

The Whispering Hill Cemetery lay behind the small white-planked Methodist Church. Young Matt knew it well. Season after season, he and Grandad had placed flowers on graves of the aunts, uncles, grandmothers, and grandfathers who rested there. Matt's father laid his weathered hand on the boy's shoulder and directed him to a mound of freshly-dug clay in the last row.

Matt slumped down on the grass beside it and listened while his father walked along the row reading aloud the poetry carved into the old tombstones.

Unable to concentrate on the words, he turned his head toward the woods and raked his fingers through the loose red dirt.

The sun lowered and a scent of jasmine drifted on the breeze. Squinting at the figure in the distance, Matt jumped up. There was Grandad at the edge of the woods standing in the first row of black gum trees. *I knew it! Come on. Let's go home. Weather's warm enough to sit on the porch. You can tell a story. We'll sing.*

Matt's father grasped his shoulder and shook it. "Son, listen to me. It's getting dark. We have to go. We'll come back tomorrow."

Young Matt pointed toward the woods and with a trembling voice told his father to look. But he was too late, and Grandad had gone.

The back door slammed. Matt heard the children's voices. Lillie was bringing them in. He stayed quiet and kept his eyes closed.

"MARCH, TWO, THREE, FOUR," LILLIE SAID. THE TWO GIRLS were in front, swinging their arms like soldiers on their first day of training. She followed, carrying a baby in the crook of each arm, through the kitchen and into the playroom.

Gently, Lillie placed a sleeping baby in the Pack and Play. She changed the other baby's diaper and washed four small hands before turning on the girls' favorite Baby Mozart CD. While they listened to the music, she stepped through double doors into the living room. There she folded two blue blankets to fit the size of each girl and laid them on the floor to the right of the couch. On the blankets, she placed small pillows embroidered with the names Bella and Rachel.

"Pick your book, girls," Lillie said as she lowered herself to the floor between the pallets. Lillie read to them, changing her voice to fit each character. The girls giggled and joined in, adding their own versions. When the stories were over, they lay down on their blankets. Bella slipped her thumb in her mouth.

Lillie glanced at Matt in his chair, thanking God he was asleep, for she hadn't yet figured out how to get her body off the floor without thinking she looked like a pig trying to raise itself out of the mud. Twisting her legs back, she threw herself forward to land on her hands and knees. Then she crawled three steps to the couch and pulled up. It was at this point she had to be careful. Once, she had ended up facing the back of the couch and, while trying to turn over, rolled onto the floor. When people asked how she had bruised her nose, she said she had run into a door. It was easier that saying, "When a fat lady starts rolling off a couch, she can't stop."

AS LILLIE AND THE CHILDREN SLEPT, MATT RETURNED to the past. Although others described the past as a time that no longer existed, that had never been true for him. The events of his life were as real and present as snoring children on their blankets and a wife on her couch. But some situations confused him like his current one. He didn't understand what was happening or why. It was like photographs scrambled in a box.

Lillie had said he shouldn't try so hard to understand. God was in charge, knew what He was doing, and had His reasons for everything that happened. Matt glanced at his wife. If she were awake, he would ask two questions: Why did God give me a brain and the ability to think and work if He didn't want me to have control over my life? And how can I, if I don't understand what's going on?

On November third, five months to the day after his grandfather died, twelve-year-old Matt jumped off the school bus, wondering what his mother had baked that day. His appetite had been poor since Grandad's passing, so she coaxed it to life every afternoon with one of his favorite desserts. He was tall, and she said he looked scrawny—too much like a plucked chicken.

Entering the yard, Matt lifted his head and sniffed, searching for the scent of caramel cake, banana pudding, or fried apple pies. But there was nothing. He opened the back door and saw an empty kitchen table. "Mama?" Listening for sounds, he crept through the dining room and stopped at the bottom of the stairs. There were footsteps in his mother's upstairs bedroom.

Matt's father lay in bed with his eyes closed. His mother looked up, put her finger to her lips, and motioned for him to follow her downstairs. They sat at the kitchen table.

His father had collapsed that morning at work. The doctor believed the problem was diabetes but wouldn't know for certain until he had the blood report from the laboratory. His father would probably be fine, if he took good care of himself. They would need to help him.

As his mother climbed the stairs, Matt tiptoed to the living room and picked up the picture of his father and grandfather from the mantel. He stared at the two men—his grandfather broad-chested, six-feet two-inches tall, and his father five-feet nine-inches, weighing no more than a hundred fifty pounds. Matt had often wondered how a man strong enough to pull his own plow could have a son barely able to walk behind one. Perhaps this was the answer to that question.

Three months later, Matt's father's heart started acting up. Everyone was surprised except him. When he had tried to join the army after Pearl Harbor, he was rejected because of his heart but kept it a secret so no one would worry. He figured whatever happened, happened; he would go on with life and do the best he could with what it brought.

Matt smelled bacon. Shifting in his chair, he opened his eyes. Lillie and the children were still asleep. Then he remembered. His mother had been frying bacon the last day he went to school before his father died. That morning his father had been sitting at the kitchen table, dressed in work clothes. The skin on his face was pearly white and his lips a light gray-blue. As Matt said goodbye, his father reached for his hand. "Son, I want you to work hard, do right by people, and trust God's ways."

His father didn't finish work that day. He spent the next year at home in bed and then three months in the hospital, gurgling as he inhaled and exhaled, too tired to eat or talk. He lay with deep dark eyes closed, practicing eternal rest.

Matt refused to go to school while his father was at home, saying, "No," to his mother, and then to his teacher, and, finally, to the principal. He hoed the garden and ran up to check on his father. He worked in the kitchen and ran up to feed his father. He spread grain for the chickens and ran up to give his father water.

At night, Matt tended his dreams. He saw his daddy, mama, and granny sitting on the porch with their heads turned toward Grandad as he told his stories. Their faces beamed as they murmured, "Oh, my. Isn't that something." They sat in twilight, then in darkness, no one turning on a light. The images Matt had created for his grandfather's stories appeared. Ocean waves rose and fell as Grandad and his friend sailed on the troopship to Europe. His ears rang with the explosions in France. Heat from the bonfire made his face flush and his shoulders tighten when the woman cursed the Kaiser. Night after night, the pictures came and Grandad's memories saved his place in life.

His mother took a job in the Erlanger cotton mill. Five days a week, she returned home with lint-streaked sweat running down her face and arms, so tired she could barely hold her head up. Her warm smile disappeared; the light in her eyes dimmed. Matt watched and worried.

When his father died, his mother sold their house and rented one in the mill village. They moved to a place where Matt couldn't see Grandad's house: where there were no woods, no birds, and no father. Where there was no room for a garden and when he walked out his door, he saw only strangers.

Matt returned to school when he was fourteen. The principal started him in ninth grade, allowing him to skip seventh and eighth, because he was tall. He discovered that he had forgotten most of what he had learned. Dealing with numbers was like speaking a foreign tongue. And he noticed something new about himself: he was able to describe an event, without error, days after it had occurred. He could say whether there was the smell of lightning in the air or a leaf hanging from a spider web twirled clockwise or counter-clockwise in the wind. He remembered whether a boy had worn a green shirt or a blue one the Friday before. He could tell by the sound of the front door slamming when his mother returned from work, whether she had one of her bad headaches or was just tired.

The boys at school spoke the unfamiliar language of beer, girls, and cars, and Matt had no desire to learn it. He was content being alone, until Lillie came along. "Lillie saved me and she's doing it again," Matt said aloud. Opening his eyes, he looked around for her and the children. Their voices drifted in from the yard.

Sixteen years old, and the prettiest little thing I'd ever seen. Matt laughed. *Well, not so little. Eyes the color of grass with skin like spring sunlight. A cute pug nose and a smile that reminded me of life before Grandad died. Ah, Lillie. My heart beat again the first time I saw you.*

But feisty! Our first date at the Youth Fellowship hayride, and there I was pushing you up into the wagon. We both fell, you landed on top of me, and everybody laughed. Boy, what a temper! I thought you were going to jerk a knot in me.

But to tell you the truth, I didn't care. I just wanted to wrap my arms around you and roll over. That was when I understood what the boys were talking about. There was no mistaking it. It was real different from anything else.

Matt shifted in his chair and rubbed the insides of his thighs with both hands. *Um, hmm. Will we ever get it back?* He felt the smile fade from his face.

5

IT WAS THE KIND OF DAY EVERYONE CALLED PRETTY: there was enough warmth to have the doors and windows open but not so much to need a fan. That rare day when hot air and cold air were at peace. To make it even finer, it was a Sunday, giving people time to enjoy it.

The soft breeze moving the curtains lazily in and out made the house appear to be breathing. Matt sat in his living room chair, his thoughts alternating between the curtains and a television program about the migration of wildebeest and zebra herds in East Africa. Then he heard the crunch of gravel. Using both hands, he smoothed down his hair and wished he had brushed it that morning. A minute or two later, Bobby and Myra opened the screen door and stepped into the room.

"Hey, you lazy bum," Bobby teased. "Let's go for a ride."

Matt wanted to smile and then toss something back at his cousin but didn't have the energy. "Wouldn't I like that. Four months, and I'm still in this chair or the bed." When Bobby and Myra sat down on the couch, Matt noticed how much it slanted toward one end. Bobby had to brace himself with his right arm to keep level.

Lillie's voice reached them from the kitchen. "I hear you! Be right there."

Matt felt his cousin's stare before Bobby asked, "Boy, have you lost weight?"

Lillie answered for her husband as she entered the room carrying a tray with four tall glasses of ice water. "Has he ever." She nodded toward the tray. "Sorry. We don't have any tea."

Myra rose from the couch, lifted two glasses from the tray and handed them to her husband and Matt. Then she took Lillie by the arm. "Let's leave these boys alone and go see your strawberry patch. Mine got hurt by the cold this winter. Maybe you can tell me what to do."

Matt's cousin had a gift of gab that exceeded even his own. When the two talked about politics, they could go on for hours, each raising his voice louder and louder to make sure the other understood his point. Bobby had stomped off more than one time, yelling that Matt was a "damn know-it-all." As soon as he got home, he would call to finish the argument.

Knowing what was expected of him and figuring he might as well get the jump on Bobby, Matt asked his question quickly. "What do you think of our new governor?"

Bobby leaned forward. "I've never been to this house when I didn't get a glass of tea. What's going on?"

Matt wanted to jump up and run from the room but couldn't. And he knew there was no point in trying to convince his best friend that something so obvious was not true. "Things are tight just now."

As Bobby shifted his weight from his right leg to remove the wallet from his back pocket, he nearly fell over. He thrust two twenty-dollar bills toward Matt. "Here. Take this."

The breeze that soothed Matt earlier had disappeared. His face felt hot. Shaking his head, he looked away. "No, we're fine. We don't need tea."

Bobby lurched toward him and stuffed the bills in the right pocket of Matt's jeans. "Listen to me." He leaned over his cousin. "It's time to go to another doctor. This one's not doing you any good."

Matt was shocked and embarrassed to feel tears rising toward the surface. "I've been thinking about it."

Bobby sounded angry. "Wait a minute. How much do you have to think?"

Tilting his head to the right, Matt stared into space. He hadn't realized until his surgery how difficult it was to make himself understood by another person. Daily communication and banter hadn't required it. He had the urge to say, I'm scared and don't even have the gas money to get to another doctor, but that made him feel weak and foolish. "I hear you, but the one I've got is better than nothing. I can't drive to another town to find somebody else."

Bobby's anger kept coming. He held out his hands, as if grabbing Matt by the shoulders and shaking him. "Have you lost your mind? Get a name. Myra will drive you anywhere, anytime. And send Lillie to the grocery store. I'll bring more money tomorrow."

UNLESS HE HAD AN EMERGENCY TO DEAL WITH, DR. ED Latham began every morning in his second-floor office the same way: sipping coffee and leaning against the oak facing of his large window while looking down into the town square. His nurse perched on the edge of his oversized leather desk chair and reviewed aloud the conditions of the patients he would see that day. It had become harder to keep his attention on what Louise was saying because he knew his patients so well. He rarely saw anyone he hadn't treated for ten, twenty, sometimes thirty years. Sometimes he wondered whether he should continue the routine, but decided that, at the very least, it gave him a chance to have another cup of coffee and to catch up on the latest gossip. Louise knew it all.

Louise was talking, "And your eight-thirty is Matt Bradfurd. Said he wanted some advice from you. His surgery was four months ago."

"What?" Ed pressed his forehead against the window hoping for a closer look.

Louise looked out the window. "Oh, there he is on the sidewalk. My, he looks bad."

Ed set his coffee on the bookshelf and pressed harder against the pane. "Good grief." Turning quickly, he reached for his cup and said, "Let's cut this short. Get him in here as soon as you can." Tension gripped him. That made him want to hit somebody.

As his nurse closed the door behind her, Ed headed for the reclining chair in the corner of his office. Pushing on the back to raise his legs, he closed his eyes, separated his clenched teeth, and took several long, slow, deep breaths. Thinking of his wife's comment—"Okay, Buddha, go to it."—the first time she saw him in his relaxation routine made him chuckle, now that it had become a rather accurate description of his appearance.

After several minutes, when his body felt less tense, Ed began the often repeated summary of his life, beginning with the pictures surrounding him. Those of Ellen, their four children, and grandchildren stood on his desk with their backs to him, but he could see their faces clearly. His mother and father looked down at him from the top of the bookcase. The friend he had known since first grade, until he dropped dead of a massive coronary at fifty-six, sat on the file cabinet.

Ed rested his gaze on the oak file cabinets that held his life's work, his notes on his patients. Then it drifted to the bookcase containing medical books, biographies he couldn't bear to part with, and the poetry and philosophy books he had tried so hard to understand.

His fishing poles leaned against the corner beside the bookcase. It was hard to explain why they were there instead of in his camper-pickup. Occasionally, a patient would wink and make some comment, but Ed never responded. All he could come up with, even to himself, was that they held him to the banks of High Rock Lake and the Yadkin river, and it was those places that gave him the courage to live life the way he wanted.

When Ed's childhood friend died, he had changed his life. His wife called it a mid-life crisis. He called it coming home. His first act was to learn relaxation exercises, and then he started fishing. Soon after that he quit the country club, resigned from his board positions, and stopped accepting social invitations. Then he changed his office: he fired every employee he didn't respect and put the word out that he wasn't taking new patients, even though he was. He wouldn't allow himself to abandon anyone he was seeing but was very selective when accepting a new one.

He heard two taps on the door, Louise's signal that a patient was in the exam room.

Matt's head nodded up and down as he described in a high-pitched voice what he had been like since his surgery. "Now, you believe me, don't you? I'm not saying I don't trust your judgment about Dr. Ramsey."

"Don't worry." Ed imitated the movement of his patient's head in an attempt to reassure him. "I don't like your progress, either. I want you to call Dr. Ramsey and ask for the name of another ortho-pedist. Tell him I said so." Ed slipped his shoulder under Matt's arm to help him from the chair. "But I don't know about your idea of working, even sitting and part-time. Let me think. Maybe I can come up with something."

ED PICKED UP HIS CUP OF COLD COFFEE FROM THE bookcase and gulped it down. *To hell with the caffeine.* He raised the sash as high as it would go, and then grunted as he dragged his heavy desk chair close to the window. The scent of hyacinths drift-ing up from the square nearly overwhelmed him. He glanced at his watch—ten minutes to think before the next patient.

Visually, Ed searched the square as methodi-cally as he would the body of a critically ill patient, as if the answer to Matt Bradfurd's dilemma lay un-der one of the dozens of red, white, and pink azalea shrubs. He started at the quadrant that held the World Wars I and II monument. His mother's broth-er's name was engraved there—"Iwo Jima" beside it—and his father's uncle, killed in France. All the local names of those killed were on them, but the red azaleas had grown so thick that it was hard to get close enough to read them. He assumed the city hadn't bothered to cut the bushes back because most people had memorized the names.

Ed's gaze followed a clockwise path to the corner where the Vietnam War memorial stood. It was a small copy of the one in Washington but only held local names. There were three Lathams on that one—a first cousin and two more distant ones. Broken forsythia branches lay in front of it and to the left, a faded artificial wreath.

Although he tried not to focus on it, it was the statue at the center of the square that drew his attention. The Confederate soldier stood on a pedestal facing north, his rifle held high. White azaleas, some as tall as seven feet, covered the lower half of his body. The old brick pathways within the square—perhaps the entire town—led to the conflicting emotions aroused by that memory. Around it were iron benches, recently painted forest green, with daffodils and hyacinths leaning against them.

Across from Ed's window was the Allen County Courthouse, built in Greek Revival style in 1858. Although Ed admired the old building with its four marble columns and clock tower, he often wondered how the county had afforded it. The population couldn't have been more than a few thousand at the time. Even now the town had only about eighteen thousand. The whole thing seemed like a waste of money to him.

At that moment, a man descended the courthouse steps. Ed straightened in his chair. *That's it! George Russell. He's the one who could help Matt!* As quickly as his excitement rose, it faded. *No, no. Don't want to be indebted to him.* "Damn!" Ed shoved hard on the sash, causing the window to rattle as it slammed down.

George Russell had become a patient of Ed's fifteen years before—two years before the big shake-up. Ed didn't like him. Russell owned a large accounting firm that drew clients from the entire tri-city area. He was active in the Rotary Club and on the boards of other nonprofits. His picture appeared in the newspaper often, either for activities at the country club or for fund-raisers at the First Presbyterian Church.

Ed heard two taps on the door. "Thank you, Louise. I'll be there."

That afternoon, between each patient, Ed searched for resources to help Matt Bradfurd. He flipped through patient files for ideas, asked Louise to make some calls, and talked to County Social Services.

At four o'clock, realizing he was in a horrible mood, Ed knew he might as well get over with. He had a few friends and many good, loyal patients but none with the influence and power of George Thomas Russell.

When the courthouse clock struck a single brazen note at four-thirty, Ed laid his hand on the telephone. *Stop whining and do it! Dial the damn number.*

6

GEORGE RUSSELL REMOVED HIS WIRE-RIMMED GLASSES and tossed them on his desk. While he massaged his forehead with one hand, he picked up the silver frame holding his calendar and stared at the blurry red circle. Although he no longer prepared tax returns, the stress of April fifteenth got to him. His accountants saw to that by pushing their problems up to his office. The only way to avoid it was to leave town—precisely the reason he and his wife held first-class tickets on British air to London on April tenth.

The ringing startled George, causing him to drop the heavy frame on his French Provincial antique desk. Ignoring the phone for a moment, he rubbed the deep indentation it caused with his thumb and mumbled about the thousands of dollars he had spent on that desk.

"No, Mrs. Barbee. You're not disturbing me. *Dr. Latham* wants to talk to me?"

George was confused. He had seen the internist for an annual physical three weeks before, earlier than usual, because of cramping in his legs. The cramping had turned out to be a side effect of his blood-pressure medicine and was resolved by switching to another. The nurse had called with the results of his routine blood work and said everything else was fine. Then it occurred to George that maybe something had been discovered, and the doctor was calling to give him the bad news.

Reaching for his glasses, he shoved them on and sat up straight. "Yes, sir, Dr. Latham—yes, *Ed*—I'm fine. What's wrong?"

George found it hard to believe what he was hearing: Dr. Latham wanted a favor from *him*. "Of course, *Ed*, it would be an honor to help that unfortunate man. Let me see what I can do. It was a pleasure talking to you, too."

Releasing the breath he had been holding, George sank back against the soft leather of his desk chair. He felt relieved, amused, and irritated. *You want me to find work a couple hours a day for a guy who can't walk or stand and isn't trained for anything except factory work. Or find food and financial help—maybe a club to sponsor the whole family until he gets on his feet. Right!*

A hard push with his foot swiveled the chair around to face the floor-to-ceiling window behind George. The light blue of the foothills—created by a haze that Native Americans had called smoke—had deepened to purple. It was a view that made him feel happy and content with the world, but suddenly, he felt somber. *Latham doesn't even like me. He smiles and greets others by taking their hands or putting his arm around their shoulders. With me he's cool and stiff.*

About five years before, George had realized the discomfort he felt with his doctor and asked around the Club for the name of another. But people told him he'd be a fool to leave the best internist in town—saying he was lucky to have him—because he had stopped taking new patients. So George had decided not to worry about the man's feelings for him: not everybody needed to like him. There were plenty in his life who did.

Then George's sadness turned to anger. He smacked the black leather arms of his chair. *You know a lot of people in town. Why dump this on me?*

Turning back toward the large wood-paneled office, George laughed and spoke aloud to his doctor. "Why should I feel uncomfortable with you?" He raised his arms. "Look at who I am!" Jumping from his chair, he strode across the antique Persian rug to the calf-skin sofa he'd imported from Italy. He grinned when he reached the five certificates hanging above it from service organizations. They were filled with praise and thanks for his contributions to the community. Continuing to survey his grand realm, George settled on the Ermenegildo Zegna suit jacket hanging on the coat rack in the corner. Holding it up to an imaginary foe, he asked, "Do you have clothes like this?"

George turned to the window and noticed strands of clouds drifting across the mountains, merging with the fog. He knew what would soon follow: the mountains would vanish. That shift from green hills to blue to rich purple to none reminded him that people rarely knew the truth of anything—whether mountains existed behind clouds or what a man was like. All things were subject to alternate interpretations at any moment. *Latham doesn't really know me!* Angrily he turned back to his desk. *I'll show him—become useful to him and he'll change his tune! He'll see.*

Noticing the time, George grabbed his jacket. He and his wife had invited the new accountant to the house for dinner. *My manicure appointment. Rosalyn will be pissed if I'm late.* On his way down the back stairs to the garage, George reminded himself to deal with Latham's request the next day.

As George stretched his legs in his Mercedes 500, he thought about how perfect it was for his six-foot-one frame. His cell rang as the car surged out of the garage.

His wife's voice was cheerful, as always. "Hi, T. My tennis game lasted longer than I expected. But things are lined up. Don't be late."

"On my way." George chuckled and grinned. It was funny that Rosalyn still called him T after so many years. It was short for Tree Trunk, the name his football teammates had given him in college. Although his weight was the same—two sixty—his shape was no longer straight from ears to feet. At fifty-six, his body looked less like the trunk of a tree and more like the apple hanging from a branch.

During lulls in his conversation with the manicurist, George searched for ideas to help Latham's man. Two or three organizations and a church committee might do something if he made a personal pitch. He didn't think that any group in town had tried sponsoring a family until they were back on their feet, but it was an interesting concept that might work. The trouble was, it would take someone like him—skilled at organization and persuasion—to pull it off. But the timing was bad since he was leaving for London in five days.

George slowed as he approached the iron-scrolled gates of Clear Creek Estates. While waiting for them to swing open, he returned the guard's salute. Each evening, it was a signal to put thoughts of work and cares of the world aside. The remainder of the day belonged to him, his wife, and their friends. During the five or six evenings a week they entertained or had engagements at the Club, George and Rosalyn allowed no unpleasantness to trouble them.

Solutions for Latham's man would have to wait until the morning. He would begin the process by having his receptionist find out what programs existed and let Latham know. The girl was new in town—he had hired her as a favor to someone—but seemed resourceful. If more was needed when he returned from London, he would follow up.

Before turning in his driveway, George stopped to admire the deep veranda extending across his 7,100 square-foot colonial home. He liked the look of the white wooden rockers grouped on each side of the door and reminded himself to sit in one soon. After a deep breath, he exhaled slowly. *Just like I tell people—work hard, and God will reward you.*

Beeping the car horn twice to let Rosalyn know he was home, George then went directly to the wine cellar. On his way down the stairs, he hummed his football fight song. Choosing a wine for each course took only a few minutes because he studied the *Wine Enthusiast.* That night he wanted to surprise his guests with a discovery from Babcock, a new California winery. Running up the stairs with four bottles, he decided to send a server down for the rest.

Rosalyn stood in front of the refrigerator talking to the caterer. She was dressed the way George liked: a navy and white St. John knit with her blond hair pulled back into a smooth bun and fastened with a diamond clasp. He shook his head. *Cost me a fortune but worth it.* The style was perfect for her— it narrowed her hips and flattened her stomach— making her look younger than fifty-six.

She blew a kiss and waved a few fingers, as he approached. "Hi, T, everything's on schedule. Raquel's serving and cleaning up. You decanting the wines?"

George nodded, set the bottles on the counter, and turned away to gather the ingredients for his special pomegranate martinis.

7

MATT AWOKE FROM HIS LIGHT SLEEP TO AN IDEA: THEY would sell Lillie's car—that would bring seven or eight hundred—and have a yard sale. They would get rid of everything they could do without. Except his father's rifle.

Lillie waited at the kitchen table for Beth. The smoke and heat from cooking supper drifted about. Looking up at the lace curtains—limp with the weight of dust and grease—she fussed at herself for not having washed them recently. She hadn't considered their practicality for a kitchen when she chose them. But even if she had, this room was her sanctuary, and she loved the way they framed the pink-tinged peach tree beyond the sink and the graceful limbs of the hickory tree over the table. And they softened the stark metal block of the electric stove behind her.

Beth dashed into the kitchen and leaned over the honey-colored maple table, before raising an eyebrow at her mother. "Notebook paper. That's all we've got, Mama?"

Lillie turned the palm of her hand to her daughter. "That's it. Tape four together. The sign'll be big enough."

Beth's thick chestnut-colored hair fell over her eyes. The fourteen-year-old dropped her head forward and—with a jerk of her neck—flipped the wavy hair to her back. "But we need *two* signs."

Her mother nodded. "Right. One at the end of the driveway and one by the highway." Lillie slipped a red felt marker between Beth's fingers. "Okay, darling, go ahead and print. Garage Sale. Saturday. 152 Hill Road."

Beth allowed the marker to fall to the table. "We don't have a garage." She whirled around to face her mother. "*Why* do we have to do this?"

Lillie struggled to tape four pieces of paper together. Looking up for help, she saw anxiety on her daughter's face and softened her tone. "Daddy thinks we need to. I agree with him."

Placing hands on her hips, Beth stepped back from the table. "*What,* Mama? *What* will you sell?"

Although Lillie sighed inwardly with frustration, she tried to hide it when she wrapped her arms around her daughter. Since the two were the same height, she could look directly into Beth's eyes. "I'm sorry, darling. Sometimes, I forget you worry, too. But Daddy is, we're, sure of what we're doing." Lillie tried to sound casual and light-hearted. "We're just cleaning out—selling things we don't need. Knickknacks, extra set of sheets, that lamp in my bedroom. Pots I don't use. Old clothes."

Beth wrenched away from her mother's embrace, a look of horror on her face. "*All* your clothes are old. And you need them!" She looked away and whispered, "You want mine, Mama?"

The pain that arose in her chest made Lillie certain that her heart had split in two. "Bless you, no. Please, please, don't worry. We'll be all right."

BETH NAILED ONE OF THE FLIMSY SIGNS TO THE telephone pole at the foot of the driveway and watched it swing from side to side. Imagining it was shivering, she pounded the nail as hard as she could, while shouting, "Don't be a baby!" Tears streamed down her face. She threw the hammer to the ground, sank down beside it, and wiped her cheeks with the bottom of her T-shirt. When a car passed, the driver waved and beeped, causing her to jump up and head out to the highway with the other sign.

On the way, she created a plan for helping her parents and described it aloud. "Okay. Hurry home from school to help Mama with the children. Get house cleaning and babysitting jobs. Give her the money. Sit and talk to Daddy to keep his mind off the pain. Jump up when he asks for something without saying, 'Wait a minute.' Don't talk back when he's irritable and fusses at me." She spotted the telephone pole on the corner and pushed aside the wild yellow rosebush to hang the second sign. Then she stood and looked toward her home.

LILLIE AND BETH HAD TO PUT DOWN THE HEAVY WOODEN kitchen table three times before reaching the mimosa tree in the front yard. There they set it beside a battered coffee table they had brought from the shed. Lillie spread her quilt with the brown and red leaf design over the larger table and arranged household items on it. Beside them, she placed two carefully folded stacks of clothes. On the coffee table, she lined up tools that had belonged to Matt's father and grandfather.

"Mama, we should put the tables over there." Beth pointed to the corner of the yard nearer the road. "How about under the hickory?"

Lillie nodded. "Thank you, honey. Now go on back to the house and do your homework. I know you're behind."

Beth spun around. "Wait a minute. What about price tags?"

Lillie shook her head. "I'm going to let them make me an offer. Don't have the slightest idea what to charge. Now, go on."

Beth didn't move. "Mama, what about your anniversary trip? You're not going to use *that* money, are you?"

She gave Beth a little shove. "Go! We'll get our trip." Lillie tried to tell her daughter the truth and sound confident at the same time. But with that answer, she edged up close to a lie.

Lillie's thoughts turned to her tenth wedding anniversary, when she, Matt, and Beth had been holding hands and dancing in the living room. Beth was eight years old. Matt let go of Beth's hand and put his arms around Lillie. Lightly brushing her lips with his, he said he wanted to take her someplace special on their twentieth.

For half an hour, the three talked about places they had seen in *National Geographic* until Matt stopped them, insisting it was Lillie's decision alone. She remembered blurting it out. "Drive across the country in a motor home. And go to Mount Rushmore." Then she had pointed to Matt. "You want to see the Grand Canyon. Let's go to both." Matt had run outside into the dark of the shed and brought back a bucket. After carefully washing it, they placed it in the bottom of their closet. Lillie and Matt each took a dollar from their wallets and tossed them in. Beth added two nickels from her dresser drawer.

When the bucket was full, Lillie had deposited the money in a savings account at the bank. The bucket had been emptied five times during the previous six years. The last statement had read $830.62. But Lillie had a feeling the account wouldn't last much longer.

Straightening the quilt on the table one last time, Lillie—feeling satisfied with her display—sat down and looked at the clock she had placed in the middle of the table. It was 8:00 a. m.,still time to catch the early risers.

The day looked perfect for a yard sale: the sky Lillie's favorite blue,what her grandmother had called a "robin-egg sky." A soft, warm breeze wound through lacy mimosa branches above her. Her grandmother had told her that mimosa branches were like the wings of the angel that sheltered her. That was why she had insisted on putting the tables under them.

It was nine-twenty when the third customer pulled into the driveway. The woman lifted the iron Dutch oven and set it aside. Then she turned to the stack of Lillie's clothes. She picked up the neatly folded pink sweater on top and held it by its shoulders. With an expression of disdain, she looked at the sweater, and then glanced at Lillie, before lifting her little fingers and dropping it. Each item of clothing endured the same scrutiny and ended up in the same heap. Finally, she paid Lillie three dollars for the Dutch oven and left. Remaining motionless until she drove away, Lillie sprang from her chair faster than she realized she was able and rummaged through the clothes until she found the sweater. She tugged and pulled the tight sleeves over her sweaty arms until she got it on. Then she sat down and waited.

Two more cars stopped. Lillie stayed seated while the women glanced at the items on the table and left. She leaned back on two legs of the straight wooden chair,hoping it would hold her,and rocked. Heat was settling in. The mimosa branches were still.

She tried to lift her mood by humming any tune that came to her mind, but thoughts of failures intervened. Her biggest one,she believed,was in trying to get a daycare license six years before. Matt had tried to discourage her from that. "Why bother?" he had said. "You don't need one unless you keep six children."

She had almost jumped on him. "I'll tell you why. This is my work, and I'm good at it. I want a paper to hang on the wall saying I've accomplished something."

The visit from the state inspector had gone wrong from the moment the woman stepped across Lillie's front threshold. "Mrs. Bradfurd, you have five children here, and you're only allowed *four* without a license. One has to go today!" With pen and pad in hand, during the next hour, she scrutinized the house and yard, listing the changes needed for it to qualify as a state-certified daycare setting. The most expensive was an automatic sprinkler system. Before the woman had left, Lillie knew it was hopeless.

Flies buzzed around her ears. She struck at them. *It was silly to try to get it. As foolish as dreaming of going to college. Shoot! I'm lucky I graduated from high school.*

Turning her attention back to the road, Lillie watched two young women climb down from a vehicle that resembled a shiny yellow tank. They were wearing similar sundresses and large pastel-colored stone necklaces and bracelets. Unable to imagine having anything they would want, she smiled and greeted them but remained seated.

The women surprised Lillie with their methodical examination as they picked up each of the tiny colored glass vases and the ceramic items, turning them over to read the stamp on the bottom. After putting aside a vase, ceramic shoe, and four of Grandad's tools, they turned their attention to the brown and red leaf quilt covering the table.

Lillie took a step back and shook her head. Her voice cracked. "Oh, no. It's not for sale. My grandmother made it for me."

The shorter woman slipped her purse from her shoulder and took out four twenties. "I'll give you seventy-five dollars."

Lillie was stuck. That amount of money could buy a lot of groceries. She folded the quilt and held it against her chest before handing it to the woman. "Take good care of it."

As they drove away, Lillie turned her gaze—eyes filled with tears—to the mimosa branches. *Tell Grandma I'm sorry.*

AFTER DRYING THE LAST PLATE FROM SUPPER AND putting it in the cabinet, Beth stood ready to open the screen door before calling out. "Going to see a neighbor, Mama. Back by dark." Her mother's voice reached her as she rounded the corner by the fig tree. "What about Heather?" Pretending she didn't hear, Beth ran, turning left out the driveway. *Huh. What about Heather? I don't have money for a movie.*

One of her rubber flip-flops slipped off, causing her to stumble, and then slow to a walk. She wondered whether her mother would encourage her to go out on Saturday nights with her best friend if she knew Heather had started smoking pot on her fourteenth birthday. Three other girls had been with them, and when Beth was the only one to refuse the marijuana, Heather had pushed. "Oh, come on, you baby. This is cool! Makes you feel great." Beth had taken two puffs, pretending to like it, but was determined not to do it again. *Daddy would* kill *me if he found out.* She sighed, feeling tears well up. *Will he even be here?*

Beth was on her way to the Johnsons' house. She had met the two women—old enough to be her mother and her grandmother—at another neighbor's when she had stopped by after her father's surgery to wish them a happy Thanksgiving. Mrs. Johnson and her daughter, Miss Caroline, asked her to visit and let them know how her father was doing. She liked their upbeat nature, their laughter and joy, so much that she found herself dropping by their house once a week or so, staying between ten minutes and an hour. She didn't know why she hadn't told her parents about them, but now it seemed important that she not.

The small house came into view at the point where the road turned downhill. It looked like a building from an earlier time—unpainted wood, square with four rooms and a porch along the front. The back rested on the slope of a hill and the two front corners on columns of bricks. Double clothes lines that bordered the two sides were filled most days with the wet clothes of their customers. At each end of the lines, the ladies had planted hydrangea bushes.

As usual, the front door was wide open. Just beyond it, Mrs. Johnson stood before her ironing board in the middle of the living room. Her blond and gray hair flew about her head in large, loose curls. "Hey there, girl!" she called out as Beth climbed the creaking wooden steps.

Beth grinned in response to the half-smile, half-laughter of the woman's greeting.

Across from Mrs. Johnson, standing in front of her own board, was Miss Caroline. Except for the older woman's thicker waist, extra wrinkles, and grayer hair, they were identical. Glancing from woman to woman, Beth imagined the daughter springing, fully grown, like a Greek goddess, from her mother's head. She hoped that had happened, so they could go on forever, each daughter in her maturity bringing forth another person just like Mrs. Johnson.

At the end of the boards, a table was piled with small tight rolls of damp clothes, each awaiting its turn to be tended and smoothed by the women and their irons. A fan whirred from the corner of the room, turning first to mother, and then to daughter, cooling them by air and sound. Each time Beth visited, the two stood in the same positions, talking and ironing, their faces gleaming with a light covering of sweat.

"Hey there, ma'am." Beth stopped just inside the door. She wanted to rush in and say, I need to talk to you, but other words came. "I, well." She paused and smiled. "I came to say hello. And see how you both were doing."

"Have you lost weight?" Mrs. Johnson asked. "It's been two weeks since we've seen you. Tell us what's happening, darling."

Beth responded to the question in a voice like a song; it climbed the scale, and then dropped, continuing up and down, cheerfully, casually, imparting no distress. "I'm fine. School is good. Nothing new." Smelling starch in the steam drifting upward, Beth picked up a clothes hangar and reached for the finished shirt that Mrs. Johnson lifted from her board.

Beth buttoned the shirt, struggling some with the small buttons, and then stood with hands behind her, squeezing them together, pinching the area between thumb and forefinger, trying to force herself to say it. *Tell them what's happening at home. Ask what to do. Tell them.* Several times, words—ready to come—sank back into her.

Miss Caroline set down her iron. "Come, honey, I want you to try the pound cake I made this morning. Tell me whether it's any good."

The living room windows darkened. Beth said goodbye and went down the creaky front steps. At the edge of the yard, she stopped and listened to the strong, happy laughter. Noticing an opening in the shrubs surrounding the area under the front porch, she peeked in. It was hard-packed dirt without walls or lattices but looked warm and safe. *If I just had a sleeping bag.*

8

WRAPPED IN A WARM BLANKET AND SITTING IN A comfortable chair in the orthopedist's exam room, Matt worried that it had been foolish to choose the physician Dr. Ramsey had recommended for a second opinion. So far, the experience had been different from that in Ramsey's office, but if the two were friends, wouldn't Dr. Carlisle just back him up?

When the door opened, his concerns disappeared. Dr. Carlisle was pleasant, short, slightly plump, about the same age as Dr. Latham, and as different from Ramsey as anybody could be. Matt took to him immediately.

After completing the examination, the doctor patted Matt on the shoulder and asked him to come into his office.

As he stepped across the threshold, Matt stopped. Surprised by the spaciousness and elegance of the office, he was suddenly uncomfortable—not sure how he should behave. He looked down and wondered whether his shoes were clean enough.

Dr. Carlisle left the slender curved wooden desk and escorted Matt to a grouping of dark green leather chairs and two matching ottomans. "Sit down and put your feet up," the doctor said. When Matt bent over to untie his laces, the doctor waved his hand, no. Separating the desk and chairs was a five-foot-long aquarium filled with orange, blue and multicolored fish.

Even the doctor's formal voice was warm. "I'm not here to second-guess Dr. Ramsey, but I will give you advice on a course of action. First, I want to hear about everything that's happened since the appearance of your pains. Take your time."

While Matt told his story, he heard himself talking faster and faster and realized how excited he was. This doctor acted like he understood and could help him. When he reached the part about the leak, Dr. Carlisle asked him to slow down and be very specific.

"The day I got home from the hospital, my wife called Dr. Ramsey's office and told his nurse my bandage was wet, and I felt like I had the flu. She said I probably did and should take some Tylenol. Said the wet bandage might be from sweat."

Dr. Carlisle raised his eyebrows.

"But it didn't help. My head was killing me. My wife called the next day and the next, and the nurse kept saying the same thing. The fourth day, Lillie half-dragged me to the car, laid me in the back seat, and drove to the office. Dr. Ramsey had left for vacation, and it was almost five o'clock, so the nurse sent us to the emergency room. The doctor there said I had a hole in my spinal column and needed surgery right then."

Dr. Carlisle stopped writing and laid his hand on Matt's forearm. "So, you had a spinal leak *four* days?"

Matt nodded. "Yes, sir. And that was *some* headache!"

When Matt's story reached the present, the doctor spoke softly. "I'm sorry for all you've been through. I know you're hurting. It's obvious from the way you hold your body. And the problem can be seen right here." He lifted an X-ray and pointed to a dark space on the lower part of the spinal column. "This MRI you had today shows it more clearly than your previous one. You have a discitis in the area where they operated—a complication from your surgery."

Matt stared at the fish tank. Taking his handkerchief from his pocket, he wiped his face and neck slowly and deliberately to give himself time to decide what to say. He wanted to make certain he understood the whole situation before he left. Finally, he started with the most obvious question. "How did that happen?"

The doctor shook his head. "We don't know what's causing the inflammation. It could be the result of an old infection that finally resolved itself. *Or* trauma from your two surgeries. Maybe a current infection or your diabetes." He closed Matt's chart. "Diabetics always have a harder time during the post-op period. We expect that. Now, my nurse will draw some blood, and that'll tell us whether you have an infection. Meantime, we'll start treating the inflammation. Once the lab results are back, I'll send my report to Dr. Ramsey, and you'll have a follow-up visit with him. Any questions?"

"Nobody said my diabetes would cause problems."

"Oh, yes. Makes you slower to heal, for one thing."

There was a question Matt had wanted to ask from the moment he met Dr. Carlisle. Unsure why he hesitated, he had waited as long as he could. When he spoke, he barely recognized his own voice. "Can I be *your* patient?"

"No, I'm sorry." The doctor reacted without meeting Matt's gaze. "I've been called in for consultation only. You belong to Dr. Ramsey." Then the doctor looked directly at Matt. "You know, I would if I could, but it's not ethical."

Turning back to the aquarium, Matt watched a fish—smaller than the others—dart from one end of the tank to the other. When it reached that end, it banged its mouth into the glass before turning to repeat the journey. *I know what getting nowhere is like, too.*

"How long?" Matt cleared his throat and turned to the doctor. "How long for me to get well?"

Dr. Carlisle hesitated, and then spoke haltingly. "I. Have to say I don't know. Guessing now. But three to six months, minimum." Tapping the pen on the chart in his lap, he faced the aquarium. "Maybe longer."

MATT, AFRAID HIS IRRITATION WOULD SHOW ON HIS FACE, kept his head turned toward the passenger-side window and rolled his eyes. Myra was driving so slowly he could see the tassels on the corn in the field they were passing. Trying to distract himself, he thought of the fresh corn and tomatoes Bobby had brought from his garden. Lillie had made the best corn pudding he had ever tasted.

"Well, what do you think?" Myra asked. It's been two weeks since you started those new pills. Are you better?" She swiveled her head back and forth from the road to Matt. "You must be glad this is about over."

He wanted to say, "I'd be a whole lot better if you sped up," but criticizing Myra wasn't right. She had spent an entire day driving him to Dr. Carlisle's office, and now, she was taking him to see Dr. Ramsey.

But Matt had to admit he had an urge to just be mad at somebody—a doctor, himself, anybody. The anti-inflammatory pills took the edge off, but pain was still the focus of his life—day and night. And it was hard to say that to people who were putting so much effort into helping him get well. Most wanted to see a positive result, and quickly. People got tired of hearing a person complain.

Trying not to look at the speedometer, he nodded. "Yeah, I feel some ease. Think I'm getting better."

"MR. BRADFURD." DR. RAMSEY'S NURSE CALLED MATT'S name and led him to the exam room. After telling him to pull up his shirt and get on the table, she sat down in a chair.

Matt tilted his head in surprise. "You worn out today, huh?"

She shook her head and picked at a loose cuticle on her thumb. "Not really. Doctor wants me to stay with you."

About to ask, "Why?" instead, Matt smiled, as the doctor swung the door open.

The orthopedist thrust a lab report toward Matt. "Here's the result of the blood test. Negative. There's no infection. Just as I thought."

Squinting, Matt read the three lines of the report and handed it back to Dr. Ramsey. He had understood only two words, *negative for.*

Confused and distracted by the doctor's apparent dislike of him, Matt wondered what to do. He got along fairly well with most people. *Maybe if I looked more dignified.* Forcing himself to sit up straighter, he raised his chest and pulled his shoulders back but was able to hold that position only a few seconds before the pain around his waist caused him to hunch over again. He started to ask the doctor what was wrong but wasn't sure that was a good idea. So, he tried another smile, and asked, "Is that good or bad?"

The doctor was flipping through the pages of Matt's chart. "Depends on how you look at it."

Then, for a moment, Matt thought he heard some compassion in the doctor's voice. "There's no bacteria in there—that's good news—but it leaves us with few options. Here's what Dr. Carlisle said: 'Inflammation of unknown origin. Treat with anti-inflammatory medication until resolved.'" Stuffing the report back in the chart, he picked it up and tucked it under his arm. "Take those pills and come back in three months."

As Matt slid off the examination table, he missed the stool and landed hard on his feet. Pain exploded throughout his lower back and his right knee buckled, but he didn't fall. Standing behind the doctor, his face felt hot. He glanced at the nurse, just as she yawned. He took a deep breath before blurting out the words. "I can't wait that long. What about my job?"

Dr. Ramsey faced Matt with narrowed eyes. "Well, maybe we ought to try some *psychiatric* help. Have you considered that?"

Matt was stunned. He wasn't certain he knew *exactly* what the word meant but believed it had something to do with being crazy. "Why would you say that?"

Rather than stepping back, the orthopedist leaned even closer to Matt. "Your insistence that you're having so much pain—that's why. And the insight I got from another conversation with your employer."

"Mr. Hartman?" Matt braced himself against the table. "Wait a minute. What's going on here?"

Pointing a finger toward Matt, the doctor said, "That's what I'd like to know. Let me ask you this. Exactly what did you tell Dr. Latham?"

Holding to the table with one hand, Matt grasped and chair and pulled it toward him. He sat down hard. "That I hurt."

Dr. Ramsey's voice was strained. "Why didn't you come here?"

The nurse got up and left the room, closing the door behind her.

Matt didn't know what to do. Outside this office, he might have cussed the guy, stomped off, or both. But he had never experienced a confrontation like this in a professional setting. Then he wondered whether there was something he had done to cause it and spoke quietly. "I've known Dr. Latham a long time."

The doctor took on the demeanor of a frustrated parent. "Here's what confuses me. Most people have pain and learn to live with it. Your employer's known you a long time and wonders whether this is exaggerated. Is that possible?" The doctor's voice sounded sympathetic. "Matthew, have you just gotten tired of working? Or are you caught with the pain pills? If you are, we can get you off them."

Holding his head in his hands, Matt looked at the floor. "God help me."

Dr. Ramsey stepped back. "Look, Matthew, *I* want to help you." His voice softened. "If you insist you're having so much pain, take more pills. Do those exercises and rest your back."

Before he reached the door, he turned to face Matt again. His voice held an emotion that Matt didn't recognize. "Don't you realize I saved you from being paralyzed? I've worked hard on your case. Now, let's get on with it."

MATT WAS LEANING BACK IN HIS CHAIR, RAISING AND lowering his right leg, and then his left. Although only nine in the morning, he felt waves of hot air pushing through the screen door. They were like his feelings toward Dr. Ramsey, smothering. And he had about as much control over one as he did the other. Then he heard sandals slapping on the front cement steps. His next door neighbor, Nell, called out, as she opened the screen. "The phone's for you, a Mr. Hartman."

Nell went ahead of Matt toward her house. He followed as quickly as he could through the high grass of his yard. When she reached her bed of dahlias, she leaned over and pulled a small weed.

Matt appreciated that. When he and Lillie had given up their phone to save money around the time of the yard sale, he discovered how much privacy he was sacrificing. Nell had made the situation as tolerable as possible. Unless she was in the middle of something in the kitchen, she wandered outside while he talked. And no matter what she heard him say, he knew she wouldn't repeat it.

Matt's throat and chest felt tight. He placed the phone back on its cradle, hoping to slip across Nell's yard without having to talk. As he closed the door, she rose from the flower bed and waved but made no move toward him.

Following the chatter and laughter of the children, Matt found Lillie in the back yard pushing one of the girls in the swing.

He laid his hand on her shoulder and whispered. "I lost my job."

She gave the swing another push before turning to him. "*What* did you say?"

"Mr. Hartman called. My job is gone!"

Lillie grasped both his hands and led him to a brown metal chair. "Sit down before you fall. And start over."

Matt wiped his face with the bottom of his T-shirt. "He claimed he was calling about my insurance, but something in his voice wasn't right. I told him that Dr. Ramsey said he called, but he kept saying he didn't know what I meant."

"Just a minute." Lillie lifted Bella from the swing and carried her to the sand pile where Rachel was playing. She checked the sleeping babies on their pallet in the shade of the hickory tree. Then she dragged over the other chair, placing it so close to Matt that she bumped his knee. Easing herself into it, she asked softly. "What else?"

He said the six months is up, and the company won't pay our half of the health insurance anymore. If I want to keep it—can you believe that? If I *want* to keep it?—I have to pay the whole $528.00."

Lillie cried out. "Oh, dear Lord." She sat back and rocked slightly in the metal chair a minute or two. Then she turned to him. "Well, we'll try."

Matt put hands in his pockets and pulled them inside out. "Yeah, abracadabra. Here's the money, Lillie. You see it?"

9

THE SPEAKER PHONE RELEASED A HIGH-PITCHED NOISE, causing Jim Hartman to jump. "What?" His secretary leaned forward and pressed a button that stopped the squeal. "Good, Tibby. Now, type that up. Spell it out. The company is no longer responsible for *any portion* of his health insurance." Jim turned away from her. "Be sure to note you were a witness. If he wants insurance, he buys a COBRA and pays the entire amount, available for eighteen months, and then he finds his own policy. Get that in the mail today." As the woman reached the door, Jim said, "And thank you."

Thank you, thank you. That's what they want down here, isn't it? I'm being polite. I am trying!

When Jim heard the click, click, he realized he was hitting his pen against the metal desk. *Stupid bastard, Ramsey.* He slammed the pen down and grabbed the phone. *I'm going to ask why he told Bradfurd about my calls. Is he a fucking idiot? Now my secretary knows.*

Jim stood and pushed his desk chair back so hard that it bumped against the lab window. *Damn!* He jerked the chair forward. *You idiots are causing me to destroy what I've made.*

He peered down into the lab. *What's wrong with you fuckers? Business is the lifeblood of this country and creates everything we have.* Shaking his head, he picked up the *Central Carolina Business Journal* from his desk and flipped it to the floor. *My sacrifice makes that happen. I live in this nowhere place— frugally. Put it all back into this company. Give up a lot of family life. And you—*Jim spread his arms toward the lab workers—*you're easily replaced. Thousands are waiting at the borders to take your jobs. I could move to Mexico—anywhere, China!— and make twice what I do now. Why don't you appreciate me?*

"Ow!" Feeling a sharp pain in his right jaw, Jim pressed his fingers against it and massaged the area in front of his ear. He had experienced this pain, intermittently, since he was sixteen. He hadn't worried about it, because it never lasted more than an hour or so.

Sitting down in the stiff chair, Jim propped his elbows on his desk and rested his head in his hands. *I never do enough. Never. What do they want?* He closed his eyes and saw his father sitting to his right at the dining table. To his left sat his mother, with her unchanging smile and eyes focused on the tablecloth. Across from him, brother Max's halo glowed. The same scene every evening from six to seven-thirty for twelve years.

Jim pressed his hands against his ears, continuing to massage his jaw with the heel of his palm. His father's words rang out. "What did you accomplish today? Your grades are low. Stop going out with those friends—they don't take school seriously. Follow your brother's example." Hunching over and turning his head to the left, Jim tried to avoid the words striking him. "You weren't accepted by the University. You'll have to go to State. How do you think a professor feels when his son is an academic failure?"

Jim smacked his fist on the desk and yelled at his absent father. "Nothing I ever do makes you happy, does it? What about my work? The money I make? Oh, no. A businessman is nobody compared to a nationally recognized chairman of a history department!"

Jerking the file drawer open, Jim pulled out a folder labeled Private, and spread the contents on his desk. Pushing aside Grand Circle Travel brochures and pictures of thirty-fivefoot motor boats, Jim picked up an architect's drawings of two houses. The one on top was a 6,000 squarefoot Tudor planned for Ann Arbor Grove, and the other a three-bedroom cabin for a lot already purchased on the lake in Charlevoix. As Jim held them up, he noticed a slight tremor in his hand, but continued talking to his father. "Look, you asshole! You'll work until you're seventy-five and never have anything like this. Why can't you give me *some* credit?"

The buzzing of his phone caused him to drop the plans. Ray. Slumping in his chair, he tried to sound friendly, though he didn't feel like talking to his partner in New York. Discussions between them were awkward because they didn't have the same goals for the business. As far as Jim was concerned, Ray was too casual about making money. Having a trust fund could do that to a person, Jim thought.

"Ray, my man, how're we doing? Made any more contacts?"

His partner sounded irritated. "Don't push. I'm working hard."

Wanting to say, "Hell, no, you're not," Jim didn't. "I know, I know. But I have to deal with the hard part of our business—the employee crap." Jim heard a sigh. "Here's one from the Chamber meeting yesterday: McDonald's hired this scrawny sixty-eight-year-old woman to wipe tables and clean up in the back. She fell over a crate and broke her shoulder. Turns out she had osteoporosis, and the fucker wouldn't heal. Think about the bucks that cost them, man."

Ray made some vague response about there being nothing one could do about that.

Jim yelled. "Sure there is! Get rid of them when they turn forty *before* their bodies fall apart."

"You're crazy! How?"

"All kinds of ways. Switch their hours around. Don't give time off when they want it. Insist on overtime work. Reduce benefits. A big supermarket chain did that and it worked! Remember, union's weak down here. And...Yeah, I'm busy, too. Later."

Slipping a cigar out of its box, Jim clipped off the end and lit it. Being careful not to disturb the end-of-month numbers he was working on, he leaned back in his hard chair, put his feet up on the desk, and drew deeply. His conversation with Bradfurd, and his father's attempts to make him feel like a failure, swirled about like his great rings of smoke.

Dropping his feet to the floor, Jim slapped the surface of his desk. *Okay, people. You need to know this. No one will interfere with my plans. Buddy Ray, you need to get off your ass and work harder. Dear old Dad, stay out of my life. And you, Matt Bradfurd, will not suck my company dry with your benefits and claims. I created this company and it'll pay off big. Don't mess with me!*

With a jerk of his head to the left, he picked up the phone to call his secretary. "Tibby, type up a dismissal summary for Matthew Bradfurd. No. Not dismissal. Say this. 'Employee resigned. Reason for leaving, unclear. Unsure about work motivation. Some question of mental stability.'"

10

George Russell hadn't been himself since returning from London four weeks before. His energy and enthusiasm were gone. He hadn't once saluted the guard at his gate. Hadn't laughed with the boys at the Club or slapped them on the back. At the end of dinner, his wine glass was half-full.

Even Rosalyn, who noticed little about him, had asked if he felt well.

"Jet lag," he replied, but her question had started him thinking: the word that kept coming to him was "shabby."

Sitting in the straight-backed wooden chair to the left of the First Presbyterian church altar, George looked up at the one stained glass window and shrugged. He had been so proud of this church until he realized it was a canvas tent compared to Saint Paul's Cathedral, his own house, with its expensive antiques and marble, a tarted-up barn beside the crystal chandeliers, satins, and *true* antiques of Buckingham Palace.

He—George touched the smooth fabric of his Zegna suit—was nothing to brag about either, his fabric a tad bright. Remembering the elegance of those rushing along the grand streets of London made him want to hide. Each trip along King Street had made him feel less and less significant. Although people referred to him as Mr. Cross Hill, George realized he wasn't the leader of a real city, just a rube from a small town. He was fifty-six years old and still a hick.

Facing the congregants from his place of honor, George saw that he wasn't the only person ready to leave. Several people shifting in their seats, women looking through their purses, men checking their phones—one clipping his nails! An old man dozed in the second row.

In the front row, Roz whispered to the woman beside her. Glancing at the minister, George wondered why a man trained to work with people couldn't see what was right in front of his face. *We're bored stiff, you idiot!*

When the preacher called his name, George was shaken out of his gloom. Sucking in his stomach, he stood and winked at Roz. As he held the plaque with his name on it that would be placed beside the entrance of the new building, he wanted to sail it like a Frisbee across the heads of the congregants.

Instead, he smiled, when the minister laid a hand on his shoulder. "George, almost single-handedly, you have raised the money for our new fellowship building, furthering God's work more than any other person in this community. You have enough stars in your crown to take you through eternity."

FRIDAY BEFORE MEMORIAL DAY WAS THE DAY GEORGE gave his accountants and their secretaries the afternoon off to thank them for their work during tax season. In the past, he had invited them all to the Club for lunch, but the five accountants had sat together talking about business, leaving the women to entertain themselves. So, for the past two years, each accountant had taken his own secretary to a restaurant, while George took the receptionist and his secretary, Mrs. Barbee, to the Club. He had enjoyed the treat in the past. Today he dreaded it.

George made streaks on the inside of the windshield as he leaned forward and wiped it with his handkerchief, gripping the steering wheel with his other hand. The wipers struggled in their losing battle against the rain and he was able to see no more than five feet ahead. He kept his eyes focused on the yellow line. All he could think of was that the Club had no valet service at lunch, he would have to sit for two hours in a drafty dining room with wet pants and feet, and the air conditioning would be on no matter what the outside temperature. "Bad start to a useless day," he grumbled.

He went up the back hallway and headed directly to the reception room. When he entered, Emily looked up from her desk and smiled. George paused, realizing he hadn't noticed how pretty his new receptionist was. Her body was full and voluptuous, as asset when working with older male clients. She was about twenty-five, fairly intelligent, mature, with an AA degree in office management.

"Good morning, Emily. You remember our lunch today?"

Jumping up from her chair, the receptionist rushed over and rested her hand on his shoulder. "Let me take your coat, Mr. Russell."

George pulled his coat closer to his chest and sniffed. *Nice perfume.* "You probably know Mrs. Barbee won't be able to join us for lunch. Her husband's recovering from gallbladder surgery. If you'd rather, we could postpone it."

She looked up, shaking her head, no. A strand of curly hair dropped in front of her left ear. George noticed how blue her eyes were.

"I've been looking forward to it all week."

Nodding, George turned away toward his office.

In the center of George's desk, lay the neatly written schedule Mrs. Barbee had prepared for his day. At the bottom, she had written, "Dr. Latham saw your picture in the newspaper about the dedication of the new building. He sent his congratulations and asked if you found help for Matt Bradfurd."

George dropped the schedule. Picking up his memo pad, he wrote: "Ask Emily what she found for Bradfurd. Call Latham. Visit Roy Barbee on way home." Then he tore off the sheet and slipped it into his jacket pocket.

THE FIREPLACE IN THE CLUB DINING ROOM WASN'T LIT, but George had chosen a table beside it, hoping just the idea of a fire would make him warmer. He and Emily were the only people at that end of the sparsely populated room.

She set down her wine glass. "Umm, Mr. Russell, I've never had such delicious wine. Will you tell me about it?"

Although his socks and the lower part of his pants were damp, George felt cheerful and relaxed, excited to be pleasing this girl. She was interested in what he had to say and seemed to love his sense of humor. He held up his wine glass. "Well, my dear, this is a 1997 California Merlot. Can't go wrong with a ninety-seven from a good wine maker—it was the vintage of the century. See what flavors you can taste in it." He cautioned, "Sip slowly, now."

Emily licked her lips, took a sip, and then licked them again more slowly. "Umm, blackberry? Maybe, some mocha?"

"You have a sophisticated palate." Swirling the red wine in its glass, he continued. "Now, you see the color? Deep and rich. *Wine Enthusiast* gave it a rating of ninety-three." He lifted his chin and index finger to signal the waiter. "Let's try something different."

After the waiter cleared their plates, Emily leaned forward, resting both elbows on the white tablecloth. Since the top buttons of her blouse were undone, it folded back, exposing a rose tattoo about the size of a silver dollar on her left breast.

A few seconds after George began describing the second bottle, he realized he was staring at Emily's breast. He sat up straighter, trying to keep his eyes focused on her face. She asked what vineyard had produced the grapes, but he couldn't remember because he was trying to decide whether the rose was a light red or an intense pink. Hearing himself mumble, "Oh, probably Santa Rita," he wondered why he had thought of Emily as a girl. She was a woman—beautiful, with large rounded breasts and soft full lips.

Then George noticed Emily raise her right eyebrow, shift in her chair, and cross her legs. He saw the long slim legs for the first time. Just as he decided the rose was pink, he felt Emily's leg touch his and warmth rise to his face.

"I was going shopping this afternoon, Mr. Russell, but it's raining too hard." Her breasts rested on the table. "Now I'll be bored. Do you have plans?"

THEY LEFT EMILY'S CAR AT THE FAR EDGE OF THE hardware store parking lot and drove together to Clement, the town where she used to live. As water splashed up from the flooded street, covering the windshield, momentarily George couldn't see ahead. When Emily lowered her window and told him to turn right, George turned left.

"Are you okay, Mr. Russell?"

Although he nodded and said "Of course," he wasn't certain. Feeling light-headed and unfocused, he doubted that he could add a column of numbers if he had to.

When he pulled his Mercedes under the overhang in front of the Piedmont Motel, Emily laid her hand on his arm. "Mr. Russell, you may want to use your business credit card when you pay for the room. That way the charge won't show on your personal account."

Fastening the top button of his raincoat and hoping the clerk wouldn't notice he was wearing a suit and tie, George said, "Exactly."

"And you don't have to register with your home phone and address."

He turned his head and looked into her steady blue eyes. "Umm. Yes."

George stumbled at the threshold of the motel room. *What am I doing here?* For a moment, he was startled to see a young woman standing beside him instead of his wife. *Will I know what to do next?*

Emily tugged the tight rain coat from George's shoulders, hung it in the closet and turned to face him. Without speaking, she slowly unbuttoned her blouse and wiggled out of her skirt, allowing it to fall to her ankles. Feeling a surge of energy, George picked her up, placed his cheek against the rose, and then tossed her on the bed.

THE HOT WATER FROM THE SHOWER STUNG GEORGE'S neck. His groin throbbed. Emily stepped in and pressed her body against his.

"Better make sure you wash off my lipstick and perfume." She nuzzled his chest and stroked his hips. "Or maybe I should put more on you."

George shook himself free. "No, no. Have to get home." He shuddered. "I liked it. But it's late." *What else? Dry hair. Brush teeth. Change clothes before Roz sees me. Shred motel receipt.*

Emily's car waited in the twilight among the large puddles in the parking lot. George turned off his car engine and kept his gaze ahead. He reached for her hand and fumbled with her fingers. "I don't know what to say." Peeking sideways, he continued. "Should I apologize? You do know I'm married, don't you?" Then—all his confusion gone—George felt like himself for the first time that afternoon, speaking with certainty. "We have to forget about this."

GEORGE'S SATURDAY MORNING GOLF GAME WAS cancelled because of the soggy course, and the party at the Club that evening broke up by nine. He would, ordinarily, have been disappointed but, instead he felt relieved. Conversations had been difficult. In the middle of a sentence, his thoughts drifted to a question: *did I do that?* Saturday night, he dreamed he was lying beside Emily, his hand following the curve of her naked body from her shoulder down past her thigh.

Sunday morning, he prayed. When the minister called for a moment of silence, George confessed to God that he had betrayed his wife, and he begged forgiveness. When the congregation sang the hymn that signaled an end to prayer, George kept his head bowed and lips pressed tightly together. He told God he had taken advantage of a woman younger than his own daughters and that she was an employee—an inexcusable act of betrayal toward his business. He confessed to being a hypocrite. If his accountants had done that, he would have fired them on the spot. George raised his head. *I could get sued!*

Sunday afternoon, George stood beside Rosalyn at the wedding of a friend's son. As the young couple spoke their vows, he grasped his wife's hand, leaned over, and kissed her cheek. During the reception, he stayed by her side. He winked at her and she laughed. He twirled her about the dance floor and held her against his body when the music ended. After toasting the newlyweds, he raised his glass to his own marriage of thirty-four years and was grateful that Roz didn't criticize him for slurring his words.

GEORGE CLIMBED THE BACK STAIRS TO HIS OFFICE Monday morning. He felt tired and wondered if he was coming down with something. He praised himself at the end of his second appointment for not having thought of Emily. While working with his third client, he decided to make sure she was all right. Instead of following his usual custom of saying goodbye to his client at the door of his office, he accompanied him to the reception area. When George closed the front door behind the man, he caught Emily's eye. She blew a kiss and mouthed, "I miss you." Although he tried not to, George grinned before ducking into the hallway that led to his office.

At the end of the day, Mrs. Barbee buzzed to tell George that she was going home. He waited exactly ten minutes before opening the door to the reception area. Emily smiled, winked, and whispered, "I had a wonderful time. I thought of you all weekend."

Nodding, George tried not to look down at the rose peeking from behind her blouse lapel.

Emily moved closer, resting her left breast against his arm. "Let's do it again."

Shivering, George took a step back. "Emily, I'm a Christian."

Tears welled up and she grasped his hand. "Just one more time."

They met at one o'clock on Saturday in the same motel as before. And the next Saturday. And the next.

11

LILLIE PUSHED THE WINDOW SASH UP AS FAR AS IT WOULD go. The branches of the hickory outside had begun to stir slightly, and she hoped to entice the little breeze to join her in the kitchen. Turning back to the hot stove, she poured the heavy pot of beans into her biggest bowl, and then set it on the table under the window to cool before calling Matt and Beth to supper.

Matt bit into the cornbread a second time and wrinkled his brow. "Tastes different tonight."

"Couldn't fool you, could I?" Lillie shrugged. "Well, I'm sorry, but we don't have milk or eggs. I thought it would taste all right without them."

Beth spoke quickly. "You make good pintos, Mama."

"I'm glad of that! It's about all we've got to eat."

As soon as she heard her words, Lillie was appalled. She hated worrying Beth, and Matt was defensive, taking it as criticism anytime she referred to their money situation. She glanced at him, but he didn't look up.

After the dishes were washed and Beth had gone to her room to study for an algebra exam, Lillie took the bills from a cabinet drawer and piled them in the middle of the kitchen table. Then she went to the bedroom to get Matt.

"Come on, we have to look at the bills and figure out how we're going to live. Putting it off won't fix anything."

Matt threw his legs over the side of the bed and unplugged the heating pad tied around his waist. "I don't know what you expect me to do," he growled, following her out to the kitchen.

Lillie softened her tone. "Now, don't get your feelings hurt and don't act hateful. This is not your fault. But I need to know how much money I can spend for food. Let's just sit down here and look."

Roughly pushing the pile to one side of the table, Matt sorted the bills into groups. "All right, here. Medical's $528 a month for COBRA insurance, plus these co-pays we owe the doctor. Car, seventy-five for the payment, plus insurance and gas." The words rushed out of him. "Water, light bill, heating oil. Property tax, your self-employment tax. Then there's food and Beth and God only knows what else." He flipped a bill across the table bouncing it against the wall and raised his voice to just below a shout.

"You bring in about two hundred-fifty dollars a week. What's the point of this? We can't pay these. And who do you think will sit and wait? Insurance people? Utility companies? Grocery store?"

Lillie wanted to jump up from the table and storm out of the room, but felt an urgent need to calm Matt. "It's all right. Don't worry." She patted his hand while she reached for the envelope that had landed on the floor. "Let's try it this way—pay health insurance, taxes, part of the utilities. Won't that leave a little for food?"

He threw up his hands and glowered at her. "What about the others?"

"I'll call them and describe the situation."

Matt slammed his fist on the table. "Lillie, the damn government will throw us in jail or take the house if we don't pay our property tax." Then he laid his hand on her arm. "Sorry. I know I failed you. Let me go back to bed. Maybe I'll trap rabbits and possums to eat—like Grandad did."

BETH SAT ON HER BED HUNCHED OVER THE ALGEBRA book. It was the only place to sit in her bedroom. The wooden desk chair had come apart where one of the legs joined the seat. She didn't know how to fix it but had no intention of asking her mother or father to do one more thing—nothing large or small.

To think she couldn't ask something of her father—her best buddy when she was a young girl—was a new experience for Beth. They had done so many things together, like those walks in the woods when he tried to teach her about trees, the trips to see his silent friend Little Red, and all Grandad's stories.

With elbows propped on her thighs, she pressed her hands against her ears and read the formulas over and over in an attempt to memorize them. She pushed harder against her ears, trying to block her father's words. "Then there's food and Beth.... The damn government will take our house . . . Sweat rose on her face. Throwing the book aside, she turned toward to the window and looked up at the night sky. *Please tell them to stop arguing—to just shut up!* Although the stars didn't answer, she stared at them until she staggered backward and fell onto the bed.

Beth awoke shivering in the early morning. She was still on top the bedding. Her algebra book lay on the floor where it had landed. The only sound she heard was a cardinal's whistling in the dogwood tree just outside.

She pulled the spread over her and wondered what to do. Her earlier plans to help financially hadn't gone far. She had found some babysitting but hadn't known where to look for housecleaning jobs. The neighbors did their own work. Then she remembered something her homeroom teacher had told the class at the beginning of the year: they should come to her if they had a problem—*any* problem.

Once out of bed, she wriggled into one of the three skirts that still fit and picked up the small round mirror from the top of her dresser. She took a deep breath, sucked in her stomach, and held the mirror out to the side. *Yuck. Tight.* Then she held the mirror in front of her. Two buttons on her blouse pulled open across her breasts. *Maybe they'll think I'm sexy. Cool.* She looked down at the size nine shoes her mother and father had given her for her fifteenth birthday and laughed. *No, not sexy.*

Laying the mirror down with a sigh, Beth grabbed her hair brush and began counting. When she was seven years old, her father had told her that her hair looked like a chestnut-colored ocean with the sun shining on it. Since then, fifty strokes every morning had become a ritual. She tossed her head and tucked the thick waves behind her ears.

TWO GIRLS STOOD BESIDE THE TEACHER'S DESK WHEN Beth arrived; another walked in behind her. Moving to the side, Beth motioned for the third girl to go ahead. When they all left, her words rushed forward.

"Ma'am, do you know anybody who needs their house cleaned? Or anything? I can work in the yard, keep children, iron. I'll work hard; you don't have to worry about that. I can start the day after school's out. If the bus goes to their house that'd be good. If not, I'll get there somehow. I'll take as many jobs as I can get, days and hours don't matter."

Mrs. Long looked like she wanted to say something. Beth took a deep breath and exhaled. "Sorry, ma'am. People say I talk a blue streak like my daddy."

"Why do you need so much work, honey?"

Beth was leaning over Mrs. Long's desk. The sweat trickling down her sides reminded her that she had run out of deodorant and hoped she didn't stink. She raised her head and focused on the chalkboard, not wanting to meet her teacher's eyes. Asking people for help outside her home was a new experience and having to reveal family secrets made her feel like she was doing something wrong.

"Daddy's sick and can't work. We just don't have enough money. It's been going on all year." Her throat tightened. She feared she was betraying her father. "He—I mean, *they*—try not to worry me, but I've got to do something."

Mrs. Long reached for Beth's hand and squeezed it. Then she stood and hugged her. Beth worried that the hug would make the sweat show on her blouse. "I'll find work for you. Try not to worry, darling. But." The teacher took a step backward. "Have you been able to study for finals?"

THE ARRIVAL OF A WOMAN FROM THE CHURCH HOME Visitation Committee caught Lillie off guard. She tried to smile and be polite, as she looked around the living room and picked up anything out of place that was within reach. She was glad it was a Sunday, so she was wearing clothes that weren't stained.

The woman apologized for coming without calling. She said she had tried to, but a message said their phone had been disconnected.

Lillie nodded, offered her a glass of cold water, and invited her to sit on the side porch where it was a little cooler. "I'm sorry, but electricity is so expensive that we're trying not to use the air conditioner."

Wishing she'd had time to dust the metal porch furniture, she thought about the first thing her mother's mother would have done in this situation. She would have left the woman standing and dashed to the bathroom to rinse the snuff out of her mouth. Lillie chuckled. At least she didn't have to do that.

Matt followed them to the porch. "I served on your committee a few years ago. There're a lot of people out there who need you—housebound, lonely. We sure appreciate you coming. A new face cheers us up."

The woman cleared her throat. "Well, we've changed it a bit. Now, the committee's purpose is to try to help financially. We provide food every two weeks until people are back on their feet."

Lillie noticed that Matt didn't respond but couldn't contain herself. She leaned forward in her seat. "Did I hear you right? The church wants to send us food?"

The woman nodded. "Two bags of groceries every two weeks, starting tomorrow."

Lillie felt like jumping up and hugging her. "Well, Lord have mercy! Are you serious?"

The woman's head bobbed up and down while Lillie talked. "I just *knew* God wouldn't forget us. And tell everybody, thank you, thank you! *Nobody knows* how much we appreciate it."

Matt stared at Lillie and remained silent.

Following her to the bottom of the porch steps, Lillie waved and yelled, "God bless you!" when the woman opened her car door.

As she stepped back into the living room, Lillie felt giddy with excitement, imagining herself unloading two full bags of groceries at one time. Dropping down in her chair, she rocked as fast as she could, nearly shouting, "Can you believe this? Our good luck?"

Matt leaned back in his chair and covered his eyes with one hand. "No, Lillie, no. We can't do it."

She stopped the motion of her rocker. "Can't what? What's the matter?"

The words came slowly, sounding like Matt had just climbed a mountain. "I cannot take a handout."

Lillie jumped up and pulled his hand away. "Have you been in that kitchen, lately? Have you *opened* the refrigerator?"

Matt had a hard glint in his eyes. "I can't let myself go down that low! You want me to beg for food? Why don't I just stand on a street corner?"

She staggered back to her chair wanting to ask, "What about me?" but said instead, "No, Matt. We never begged—they're giving it because it's the right thing to do."

As she rocked, Lillie's thoughts turned to a time before Matt's pain had begun. She heard him whistling on a Sunday morning, while he shined his shoes and brushed his sport coat for church. She saw her handsome man standing tall and straight, wearing a smile and looking people directly in the eye. She listened to him explain things she couldn't begin to understand.

She nodded and murmured to herself. *That's right.* Their family dignity had come through him. He had cleared a path wide enough for the three of them. She, too, was afraid to lose it. But was pride more important than food?

Crickets chirped and there was a light coolness in the air. Lillie opened her eyes. She saw lightning bugs blinking outside the window. Although darkness had nearly closed in, the outline of Matt's body was still visible. When she leaned forward to stand, he spoke.

"*I'm* the one who's supposed to feed this family, not the church. Not even you. I can't be like those bums who don't take care of their families. What do you think I am—a welfare person?" His words became a whisper. "I'd rather starve."

She sat on the arm of his chair, pulled his head to her breast, and kissed his cheek. She smoothed down his hair and rubbed his neck. "Don't think about it anymore. Please, don't. You're the man of this family, and you *do* take care of us."

His arms surrounded her holding her like a drowning man might hold onto a lifeguard. She stayed there until her body ached. Then she put her hands under his arms and pulled him to his feet. "Come on, we need to go to bed."

The next morning, at exactly nine o'clock, Lillie called the church secretary. She told her there had been a misunderstanding—they didn't need food after all. Praising the committee for their good work, she thanked them from the bottom of her heart.

Two hours later, Lillie heard a rattle at the front screen door. Then the minister walked in and past her holding a bag of groceries in each arm. He placed them on the kitchen table, nodded, said, "Hey!" and turned toward the bedroom. There he sat on the edge of the bed and took Matt's hand in his. Lillie listened from the kitchen. "This food is not from me. And you, of all people, know it isn't from the committee. It's from God. You won't refuse Him, will you?"

12

WHEN A CHURCH MEMBER BROUGHT GROCERIES EVERY
two weeks, Matt wanted to pull a sheet over his
head or to hide behind a closed door. Instead, he
endured the humiliation, forcing himself to stand,
shake hands, and say, "Thank you."

But even with the donated food, he and Lillie
weren't making it financially. They owed money on
every bill except health insurance and electricity.
People with sharp, nasty voices called to find out
when they would be paid. Lillie described what they
were going through, how hard they were trying, and
that the ten-dollar check she had sent was all they
could afford. Matt studied her face as she walked
across the lawn after one of those calls. Like the
delicate petals drifting off the dogwoods, her spirit
was falling away.

Wincing, Matt pulled himself to a sitting position and saw his reflection in the window beside
the bed. The long scraggly hair startled him, making him wonder what others thought when they
saw it. Outside the window, he noticed the tall

grass in the yard. *What do people think when they drive past?*

"Why do you care?" he replied. Matt had begun talking to himself as if he was having a conversation. Hearing his words spoken seemed to make them clearer and gave him the advantage of a discussion with another person without having to reveal his thoughts. Recently the friends who visited had found his ideas alarming, and he didn't have the energy to deal with their responses.

"You've got the important things in life—family and friends. Why aren't you satisfied? Why do you need more?"

Matt shivered. "I want things to be the way they were. Don't want to lose what I've worked for."

He rubbed his hand along the windowsill. How long would it be until that would no longer be his—until the house would be taken to pay his debts? Only middle class people owned houses, and his membership in that group was being cancelled. He had heard the middle class referred to as the backbone on the country. His backbone was injured—maybe beyond repair—so, what would he become? Not the head or the arms. Then what?

And where would he live? In a trailer park? People on television called those living there trash. He had never thought about what it actually meant. Were all the people ignorant bums, drunks, drug addicts? Did they sit around cussing all day? Lillie would never be able to keep children in a place like that. That would mean no income at all. Then what? Would they live on a sidewalk?

Matt lurched toward the dark closet, driven and wanting something. On the top shelf against the back wall lay his father's hunting rifle. He lifted it from its resting place and circled the end of the barrel with the fingers of his right hand. Very slowly, he slid them along the metal shaft. When he reached the trigger, he curled his finger around it. *Must be a reason I didn't sell this.*

Lillie called from the kitchen. "Hey, boy, can't you smell these hamburgers and onions? Hurry. You don't want me to eat yours!" She was cooking meat for the first time in six weeks, and Matt heard the pride and excitement in her voice.

Holding the gun's wooden handle against his chest, Matt caressed it, before slipping it under the clothes piled on the front of the shelf.

After supper, while Lillie washed and dried the dishes, Matt stayed at the kitchen table. An unusual feeling of satisfaction and relaxation had come over him, and may have prompted him to ask two questions he preferred discussing only with himself. "Are you *sure* this is not all in my head? Could I be making it up?"

Lillie whirled around. "Making *what* up?"

He stared at the cracks in the raised areas of the linoleum floor. "You know. My pain." Matt's face felt hot. "Well, I mean, you remember what people said about Little Red after he came back from Vietnam?

Maybe this is just in my head, too."

She hung the dish towel from a cabinet knob. "Come on, let's go to the porch. We need some fresh air."

They sat beside each other on the metal glider, tapping the floor with their toes to start it moving. Lillie grasped one of his hands and held it in hers. Her voice was filled with frustration and compassion. "How *can* you ask such a question? Even pills don't take your pain away. When have you slept more than an hour or two at a time in the last ten months? Stop doubting yourself! Rest until you get better." She chuckled. "Funny. Here I am telling *you* what to do."

Matt had the urge to find a broom. During the years his father was sick, he had swept the house every day after supper with his mother's tall, stiff broom, not missing an inch of the floor. He had dug into corners so hard that when he finished, he had to pick up pieces of broken-off bristles. Years after, he realized that keeping the floor clean gave him a feeling of control over his life, but now he knew the broom had been as useless as he was. Whatever power existing in the world to heal and restore hadn't belonged to him and still didn't.

He turned away from the little trace of fear in his wife's eyes. It wasn't possible to rest. His worries had created a tangled chain. Each time he tried to straighten it, he created another knot. Only one thing made sense to him. *She'd be better off without me.*

13

"WAIT!" MATT SHOUTED. "STAY. DON'T LEAVE ME." HE opened his eyes, but the bedroom was pitch black, and he was unable to see even Lillie's form lying beside him. He felt his arms lifted like those of a child wanting to be picked up. His heart pounded in a chest that felt heavy and empty.

Lillie rolled over. "You all right?"

Pulling himself to a sitting position, Matt inhaled as much air as he could and blew it out. "Just dreaming. Go to sleep."

He shivered, fell back on his pillow, and told himself to calm down. He squeezed his eyes closed and hoped to return to where he had been. He knew, without a doubt, it was someplace other that this bedroom. Although he kept his body motionless, his mind wouldn't cooperate: thoughts tumbled about, demanding attention.

The first two times he came, I opened my eyes, looked at Lillie, and he disappeared. Third time, he said, "Let me stay. I need to talk to you." Matt wiped away tears. *This is crazy, it can't be—I was lifted up, taken somewhere. To a place so silent I couldn't even hear a breath.*

Matt gave in to the memory flooding his mind. The man in his dream was surrounded by soft blue light. He wore overalls. His face was mostly covered, but the shape of his body—tall and strong-looking—was like his grandfather's.

But it was the voice that made Matt certain Grandad was standing before him. "Having a hard time, aren't you, boy? Your body's giving you a fit." His grandfather extended a hand but didn't come close enough to touch him.

"I grieve over your suffering and wish I could repair your body." His grandfather shook his head. "Just do the best you can and see where it goes. I'm here to talk about your other struggles. Tell me what's wrong, boy."

Matt remembered being soothed by his grandfather's presence. "Grandad, are you real?" Words came, filled with tears. "I've missed you more than you'll ever know. A hole opened in my heart when you died. *Are* you dead?"

His grandfather raised his right hand. "Go on, son. Talk to me."

Where should he begin? "Well, Daddy got sick. Mama died. Guess you know that. And I'm a mess! Can you believe I turned out to be a weakling? I thought I'd be like you—strong, able to take care of my family and figure things out. But look at me! I'm ashamed of myself."

As the man moved closer, Matt tried harder to see his face but couldn't. "Son, listen. I'm proud of you. Every person has both strengths and weaknesses. It's not only one or the other. And behavior that looks weak isn't always what it seems. Same with strength. You have to understand what it is you're seeing. This is a time of struggle for you. And that's all right. It gives you a chance to learn. And remember this—it's not just relying on yourself and having a lot of money that makes you a man."

Matt was frightened at this point. Some of his grandfather's words weren't familiar. He wanted to pull the covering from the man's face but couldn't move. He was certain he wasn't breathing and wondered if he was dying.

His grandfather continued. "I have a story to tell you. You heard it as a boy; I want you to hear it again. It'll help you remember what I said and will be important in the future.

"This happened in 1867, to my daddy, Joseph, when he was fourteen. It was October, two and a half years after the War Between the States, and Joseph was hunting for game. He saw bushes move and was seconds from pulling his trigger, until he heard a groan. 'Come out and I won't shoot,' he called.

"Not getting an answer, he crept behind the sound and saw a man dressed in a suit. Blood had soaked through his right sleeve and the front of his shirt. One leg was twisted. Neither hand held a gun. As soon as Joseph said he wouldn't hurt him, the man passed out.

"Daddy Joseph considered the blood and the fading sunlight and knew he had to move fast; the man couldn't survive overnight in the woods. As he ran for help, he worried about his father's reaction. Since his father had returned from the War, he had spoken only when necessary and wanted nothing to do with people outside the family.

"His father shook his head. 'No, we don't need somebody else's trouble. We've got enough of out own.'

"Joseph hesitated. He had never talked back to his father. 'The Bible says, "Thou shalt not stand idly by when a human life is in danger." "That's Leviticus 19:16. Mama read it to me. Want me to drag him here by myself?'

"His brothers lowered their heads, and his father stared with narrowed eyes. Several minutes passed in silence. 'Go on, we're behind you.'

"When they got him back to the house, Grandma dug a bullet out of the man's shoulder and set his broken leg. Then she pulled her rocker by the bed and held his hand the rest of the night.

"When a narrow rose stripe showed on the horizon, Grandpa shook the man awake and demanded answers, but he wouldn't give any. He kept saying he wanted a doctor. Jerking him to a sitting position, Grandpa leaned close to his face. 'Our doctor died of the fever. I've got a wagon, but all my animals have been stolen, starved, or killed. Now, let's start over. Give me the truth.'

"He was a twenty-two-year-old teacher sent by The Freedman's Aid Society to open a Quaker school and teach former slaves to read and write. He had gotten off the train at Clement, bought food and a horse, and asked for directions to Winston. Three men on horseback followed. When they started shooting, his horse turned into the woods, dumped him, and kept going.

"When Grandpa heard that, he knew trouble was coming. Talk in town had told him people were determined to keep more Yankees from coming in. He walked down to the Yadkin and watched it swirl out of control. The river reminded him of his life during the past six years and made him mad. How had he been so stupid? Since Bradfurds had settled his land in 1750, it had never been touched by the foot of a slave. Yet he had taken two of his sons to war and had let one be killed. Why hadn't he followed his younger brother to Indiana when conscription started?

"Then again, why hadn't the teacher stayed where he belonged? Did everybody in *his* town up North know how to read? Why mess in other people's business? What should he do with the man? Turn him over if they came for him? Grandpa slammed his fist against a tree. He was certain of only one thing—he wouldn't sacrifice another son for God Himself.

"When they heard the horses, Grandpa picked up his rifle for the first time since the war's end. His second son, who had stood beside him during the war, pointed his gun at the three men. Grandpa recognized the one who worked at the depot.

"The men said they were members of The Pale Faces and were looking for someone who had gotten off the train at the wrong place. They wanted to put him back on, heading north.

"Grandpa started talking, still not knowing what he'd do. He had never figured lying served a man well but heard himself doing it until the men started telling him who he was and how he should act. That made him mad and lying stopped working.

"He told them he'd been in General Johnston's Army until the day peace was signed with Sherman. He asked what they'd done during the war, since it didn't look like they'd suffered much. And said, 'I don't think much of the group y'all are in. When the War was over,' he told them, 'Davis had called for soldiers to hide in the mountains and swamps and keep the fight going. Said they'd wear the Yankees down. But Lee and Johnston put a stop to it.' Grandpa told the men they reminded him of Davis keeping up a bad fight, and he wanted them off his land.

"When the sound of horses' hooves disappeared, Joseph and his sisters carried the schoolteacher on a quilt to a cave Joseph had discovered as a boy.

"They returned to the house just as their mother put the midday meal on the table and minutes before a group of ten men rode up. One of the three who had been there that morning rammed the muzzle of his rifle against Joseph's older brother's neck and swore to pull the trigger if Grandpa didn't turn over the Yankee. Grandpa sneered. 'You know how many Yankees this boy *killed* in three years? Why save one now? Don't worry; I'll let you know if a stranger comes by. Make yourselves at home and look around as much as you want.'

"Those first three men showed up twice more and threatened Grandpa. Each time, he welcomed them, repeating his words.

"Joseph lived in the cave with the Yankee four weeks. When it was safe, he took the man from the cave back to the house. Then Joseph set out on foot for Winston. It took him two weeks, but he found the Methodist minister and Quaker leader the Yankee was to have met. They escorted the school teacher on the rest of his journey.

"Our family never heard from the man again. Joseph didn't know whether he stayed in Winston, whether he lived, or whether he died. He didn't even know his family name. All he knew was his given name, Silas.

"But Grandpa didn't care about any of that. He was a changed man. Until his dying day, he claimed Silas had saved *his* life. All his feelings had been deadened except hatred toward himself for allowing his son to be killed. When Silas appeared, he forced Grandpa to turn back to people and allow forgiveness to work in him.

"Here's your lesson, boy: You've helped others. Now, give them a chance to do the same for you. It's not shame: it's love. This is the way life is meant to be. And never, ever, turn your back on it."

14

THE AGENT AT THE AMERICAN AIRLINES' FIRST CLASS desk at the Triad airport whistled when she picked up the empty suitcases that George Russell had placed on the scale. "Travel light, don't you?"

He and Rosalyn started answering at the same time. George stepped back and let his wife continue. "Everybody laughs. We take underwear, toiletries, and sometimes, coats. That's all. Can you imagine how much shopping we have to do our first day?"

The agent raised her eyebrows. "Must be fun."

"Yes. But *hard work* buying enough clothes and shoes to last a year. We've gone to New York every year at Christmas since our younger daughter left for college—eleven years, now." Rosalyn swung her black Chanel purse over her shoulder and leaned forward as if sharing a secret with the agent. "It can be a hassle, believe me. But to tell you the truth, I don't think we'd know where to shop around here, anymore."

The agent shifted her gaze to the coworker on her left and motioned to the next person in line.

"Don't you think you went a little overboard there?" George whispered.

A puzzled look on her face, Rosalyn shrugged and walked ahead of him toward the gate.

George didn't try to keep up. He had no enthusiasm for the trip this year. He had hinted to his wife that they change their routine and go in the spring, instead. Before he had completed his thought, she had cut him off. "George, you out of your mind? You love it more than I do!" He had to admit she was right. So, why wouldn't he want to go?

THE BELLMAN AT THE PLAZA OPENED ROSALYN'S DOOR before the taxi came to a complete stop. George smiled. Although the rooms had become worn and slightly seedy over the years, the service and location of this hotel couldn't be matched.

As he looked out the window at Central Park, George realized his mood had lifted. Rosalyn was right: he loved New York City. Here high cholesterol, middle age, and irritants—such as a wife—disappeared. Here was a world where he was attended to, appreciated, and could do no wrong.

He slipped into his black cashmere coat and picked up his fedora just as Rosalyn stepped out of the closet. She wore the fitted black leather coat and knee length boots they had bought the year before. Her smooth blond hair was pulled back in a bun wrapped in black velvet. He winked and opened the door for her. That was what he liked—loved—about her. She could be the sophisticated New Yorker and make him proud.

On their way down Fifth Avenue, George and Rosalyn stole quick peeks in some of the shop windows, but their discipline held. Ritual dictated that they begin with lunch at Saks and start shopping there. It was his favorite store.

They sat at their usual table next to the wall of windows. While they ate, Rosalyn chatted, allowing George's thoughts to drift. Most centered on the changes in him since his trip to London last April. He felt tired now and less excited about life. Catching his reflection in the window, George raised his hand to his neck: his double chin showed clearly. Then there was the on-again, off-again relationship with Emily. He didn't know what to do about that. It raised his spirits, so he didn't want it to end but knew it would eventually.

When the waitress brought dessert, he noticed a light snow falling. Suddenly feeling like his old self, he was content, resting on his pedestal, safe and warm, all of New York City at his feet. *I am blessed. Nothing will ever change that.*

Rosalyn and George found clothes at Saks for the evening and the next day. Alterations would be done that afternoon and the clothes delivered to their hotel room. Since that took the pressure off, they walked casually up the avenue, stopping to enjoy window decorations and laughing as Rosalyn tried to catch snowflakes.

When they reached Tiffany, she motioned for George to follow her in. He shook his head, "Be there in a minute," wanting to cross the street and see the store's decorations from a distance. The building was intended to be a five-story-high Christmas tree, its façade a triangle of green lights topped with a white star. The interior of the tree contained multi-colored lights grouped to look like ornaments. Below the tree, piled in the sidewalk display windows, were giant-sized Tiffany blue boxes bordered by tiny white lights. He crossed the street again ready to go in.

A security guard said, "Good evening," and swung Tiffany's door wide open for George. As he stepped into the store, he felt he was entering Christmas itself—a fantasyland where happiness sparkled in glass cases. To obtain it, he needed only money, and he had plenty of that.

Rosalyn was nowhere to be seen. Guessing she had gone to see the more expensive pieces on the second floor, George was glad. He wanted time to look around alone. But his pleasure was thwarted each time he stopped at a case and a sales associate appeared. When the person asked what he had in mind, he mumbled, "Just looking," and moved on.

A thought followed him around the room. *That would look good on Emily.* Thinking of her reminded him of their Saturday afternoons together, and how much he loved kissing the rose tattoo.

After the Memorial Day lunch, George and Emily had met four consecutive Saturdays, until feelings of guilt had taken over and he pulled back. Half a dozen times since then, he had "fallen off the wagon," as he referred to it. Touching, soft words, and kisses in the office weren't counted. He didn't consider them a betrayal of his wife, since there was no intercourse.

Thoughts of Emily continued to intrude, preventing Manhattan's charms from captivating George the way they usually did. He had no desire to see the Monet exhibit, so he and Rosalyn didn't go to the Metropolitan Museum of Art at all. They did go to Herald Square to see the display in Macy's window, but he was disappointed. Rockefeller Center was too crowded for him to enjoy the Christmas tree, and he was too cold to watch the ice skaters in Central Park.

They saw three Broadway shows, and George enjoyed one of them. Cocktail hour in the Plaza Bar was as much fun as usual, but he ended up with heartburn after their dinners. Rosalyn begged him to take an antacid, so he could eat whatever he wanted, but he wouldn't.

On their sixth day in the city, Rosalyn and George shopped separately. He went directly to Tiffany's.

A young sales associate removed a bracelet from the case. "It's our new lace design, sir. As you can see, a combination of pearls and diamonds set in eighteen-carat white gold."

George flushed as he handed it back to her. "May I see it on *your* wrist?"

"Of course, sir." She smiled and gazed at him a few seconds. "This was created for an especially delicate and youthful wrist."

Not meeting her eyes, George gave her his business credit card. "I'm in a hurry."

The woman bowed. "That will be two thousand six hundred ninety-five."

Out on the sidewalk, George removed the flat blue box from its bag, slipped it into an inside pocket of his long black coat, and stuffed the bag into the garbage can on the corner.

He patted the box, satisfied that it was in a secure place and hidden from Rosalyn. *But why? I don't need to hide anything. It's a gift for an employee. What's the big deal?*

Anxiety distracted George the rest of the day. He entered one store after another on Madison Avenue, intending to shop, but left empty-handed each time. Once, when he found himself staring at a young woman, she stared back, and he hurried out of the store. Finally, he gave up and stopped for a drink.

GEORGE WAS EXCITED TO BE HOME AND GLAD TO GO back to work. His car was the first to arrive in the garage and his hands trembled as he removed the small, blue box from the wheel storage unit of the trunk. When he slipped it into his jacket pocket, he felt a piece of paper. It was the note he had written before the Memorial Day lunch. "Talk to Emily about Bradfurd. Call Latham. Visit Roy Barbee on way home."

"Good God!" Crushing the paper, he shook his head. "I haven't dealt with that!" Then he wondered. Hadn't he asked Emily what she found for Bradfurd at that lunch? *Yes!* Just before she asked him to describe the wine, he *had asked* but never received an answer.

George hurried to his office and placed the blue box in the center drawer of his desk. He shivered with relief that it hadn't been discovered and then turned to the window behind his desk. Most of the red and gold leaves had given way to the wind by late December, but a few still clung to maple trees. Although George knew it sounded strange when referring to leaves, he admired anything that could hold on so long. The difficulty for him was in knowing what to hold on *to.*

When Mrs. Barbee knocked on his door and handed George his schedule for the day, he looked at the first two appointments, then laid it aside, unable to concentrate. He glanced at his watch.

Five minutes later, he picked up the phone. "Emily, I need to see you at lunchtime. Wait until Mrs. Barbee leaves."

He tried to finish the notes on his last client but found it difficult to think of what to write. Finally, he dropped the pen and slapped the folder closed. His hands trembled slightly. He looked over at the certificates of accomplishment and praise hanging above the couch. There was proof of his good judgment.

Emily swung the office door open. George was startled, even though he expected her. To cover his nervousness, he picked up the blue box and held it high, like a young boy presenting a gift to his mother.

Steadying himself on the front edge of his desk, George fastened the pearls and diamonds on Emily's wrist. When she leaned forward with lips puckered, the top of her blouse dropped open and the scent of the rose made him light-headed.

She put her arms around his neck and pressed her body against his. Her hands moved down his chest and unzipped his pants. She unbuttoned her blouse and slipped out of her panties. When they pushed aside the objects on his desk, they knocked over Rosalyn's photograph.

The actions that followed made George feel like he had played a part in a movie—as if a script had been handed to him. He was neither writer nor director, but an actor impersonating the man he was told to play. The only question originating in him was whether Emily had locked the door.

15

MATT STRUGGLED TO LIE STILL, AS THE PURPLE BLACK of night slowly moved aside and gave way to the gray light of morning. He felt like a plant pushing through the topsoil in his garden, about to meet the spring sun for the first time. He wanted to get out of bed and follow Lillie to the kitchen: to sit at the table, drink coffee, and tell her everything that had happened during the night. He wanted to buy her a dress for Christmas. He wanted to smile and laugh, filling himself with new air.

Feeling guilty, he shook the mattress harder than necessary when turning over. *Come on, girl. Life's waiting.*

She blinked, sighed, and rolled over.

"You awake? Good." He grinned. "I saw Grandad last night!"

"*Who?*" Lillie propped up on one elbow.

"Never mind, Lillie, never mind. I've made a decision! We're going to find help until I get back to work."

Letting herself fall back on the bed, Lillie crossed her arms over her chest. "Well, praise the Lord."

MATT PUT DOWN NELL'S PHONE AND HURRIED AWAY without a proper goodbye. He felt like Grandad was waiting outside. When he stepped out the door, he looked up at the clear blue winter sky. *Are you? Can you hear me? Or see me? Should I talk to you like I do to Lillie?* He lowered his head and closed his eyes, his joy pushed back by a burst of sadness. *Maybe you're only in my mind.* "But, no!" he insisted aloud. "I saw you!"

Back in his yard, he used the iron railing to pull himself up the front steps one at a time. Lillie was watching from the window. He waved at her.

As soon as he opened the door, she asked, "Well? What'd they say?"

Holding up his hand, he said, "Let me catch my breath." Matt stepped around the children's toys, groaned, and slumped down in his chair. "First thing I did was talk to a computer. It kept telling me to put in an extension number to reach the social worker I wanted." He smacked the chair arm. "I asked, 'How do I know?' five or six times before a woman came on. By that time, I just wanted to reach in and unplug the thing!"

Lillie leaned over and picked up a whining baby. "Come on, tell me. What'd she say?"

"I'm getting to that. Nothing! Might as well have talked to the computer. I have to be there in person. They're open eight to five, Monday through Friday, first come, first served. Period!"

"Did you tell her you can't drive?"

"Yeah. Said she couldn't change the rules. I have to go in."

Lillie held the baby against her chest with one hand and patted Matt's shoulder with the other. "Well, everybody has their rules. Don't worry, darling." She hesitated. "I'll take you. One of the mothers will keep the children an hour or two."

Matt smiled, hoping to coax one from Lillie. He hated putting these burdens on her. Over the years, she had made it a policy never to ask a parent to help her out. She had heard too many stories about bosses getting back at them when they took days off because of child care.

Resting his head against the back of his chair, Matt closed his eyes and saw his wife carrying on her shoulders a large burlap sack like an old woman in a fairy tale. All their struggles, worries, and hunger pains turned into pebbles that leaped into the bag, each one forcing her closer to the ground as she walked the path. Matt shuddered, opened his eyes, and watched her change the baby's diaper. *Smile at me, Lillie. Tell me you're all right.*

MATT LISTENED THROUGH THE NIGHT TO THE RAIN hitting his bedroom window. By six in the morning, it had turned into a drizzle. When he and Lillie left for the Social Services office at seven-thirty, the dark gray clouds had parted and wide blue streaks crossed the sky. *An omen. A path's opening up.* Matt held onto that hope until he left the building at ten-thirty. On the way home, though the sun was so bright he had to shield his eyes, his mind was filled with failure and the new rough-cut pebbles in Lillie's bag.

Matt hid in the bedroom, while Lillie talked to the mother who had taken care of the children. There was frustration and embarrassment in her voice. "Diane, we thought we'd be first if we got there at eight, but three people were ahead of us! Finally, we told them we had to leave, because you needed to be at work by eleven." Lillie wrinkled her brow and shook her head. "We don't know what we're doing."

Diane hugged Lillie. "I can come back on Friday." As she ran down the front steps, she called over her shoulder. "I'll stay here until you're home or every last child's been picked up."

Matt's mind had trouble keeping up with his hands. He stared at the clock on his bedside table, rubbed his legs, scratched his arms, and ran his fingers through his hair. He shifted his body in an attempt to scratch his back and clawed at his chest. He felt like bedbugs had descended on him like locusts from the Bible. The instant the clock turned five, he pulled himself out of bed. It was Friday morning.

Steam from the shower filled the bathroom. Matt's elbows bumped the plastic walls of the shower as he washed his hair and scrubbed away the nervous itch. He stood in front of the mirror and with Lillie's sewing scissors trimmed the hair around his ears and neck before reaching in the medicine cabinet for Beth's hair gel. But when he squeezed the tube, nothing came out. Holding it up to the light, he saw that it was empty. Why had his daughter kept it? *To pretend her life was normal?* He carefully placed the tube back in the same spot. Noticing the bottle of shampoo on the rim of the tub, he had an idea: a small amount rubbed into his wet hair would hold it down a few hours.

The Sunday shirt Lillie had pressed the night before was hanging on the back of the door. Matt put it on and tucked it with great care into his pants. When he picked up his belt, he thought of the spasms it would cause in back to wear it. But his decision had been made. He slipped it through the loops, straightened his shirt collar, and looked in the mirror. *I'll make it happen, today, Lillie. You'll be proud of me.*

When the receptionist opened the front door of the Social Services building at eight o'clock, Matt smiled and told her his name. He sat beside Lillie in a straight chair and picked up a *Time* magazine dated two years before. Two pages fell out. He started reading the article about global warming until he noticed the bottom half of the page had been torn off.

Pain hit him in the left hip and shot down his leg. He took a deep breath, shifted his weight to his right hip, and looked away. When it became less intense, he took out his handkerchief, wiped the sweat from his face, and laid his hand on Lillie's.

At nine, a case worker invited Matt and Lillie into her office. She shook their hands and smiled warmly before sitting down to read their application for public assistance.

"Mr. Bradfurd, I'm confused." She turned the application over and looked at it again. "The two of you have a combined income of about a thousand a month. That's too much to qualify for public assistance."

That was the one response Matt hadn't prepared for. He opened his eyes widely and tilted his head. "What? Too much for *three people?* Before taxes?"

"See for yourself. Here's the chart." She handed him a laminated card. "You're above the cut-off."

"Well, ma'am." Matt leaned back in his chair and glanced at Lillie. He didn't know what to say. "This is hard to believe. How can people live on that? We pay five hundred and twenty-eight dollars alone on health insurance! And then utilities, medicines, property tax, and everything else." He shook his head. "Ma'am, there's even more."

The social worker picked up the application. "All right. Let's see about your assets. You've got a car. Why not let it go?"

Matt flushed. Speaking quickly, but carefully, he tried to keep the edge out of his voice. "Ma'am, if we did that, we wouldn't be able to get anywhere—like

here, for instance. Or the doctor's office and the grocery store. We sold the other car and anything else
people would buy. We let the phone go." He heard it:
the edge was there and getting sharper. He stopped
and took a deep breath. "Our savings have been
gone a long time, now. What else can we do?"

The gentleness in the case worker's face and
voice had disappeared. "I guess you'll have to get a
job."

Matt felt like he had been hit from behind. He
wanted to yell and swing at somebody. Pushing up
from the chair as fast as he could, he turned toward
the door. When he grabbed the knob and stepped
back to let Lillie go ahead of him, she wasn't there.
She had remained in her chair, watching him. He
crossed the room and, for a few seconds, leaned
over the woman's desk closer to her face than he
should have.

The tightness in his jaw made his voice sound
like a growl. "I wrote it right there." He pointed to
the application. "My doctor won't *let* me work! You
think I *want* to be here?"

The social worker sighed, loudly, and laid down
her pen. "There must be *something* you can do."

Matt stepped back and turned toward Lillie. His
voice was no more than a whisper. "I wonder about
that every day of my life." When he held out his
hand, Lillie rose and took it.

The woman pushed back her chair and extended
her hand. "Mr. Bradfurd, I *am* sorry. I would help if

I could, but there's nothing here for people in your situation. We only serve the truly down and out."

Matt was grateful Lillie didn't talk on the way home. He didn't want to tell her how it felt being the only man in the waiting room, the only man he knew who would beg somebody else to feed him. What Grandad had said about reaching out for help made sense, but doing it was harder than he ever imagined it would be.

When they reached home, Matt went around behind the fig tree and waited until Diane left. He couldn't bear to have her see his failure. Then he went to his bedroom. After taking off his shirt and putting it on a hanger, he held it up. *That's what I'm like.* He shook the hanger. *Everything inside me is gone.*

MATT PUT ON HIS PAJAMAS, WENT TO BED AND STAYED there. He didn't see the Christmas snow that glistened in the morning sun. Nor did he feel the warm wind that brought Easter. He didn't see the daffodils blooming in the yard or the eighteen that Lillie cut and put by his bedside. He didn't see the eggs she and the children decorated in his favorite colors. He saw nothing when she pulled him to the side of the bed, fed him as she would a young child, and led him to the bathroom. He didn't feel her arms when she put them around his head and shoulders and rocked.

Lillie saw it all and worried. She wondered what was wrong and whether he was eating enough food to keep his blood sugar where it should be. Finally, she called Dr. Ramsey's office. The doctor said not to be concerned if he was eating anything at all; he was in a depression and would eventually come out of it.

But Lillie wanted to do more and hoped pushing him would help. When she and Beth could get enough response from him, they led Matt to his chair. He sat there like a man frozen in a block of ice, his once proud body slumped like a sack of potatoes. The girls ignored him as they would a piece of furniture. But Lillie never stopped talking. She told him what was happening with Beth, what the children did that was funny, and how much she loved him. She assured him that he'd get better in time, and that life would be like it used to be.

One late April evening, while Lillie was feeding Matt supper, he tilted his head and looked at her. The connection was brief but startling. It reminded her that he had eaten more the last few days and had walked to the bathroom without leaning on her as much. She called Beth. Placing his arms on their shoulders, they led him to the side porch and sat him on the glider. Then Lillie asked her daughter to go inside.

Standing in front of him, she gently lifted his chin and turned his face to her. She held it in that position and spoke in a loud, firm voice. "Look at me, darling. I'm lonesome and scared. You've got to come back." As she repeated the words, again and again, her voice became softer, finally turning into a whisper closed off by tears. She slumped down beside him and laid her head on his shoulder.

Opening his eyes, Matt raised a trembling hand and let it fall on her lap. Lillie bolted upright and took his face in both her hands. "You're here." She brushed his hair from his forehead. "I can't live without you."

His voice sounded like it came from another place. "I don't know." Although Lillie saw his lips move, she looked around to see whether someone else was there and speaking.

She held his face again. "Don't know what? What is it?"

He closed his eyes. "Can't."

Lillie rubbed his cheeks, lightly kissed his lips, and squeezed his hand. "It's okay, don't worry. Just, just stay. Open your eyes."

Matt opened his eyes, looked to one side, and then the other. There was no expression on his face. Then he stared at her a few minutes before turning toward Nell's yard. As the sunlight dimmed, a breeze picked up carrying with it the scent of sweet alyssum. Lillie watched.

When he spoke again, his voice sounded more familiar. "You remember Grandad's watermelons?"

"Oh, praised be to God. Tell me about Grandad bringing you a watermelon!"

"In the yard. I see him." Matt's arm shook as he pointed toward Nell's. His voice became clearer and stronger. "We're all there. Look. He splits it with one strike of the knife." He turned to face her. "Always gives me the heart."

Lillie could hardly control herself. She wanted to ask so many questions—where had he gone, why, and what had been going through his mind. But she wasn't sure he understood what was real right then, and was afraid of saying something wrong, and pushing him back to that dark, silent place. So she waited.

Cicadas sawed away shrilly in the high grass. Branches of the plum tree scraped hard against the porch screen. Life was insistent, Lillie saw, holding her breath, trying not to move a muscle. Occasionally, Matt said a few words: some making sense and some not. When he cried, she laid her head on his chest. She wanted to ask what was wrong—she needed to know—and she wanted to comfort him but didn't. She waited.

Finally, Matt grasped her hand and cleared his throat. "Grandad wants us to go for a ride."

"Where? Okay." Lillie jumped up. "Wait right here!" She rushed to the kitchen, grabbed the car keys, and then struggled to keep him from getting tangled in the tall weeds of the yard as they crossed toward the car. When they passed the white lilac bush, Matt paused and squeezed a clump of blossoms.

She drove where Matt directed. First, they stopped at the bottom of Grandad's old driveway. Next, they went to High Rock Lake where he and Grandad had fished, and then to the cemetery. Lillie tried to make out his words as they stood in the dark by Grandad's grave. She heard, "You're right," and "Again. Will try again." The rest of the words were too soft to hear or didn't make sense. After leaving the cemetery, they went to the factory and sat in the parking lot a long time, until Matt said, "Let's go home."

16

THE BEDROOM WINDOW SHADE FLAPPED GENTLY IN THE early morning breeze. Matt watched the day gradually turn from black to gray. The new beginning that signaled was one of the things he loved about life: every twenty-four hours, a person was allowed to start up again.

Lillie moaned and rolled over.

Pulling himself over the center ridge of the mattress, Matt pressed his body against hers. She opened her eyes and nearly shouted. "You're smiling!"

"Because of those beautiful bedroom eyes." He touched her lips with his fingers. "I feel like being with you."

Lillie giggled. "Oh, my husband's back. I like that." She nuzzled his cheek. "You think we could?"

Matt closed his eyes and moved his hand from her shoulder. "I don't know." He slid over to his side of the bed. Experiencing a rare feeling of embarrassment with Lillie, he mumbled, "I'm afraid of messing things up." Hearing a car pass on the road reminded him of his plan, and he grinned. "I'm going back to work today!"

"What?" Lillie sat up. "The factory? You're not able! Besides, you said he fired you."

"Well, not in those words. And not in writing! So, my job's still there." Grasping the edge of the mattress, Matt swung his legs over the side of the bed. "Don't say another word, Lillie. I'm going, come hell or high water."

Wearing the gown she hated to be seen in because it allowed the fat around her knees to show, Lillie ran around the bed and stood before him. "Wait a minute! How will you get there?"

Matt pushed on the bedside table to stand. Lillie grabbed his arm when he swayed. Jerking it away, he lifted the shade and gazed out the window. "I'm driving."

Lillie stepped between him and the window. "No. I'll take you. Maybe, tomorrow. Or a few days. I'll get one of the mothers to stay."

Damn! Didn't she, of all people, understand how long he had already waited? "I'm going, now! Mr. Hartman'll be there at seven."

Lillie headed for the kitchen, leaving her robe on the end of the bed. "You've got to eat and take a pain pill."

Matt called after her. "A bite, but no pill. I don't want to mess up my driving."

THE '94 STEEL-BLUE IMPALA SAT AT THE TOP OF THE
driveway. When Matt saw it, he wanted to hug it.
He would be its driver again. He loved everything
about that car except one thing: the strong ciga-
rette odor left by the man who had sold it to him.
When he bought the car, he thought it would easy
to get rid of. But sprays hadn't worked; even the
blue Christmas-tree deodorizer he hung from the
mirror hadn't helped.

When he opened the car door, Matt was surprised
at how heavy it was. Sitting on the edge of the seat,
he swiveled his body around and used both hands
to lift his left leg into place. He grinned at himself
in the rearview mirror and smacked the steering
wheel. *You son of a gun, you made it!*

Matt was about to turn on the ignition, when
he realized driving wouldn't be the same. He would
have to raise his left leg with his arms to get his
foot on the clutch, and then lean his body forward
to push it in. By the time he reached the end of
the driveway, hard pains had hit his back and his
hands were trembling.

The two-lane back road to the factory wasn't
busy. When the car stalled the first time, Matt re-
started it before anyone came up behind him. The
second time, he let it glide onto the shoulder. The
Impala growled as he forced it back onto the blacktop in second gear. Even with the downhill slope, it
refused to go faster than forty. When it rolled into
the factory parking lot, it shuddered and died.

IT PLEASED MATT TO OPEN THE DOOR OF THE RECEPTION room and see Tibby looking like he remembered with her neat, short, brown hair behind her ears and a small gold cross hanging from the delicate chain around her neck.

Having things stay the same comforted Matt. He enjoyed tradition and ritual. Repetitive tasks that others complained of didn't bother him at all. But he liked Tibby for reasons other than her sameness. She added a kindness and warmth to the office, like the contrast between an overhead fluorescent light and a corner lamp with a soft yellow shade.

She looked up and smiled as Matt approached her desk. But by the time he reached her, the smile had been replaced by a wrinkled brow.

That puzzled Matt. Although they didn't know each other well, he thought she liked him. "Hey, I sure am glad to see you."

"Well, I'm surprised to see you."

Matt steadied himself with the corner of her desk. "Didn't think I'd make it back?"

She lowered her voice. "Some days, this place confuses me."

He started to ask what she meant, but thought he shouldn't. "I'd like to talk to Mr. Hartman. Is he busy?"

She looked down. "Hard to tell, but let me see what I can do."

Matt's leg was about to give way. "I'll wait as long as need be. That all right with you?"

When Tibby's eyes met his, she reached over and patted his hand. She looked relaxed for the first time since he had entered the room. "Sit down. Make yourself at home. I'll bring you some water."

As time dragged on, Matt struggled to keep from lying down on the floor. He sat like a statue on the edge of a hard plastic chair as long as he could tolerate it. Then he walked to the bathroom, stretched his legs, and wiped the sweat from his face and neck. Going back to the chair, he repeated his actions like a man walking in a circle. Each time he stood, Tibby jumped up to refill his water.

After an hour, Jim Hartman opened his office door and smiled broadly. "Hello, Matthew. Surprise. What can I do for you?"

Matt tried to look comfortable and strong when he rose from the chair. As he moved toward his boss, Jim Hartman took a step back. Even slightly bent at the waist, Matt was half a foot taller.

Matt spoke with as much enthusiasm as he could gather. "I'm ready to go to work."

Jim Hartman stood beside his secretary's desk, feet shoulder width apart and planted to the floor. All softness disappeared from his face. "Really? You're well? Tell me what you can do."

Matt willed his body to straighten. "Anything! Whatever you want. I'll do it."

His boss leaned forward, his fingers curled on the way to clenching his fists. "You know what your job's like. Can you stand on your feet all day? Pack boxes? Carry them to trucks?"

"Well, I—"

Mr. Hartman raised his eyebrows when he interrupted Matt. "And where's the letter that releases you from your surgeon's care?"

A frown crossed Matt's face. "Nobody told me I had to bring a letter." He glanced at the secretary. Although she was looking down at her desk, he saw her face redden. He turned back to his employer. "Can't you let me do *something?*"

Mr. Hartman's voice softened. "You know, I don't have anything available right now that would fit. We had to put somebody else in your old job."

A fly buzzed around Matt's right ear. Sweat streamed down his back. Wanting to explode with rage, he realized he couldn't. He tilted his head and stared at his boss, before turning to Tibby's bright red face. Her eyes were still directed toward her desk. Then he remembered her comment when he entered the office about this place being confusing and realized he was defeated. "So, you're telling me, even if I do get a letter, you don't have work for me? And even though you said my job would be here."

"You don't look in good shape." Mr. Hartman reached toward him, but Matt pulled back before he could place a hand on his shoulder. "Try back another time."

Keeping his body straight until he closed the car door, Matt leaned over the steering wheel. When clouds darkened the car, he turned his head to look for the sun and thought of Grandad. *There!* He banged his fist on the dash. *See what I told you?* Tears filled his eyes. *And what else do I have besides this body? The smartest mind in the world? Talent to be a big racecar driver? Rich parents to bail me out?*

THE BACK SCREEN DOOR BANGED AGAINST THE WALL when Lillie swung it open to help Matt. She slipped her shoulder under his arm and led him to the kitchen table. "I'll get some food."

He shook his head. "I've been dumped."

She set a peanut butter and jelly sandwich on the table in front of him and placed an envelope beside it. "What about his promise?"

"The man doesn't know what the word means." Matt pushed the plate away and tore open the envelope.

He read the letter aloud.

Dear Matthew and Lillie Bradfurd,

It has been our Christian duty and our pleasure to help you. We hope you're doing well. We will no longer be sending you food. Our mission is to help as many people in the community as possible. Therefore, we limit the service to six months. After that time, we expect that people are back on their feet. God bless you.

The Congregation of the
First Baptist Church

Lillie put her arms around Matt's shoulders, resting her face against his. "Well, everybody has their own way of doing things. Bless their hearts."

Shoving his chair sideways, Matt caused Lillie to stagger back against the counter. He looked up at the startled expression on her face. "Sorry. Have I ever told you about Grandad's friend who went to Panama in 1908?"

Matt glanced up. Lillie was shaking her head. When he saw her eyes glistening with tears, he turned away. "Our government was building the canal and needed men to work there as policemen. Pay was eighty a month, plus expenses." Matt nodded and stared at the kitchen stove. "That was a lot of money, you know. This friend begged Grandad to go with him. Figured it'd be a good way to get out of farming a few years and see the world. They were going to New York City first for training, and then on a boat to Cristobal. Sounds exciting, huh? Grandad said he wanted to go but didn't think it was fair to leave his mama and daddy."

The sound from a lawn mower hitting a rock in Nell's yard caused Matt to jump. He looked around and lowered his voice, as if someone could hear him besides Lillie and the children. "You think the government has something like that I could do? Could they use me in some way? I could volunteer for some kind of experiment where they test things on people. Maybe, sell a kidney. I could make a little money from that."

By the time Matt finished talking, he was staring at the floor. When he felt Lillie's hand under his arms, he got up.

"Lord, help us, child. Go to bed."

THE NEXT MORNING, MATT COASTED INTO A PARKING space beside the front door of the State Employment Office. One sign on the door said closed; another listed the hours as eight to five. He lifted Grandad's watch from his shirt pocket and saw he had half an hour to kill.

Opening his car door to the warm morning air, Matt leaned his seat back and watched butterflies flirt with pink crepe myrtle blossoms in the corner of the lot. His attention then turned to the kudzu vine climbing the corner of the building. Since the plant could grow sixty feet a year, he wondered whether even the door would be left uncovered by the end of the summer. Chuckling, he remembered Grandad telling him to listen carefully when near a clump of kudzu, because a person who had fallen asleep in his chair might be under it.

The pungent odor of a dirty body accented by beer and urine reached him before the man spoke.

"Mister, can you help a fellow out?"

Matt threw his left arm toward the voice and swung his body around, feeling a deep pain stab him in the back. In front of him was a sunburned face with thick, heavily creased skin drooping below the chin. Stringy, gray-streaked black hair that looked days uncombed surrounded his face. Baggy, filthy clothes hung on the man's skinny form and he was clutching a stained sleeping bag.

"What do you want? Get out of here!" *Hair looks like mine.*

The man had taken a step back and tried to smile. "Can you spare—?"

Flipping the back of his hand toward him, Matt yelled, "Get a job, you bum!" before slamming the car door and locking it. He noticed a tremor in his hands.

STANDING WITH HIS WEIGHT FIRST ON ONE LEG AND THEN the other, Matt watched a pleasant-looking woman turn over the sign hanging in the window and unlock the glass door. He was glad she was older, believing compassion and a desire to help accompanied age. Quickly stepping across the threshold, Matt nearly bumped into her. He smiled but spoke without his customary greeting. "Ma'am, I need a job. I'll take anything you've got."

Since no other clients were waiting, the woman allowed Matt to fill out the application across from her desk. She interviewed him as she read it. "High school graduate, good." She looked up. "A year of community college work?"

He nodded. "Yes, ma'am. I'm surprised myself."

"Let's see. Supermarket and factory work during your career. And you haven't worked lately because of surgery. Will that limit you?"

He rubbed his smoothly-shaven jaw and thought about how much more normal he felt—more an accepted part of the world—when he shaved and vowed to do it every day. He looked down. "Well, not sure I could do much lifting right now."

"Is there anything you would especially *like* to do?"

The woman's manner had put Matt at ease. "Yes, ma'am, I'd like to be President of the United States." Grinning, he pulled his chair closer to her desk. "Sorry, ma'am. I know this is serious. *Any* job. I'll take anything you have."

She laid down her pen and smiled. "That's all right. A little levity helps in this office. Truth is, jobs are scarce around here. I'm sure you've heard that." She turned to the computer screen. "The only possibility I see is this delivery job for Sunrise Bakery." She looked at Matt. "And you *are* physically able?"

Matt wished he didn't have to meet the woman's eyes. He believed she knew he wasn't being completely honest and that embarrassed him. And he felt guilty, because she was trying to help. He leaned back in the chair. "Uh, yes, ma'am. I bet I can handle it."

She turned back to the computer. "Now, it pays minimum wage, about half what you made before." She frowned. "This is a small company, so there's no health insurance or paid vacation. That all right?"

In the past, Matt would have refused the job and told her it wouldn't provide a decent living, but his definition of that term had changed. Now, it meant having food and a roof over his head. He nodded. "Better than nothing."

LIFTING HIS LEGS HIGH TO KEEP FROM STUMBLING AND holding his body rigidly straight, Matt crossed the parking lot of the Sunrise Bakery the next morning.

A man, partially hidden by the warehouse door, extended his hand and said, "Name's Fred Brinkley." Matt grasped the hand and shook it firmly.

"Well, you're a big fellow; you just might do. Ever driven one of these things before?"

Matt smiled warmly. "No, sir, don't believe I have. But when I was a boy, I drove just about everything else on my Grandad's farm."

The man's face relaxed. "I did, too." He slapped Matt on the shoulder. "Well, I'm the owner of this place and like to take a ride with my drivers. Let's see how you do with these boxes. Jump on up in this truck, and I'll tell you where to go."

Facing the driver's side door of the delivery truck, Matt looked at the height of the step. He grasped the door handle and pulled, but his body stayed where it was. On the second try, he reached the step. His next task was to get the door open and work his way into the driver's seat. By the time he accomplished that, he had sweat on his face and neck and imagined himself looking pale. He hoped the man would think he was hot, but that wasn't likely at six-thirty in the morning. This man was no fool.

By some miracle, he managed to raise his foot to the clutch the first time. The second time, it got caught, and he had to free it with his left hand. Once he didn't have to change gears, driving wasn't a problem. Worry left him long enough to ask the man what he thought about the heat they were having and to enjoy the scent of fresh, warm bread.

When Matt steered the truck into a space in front of Esau's Café, the engine jerked to a standstill. The bakery owner made no comment, just jumped out and headed to the back of the truck. Looking down, Matt knew he'd better not jump. His weight had to end up on his right leg on both the truck step and the pavement. When he reached the ground, upright but swaying, he saw the owner watching. Anybody with an ounce of common sense would know he couldn't do that twenty times a day.

Matt leaned on the back bumper of the truck while Mr. Brinkley carried boxes of bread into the Café. When he returned, he shook Matt's hand. "You seem like a good fellow. Wish I could hire you, but don't believe your back's ready for this. And I can't let people on pain medicine drive."

Although his experience with the bakery truck kept Matt in bed two days, he spent the time planning his next step.

After supper on the second day, he crossed the yard to use Nell's phone. She unhooked the screen door as he approached. Her hair was rolled into curls about the size of a quarter and lay flat on her head, fastened with bobby pins. Every strand was in place. The cotton dress she wore was frayed at the neckline but perfectly slick from starch and a hot iron. Nell was seventy-one years old, entirely on her own, yet able to create a life of perfect order. Matt envied her.

Bobby answered on the second ring. After Matt presented his idea to his cousin, neither man spoke.

Silence with Bobby was unusual. Matt felt so uncomfortable that he forced himself to speak. "Sorry to put you on the spot like this. Will you teach me or not?"

Bobby sighed heavily. "Boy, how can you work as a plumber with that back? Think you can crawl around under sinks? And dig trenches?"

Under ordinary circumstances, Matt would have loudly asked his cousin why he was asking such dumb questions, but this time, his voice trembled slightly. "Figure I don't have many choices. You're the only person I know who owns a business. Got to try something."

Bobby answered gently. "I won't say no to you. Meet me at the house at seven tomorrow morning. No, wait. I'll pick you up."

BOBBY WAS A MUSCULAR MAN BUT WEIGHED LESS AND was four inches shorter than Matt. By mid-morning, he held Matt around the waist, helped him stoop to the floor, and then pulled him up. He slipped his shoulder under Matt's arm when he walked, wouldn't let him carry anything, and babied him as much as he could. He asked Matt to take some pain pills and said he'd be glad to drive him to the doctor.

The sound of Bobby's voice and the look on his face astonished Matt. He saw a tenderness that hadn't appeared in the thirty-eight years they had known each other. A few times, he thought his cousin might cry.

At noon, Bobby said it was over. He was taking him home.

Lillie cried out when Bobby half-carried Matt through the door. She jumped up from the rocker, laid the baby she was holding in the crib, and followed them to the bedroom. Bobby eased Matt onto the pillow and lifted his legs. He untied his cousin's shoes and placed them under his bedside table. As he left the room, he whispered to Lillie, "He needs a doctor."

Lillie placed her hand on Matt's forehead. "Maybe your blood sugar's low. You look like you need food."

Her hand trembled as she fed him the vegetable soup, and she sounded as frustrated as a mother with a disobedient child. "Now, don't say a word. I'm calling Dr. Latham. You've been his patient since you were sixteen, and he'll know what to do."

Matt closed his eyes. "We can't—"

"Afford it. Right now, I don't care," Lillie said, slapping the mattress. "Insurance'll pay most of it."

Lillie picked up the babies, placing them in the crooks of her arms and called to Rachel and Bella. "Come on, sweethearts. We're going to see Miss Nell. Let's make our train—choo, choo."

Nell led the girls to her kitchen, where they baked a pretend chocolate cake, while Lillie talked to the nurse. "Yes, he'll be there tomorrow. Now, you *will* tell Dr. Latham everything I've said about the last four months?"

17

JIM HARTMAN HADN'T TURNED ON THE OFFICE LIGHT when he struck the match, and the glow of its fire held his attention a few seconds. Then he remembered his promise to Melanie to quit smoking and blew it out. Leaning back in his chair, his thoughts stayed with the burnt matchstick in the ashtray. He wondered, when people looked at him, a man as bland and ordinary as that small piece of wood, did they have any idea of the fire within him? Did they know how capable he was? "Of course, they don't," Jim said aloud.

That reminded him of his college graduation. It was a warm spring day and his father and brother had rushed out of the stadium at the end of the ceremony and were lost in the crowd for some time. His mother had waited by the tunnel where the students exited and slipped in line beside him. She took his hand in hers and whispered, "I'm proud of you." A worried look replaced her smile and she mumbled, "We have to hurry and find your father." Three friends trailed Jim and his mother while making plans to meet at Joe's Bar as soon as they could stow their robes.

Jim spotted his father and brother talking animatedly in a small circle of shade. He walked up just as his father was congratulating his brother about something. At that moment, he wanted to step between them and talk about his plan for manufacturing hair products. But he hesitated seconds too long and the words wouldn't come.

Jim's mother grasped his father's hand as Professor Hartman cleared his throat and asked loudly, "Well, James, what now? Where will you go with an undergrad degree in business administration?"

Jim turned toward his friends and called out over his shoulder, "Well, Dad, right now it's taking me to a party! See you around."

Jim had done more than party, though he revealed little to his father until it was done. He had learned organizational skills, discipline, and to work hard. And it felt like he had done it on his own. He was more confident now than at any time in his life. His cleverness in managing Matthew Bradfurd had erased his last doubts about his ability as a businessman. The year was ending, and he had loosened a huge potential financial liability from his payroll, chopping off the head of the workers' comp snake before it slithered through his company. He wished he could tell someone how proud he was.

The buzz of his phone jolted Jim from his thoughts and he sighed. While leaning forward, he accidentally touched his cheek and was stunned to discover that his face was wet.

Tibby told him his father was calling.

"From Ann Arbor? You're sure?" Jim jumped from his chair and stood rigidly before his desk. He used his right middle finger to press line one and was aware of a twinge of pain in front of his right temple. "Yeah, Dad. What's going on?"

"Son, how are you? And the girls and Melanie? It's been a long time." Professor Hartman hesitated. "Is work going, um, well?"

The pain was spreading to Jim's jaw, making it hard to open his mouth. "Um, hmm. Good. Mom okay?"

"Of course, your mother's healthy and busy, as usual. Still volunteering with United Way and Planned Parenthood. I'm doing well. Your brother's made full professor. His wife's pediatric practice is very successful. Their boys are brilliant and make us all proud. And I have news! Your mother and I are coming to visit during spring break."

"Here? But why?"

"It's been three years since we were there. Don't you think it's about time? We don't want to neglect our granddaughters."

Jim felt like someone had punched him in the abdomen. "It's just. We'll be coming there this summer. To the lake. In only six months."

The professor shouted, "Splendid! We'll see you in March and again this summer. And then, well, your mother thought we should wait to tell you, but I can't. Very likely, we'll move to Cross Hill. We're planning to look at houses while we're there. Maybe a rental first."

"You're kidding! Why?"

"Jim, can you ask anything besides why?"

The two men slipped into a familiar silence until the professor interrupted it. He spoke slowly. "Let me start over. I'm stepping down as chair of the department at the end of this academic year and will retire the end of December. Seventy's old enough. Don't you think?"

Jim remained quiet.

"Our primary reason for moving there is to be with your family. We spent the last ten years with our grandsons and want to know our granddaughters better." His father's voice regained its energy. "Another thing. I've become excited about genealogical research. Remember the great-grandfather I told you about who lived near Cross Hill? His life interests me. I may write a book about him."

When his father hung up, Jim slammed down the phone. *Jesus Christ! Now, the fucker wants to be around me!* He lifted the mangled cigar he had smoked two days before from the ashtray, rummaged the bottom drawer for his scissors, and struggled to snip off the burnt end. Although he had a full box of Macanudos in the drawer, he was determined to finish smoking that one and no one could stop him. As he tried to get past the charred tobacco, Jim was forced to puff harder and harder, causing him to feel dizzy. And the taste in his mouth was bitter.

The more he thought about the reasons his father gave for moving, the less Jim believed them. Research could be done in any library or online. And to say he wanted to get to know the girls better was just plain bull. His father and brother were joined at the hip. No one mattered more to them than the other; they were stand-up comedians doing a routine that never ended. He wouldn't leave him except for something very important. *He's coming here just to make me miserable.*

Jim spit the cigar in the ashtray letting it smolder, dialed his wife, and repeated what his father had said.

Melanie cried, "Wonderful! Our children will have grandparents here. That's so great!"

Jim rolled his eyes. "Why do you say that? Anyway, we're leaving in a few years."

She didn't back down. "We're not sure we're moving. I like it here."

"Mel—."

"Can we finish this later? I have to pick up the girls. See you at six. Don't be late. I love you."

Her last words caused Jim to relax. He wouldn't be late. Since he had started going home at six, the changes in his relationship with Melanie had amazed him: She greeted him with a smile and a kiss. Her voice was cheerful. When she said, "I love you," he thought she probably meant it. The girls fought about who would sit on his lap first. Although most of the chatter about their day bored him, he had learned to listen. In the past few years, he realized just how much he loved Melanie and the girls. And knowing he had found a dedicated, insightful woman made him proud.

When the air conditioner came on, the stirring of air broke the stream of smoke curling from his cigar. *But don't mess up my plan! I'm moving to Ann Arbor.*

The last confrontation he had with Melanie about leaving town came to his mind. "What I want is important, too," she had said. "The girls are happy. It's the only place I've ever felt I belonged." Ignoring his attempts to stop her from continuing, she said that while she would never put anything ahead of her job as wife and mother, working at the Senior Center made her feel she was contributing to the world. "There's more to life than money and houses, Jim. And no plan is written in stone."

It wasn't that Jim objected to her serving old people lunch a while longer. That was harmless enough, didn't take too much time and helped his standing in the community. Small town people expected business leaders to do charity work, and hers took care of it for him. As he wondered how he'd get past her, he kicked the front of his desk hard. She could be tough when she made up her mind about something. But she needed to know he was leaving in a few years, no matter what.

He slammed the other foot against his desk. *Why can't she understand? Those people up there were wrong about me. I need to show them I can be somebody without cramming my square self in a round hole.* "And, hell, making money's good."

Jim suddenly had a desire to tell his father how clever he had been in overcoming the workers' comp problem in his company. He wanted him to see how harmful the situation could be to a small business owner. He would like to tell him that most owners caved in and supported the employee when he was tired of working, but that he had resisted! And what discipline and skill it had taken to stop it. He would admit that he had nothing against his workers personally, but that he had located his factory down South because they weren't organized and that was better for all concerned. "Look!" he wanted to say. "I give jobs to forty-five people. Give me some credit!"

Watching the cigar smoke spiral upward, once again undisturbed by the surrounding air, Jim smacked his thigh. *Wait! Mel didn't seem surprised about my father's call. Are they working together on this?*

18

Dr. Latham's smile disappeared when he saw Matt's thin, somber face. "Good lord, man. I haven't seen you this skinny since you were twenty years old! How much have you lost?"

Matt lay on the doctor's examination table with a light cotton blanket pulled up to his chin. "Haven't been hungry. Chilly in here." Matt shivered. "Can't seem to get over this surgery."

The doctor reached for his hand. His voice was playful. "What's this I hear about you staying in bed four months? You getting lazy?" He moved his fingers to Matt's pulse. "A little fast." He stepped back from the table. "Let me see you walk."

Matt gave him a skeptical look. "Okay." Grasping the side of the exam table, he pulled. On the third try, he and the doctor, together, succeeded in standing him up.

He stumbled toward the door, clutching at the door knob when he reached it.

Dr. Latham threw his arms out to his sides. "Good god. You can hardly walk! How long you been dragging that foot?"

Matt shook his head. "Don't know."

Placing a shoulder under his patient's arm, he led him to a chair. "When did you see Ramsey last? What'd he say?"

Ed Latham slipped a paper cup from the holder beside the sink and filled it with water for Matt. Then he took another for himself. His anger was about to overwhelm him; he needed to calm down before he said more. While he drank the water, he saw himself stretching out on the chair and ottoman in his office, doing his relaxation routine. Noticing the goose pimples on Matt's arms, he wrapped him in the cotton blanket before sitting down beside him.

"Now, let's go back. What did Dr. Ramsey say the last time you saw him?"

Matt opened his eyes wide and shook his head again. "Just said to give it time."

Ed clenched his fists. He rarely lost track of a patient's condition; he felt guilty and embarrassed. His voice rose. "Time my foot! You're worse off than before surgery. You didn't drive here, did you?"

Matt looked down.

"Tell me everything that's happened since you got the second opinion from Dr. Carlisle."

As Matt's story drew to a close, Ed took over. "What about your diabetes? Been checking your blood sugar and taking the insulin?"

He shook his head. "Well, haven't had—"

"Damn it, boy. You're playing with fire with this illness." Ed rubbed his forehead—knowing he had to calm down—and imagined sitting on the bank at High Rock with a fishing pole. He relaxed his jaw. "Diabetes causes heart attacks, strokes, kidney failure, blindness. Problems with your nerves, circulation, skin, even your gums. Stress from pain and surgery make the sugar rise. On top of that, you can't exercise, which is *absolutely necessary* for controlling the sugar level. What about your blood pressure? You taking those pills?"

Ed noticed his patient grasp the arms of his chair and take a deep breath, as if he were about to be hit. He turned away from Matt, wishing for a window in the room; looking outside provided some distance from people's troubles. "No need to answer. Doesn't insurance cover them?"

Matt nodded. "But there're co-pays for everything. Lillie *has* to have seizure medicine, and we have to buy a little food."

Remembering Matt's mother's struggle to support her son after her husband's death, Ed laid his hand on Matt's arm. His attachment to Matt was related to his feelings for her. When filling out her death certificate, he had wanted to write Cause of Death: Exhaustion.

Ed stared at the medical school diploma hanging on the wall above Matt's head, and thought how inadequate his education had been for dealing with all his patients' needs. "Well, let's see. What can we do?" His voice faded, blending with the air. For a minute he sat nodding and patting Matt's arm.

You've got to face certain facts. You may never be able to work again and money has to come from somewhere. I want you to go on disability—at least for a while. Go to the Social Security office. I'll send them a letter explaining everything."

Returning to his area of expertise, Ed sounded more hopeful. "Now, your most important job is to take care of your body. Watch your blood pressure and diabetes. Get enough exercise to keep yourself upright. I'd like you to have physical therapy, but you probably won't be able to afford it. I know that. You'll have to live with the pain and just stay off your feet." He slapped Matt's arm as he stood. "Go on, now, and apply for that disability."

"Well, sir. Accepting your facts is easier said than done." The harsh unfamiliar tone of his patient's voice caused Ed to back up and lean against a glass cabinet. "You want to know what that means? I can't take care of Lillie or Beth—even myself—anymore. I have to watch my wife work without being able to help. And you want me to beg the government to do it for me? I can't even pay *you*. Could you live with those facts?"

Ed watched silently, as Matt closed his eyes and lowered his head. "I'm sorry. I don't have the right to fuss at you."

The doctor picked up a wooden tongue depressor and tapped the counter. "You're correct. I've never had to live with that and might not have the courage." His voice softened. "But, I don't know what else you can do." A white plastic basin used to catch liquids sat next to the area he was tapping. "Wait a minute!" He whirled around to face Matt. "What about your workers' comp?"

Matt shook his head. "I don't know what that is."

Ed perched on the edge of a stool. "When a person's injured at work, the company—or their insurer—pays him a percent of his salary a certain period of time."

Matt continued shaking his head. "Never heard of that. I didn't get a dime from anybody. But, like I told my boss, I don't know what happened to my back. I just went home one day with pain, and it kept getting worse. Mr. Hartman said to have the surgery, and he'd hold my job. But when I tried to get it back, he wouldn't take me. He never mentioned anything else."

Suddenly, Ed Latham remembered the day he was about to run a man down with his father's tractor. He had suspected him of stealing a calf from the farm. As fear on the man's face increased, so did Ed's desire to hurt him. He often wondered what he would have done if his father hadn't come running across the field and stopped him. And he wondered what he would do if he came across Matt's boss in a field.

"Lifting heavy boxes, year after year, will wreck some backs. And then jar it with an accident..." The doctor steadied himself. "Let me give more thought to this. For now, here's what we'll do. Don't see Ramsey again. I'll take over your care. Come in again next week. My nurse will give you enough blood pressure and diabetes pills to last until then. You are not allowed to work under any circumstances. And don't drive. Too dangerous."

THE DOCTOR WATCHED MATT LIMP FROM THE EXAM room. "We'll get a brace to hold that foot up," he called. *My god, what a mess. This man's about to go under. A little more and he won't recover.* Ed went down the hall to his office, going directly to the window, where his gaze settled on the blue bachelor buttons and red geraniums blooming in the square. Ordinarily, when he looked down from his window, his reaction was "Beautiful town." Harsher thoughts came today. *Huh. One problem with this town is those who run it'd rather keep flowers alive than people.*

As Ed settled into his large leather desk chair, he glanced at the pictures of his mother, father, and grandparents on the top shelf of his bookcase. *Thank you for my good genes.* Then he focused on his father's picture. *Where would I be if you hadn't caught me?* Wrinkling his nose, he laughed. Anytime he thought of his family home, he turned his head toward one shoulder, and then the other, and sniffed. The smells of the farm were hard to get rid of and clung in more ways than one.

Propping his elbows on the desk, Ed rested his head in his hands. *This mess is my fault. I recommended the surgical evaluation, and I chose Ramsey.* He remembered a rumor he had heard at the County Medical Society meeting six months earlier about the orthopedist having high complication rates and trouble relating to patients. He dismissed it then because the man spreading it was a competitor, but now he knew he had made a mistake.

He picked up the green fountain pen his wife had given him for Christmas and wrote, "See weekly. Stabilize sugar and pressure. Chair exercises. Foot brace. Disability letter to SS." Ed tapped his pen hard against the desk pad. *Foot brace? Where the hell will he get money for that? Needs some kind of program.* Ed hissed through clenched teeth, "Program, my ass." *People moan and groan about the welfare burden in this country, but I see people working two jobs and still not making ends meet. And if they can't work, well, throw them out with the garbage. Who cares?*

Ed glanced at the fishing poles waiting in the corner and wished he could pick them up and leave everyone behind. Making his world the way he wanted hadn't worked. Thirteen years ago, when he had begun his process of "pulling weeds,"—getting rid of everything and everyone in his garden that displeased him—Ellen had warned that he couldn't live in a bubble. His wife had been correct. Poverty, misfortune, and people he didn't like sprouted up everywhere, no matter how often he picked at them.

Leaning close to the pictures of Ellen and his children on the desk, he beamed as he thought of the health and intelligence behind their handsome, smiling faces. He wondered whether they knew what they had been given. Had he ever told them how much genetic inheritance determined their lives? That they hadn't earned most of what they had? That luck existed, as a powerful force, clearing a path for some but not for all? Had he ever directly warned, "Beware the sin of pride?"

"Damn!" Ed banged his fist on his desk and shouted, "He didn't even get workers' comp." *I need help! What the hell happened to George Russell?*

His nurse's head appeared around a half-opened door. "Want anything?"

"No, Louise, thank you. Tell people I'm sorry I'm holding them up. Just give me another minute to make a call. And, do you know anybody who works for Organic Botanicals?"

19

LILLIE HUMMED WHILE KNEADING THE FLOUR, CRISCO, and milk. Then she set the bowl containing her biscuit dough aside, opened the pantry door, and frowned: only six cans of vegetables left on the shelves. As she reached for a can of lima beans, she thought of her garden. Although it was mostly dead, she hadn't checked it the last two days. Maybe something was there.

Walking along the first row, Lillie passed drooping corn stalks and yellow vines—their brown leaves lying flat in the warm sun. *They look exhausted but fed the three of us for four months and deserve to be tired.* Unwilling to give up, Lillie rolled up her pant legs and got down on her hands and knees in the crusty, rough dirt. Crawling along the row, she pushed aside skeletons of old plants to search for their offspring. At the end of the second row, she found five yellow squash, and in the last, two small, misshapen tomatoes.

Squash, tomatoes, limas, and biscuits would be enough supper for her and Matt. Beth was working at the drug store and would eat there. Lillie tried not to think about it: the only food they sold was candy and chips.

She struggled to push up, then brushed the dirt from her hands and shook her flip flops. Feeling like she had accomplished something, Lillie picked up her pile of vegetables and rushed to the living room to show Matt.

"You won't believe what I found!"

Sitting in his chair with his hands folded, Matt didn't open his eyes when he spoke. "I saw the letter from the power company. You hiding it from me?"

As Lillie dropped the vegetables in the front pocket of her apron, she noticed he wore two pairs of socks. "No point in worrying you. You cold?"

Sitting upright, he pushed down the footrest of his chair. He had pulled his heavy red sweatshirt over his T shirt. He sounded angry. "They'll turn the lights off a week from tomorrow if we don't pay. What did you think you'd do?"

She swept back the hair that had fallen from her ponytail, fastening it with a plastic clip. "Well, I'm sorry. Don't get your dander up. I'm taking that letter to Social Services first thing tomorrow morning. Myra's keeping the children for me."

Matt covered his mouth with his hand. His voice was filled with sarcasm. "Yeah, right! Good luck!"

"Now, wait a minute!" Lillie stepped closer to his chair, allowing the vegetables in her apron pocket to bump his shoulder. "They know people need to be able to cook and have lights. I think they'll pay it."

Matt raised his eyebrows and looked up at her. Feeling immediate remorse for her action, Lillie hoped he thought it was an accident. She leaned over and kissed him on the cheek. "Let's not worry so much. We're in the hands of the Lord. He knows what He's doing."

She was halfway to the kitchen when he called out. "Know what I think's happening? We've been swept into a deep, wild river. Every time we reach for a tree branch to pull out, it changes course on us." Matt's voice lost its emotion. "I don't think we're strong enough to buck the current, Lillie. We might *never* live the way we did before." He slumped down in his chair. "Maybe even drown one of these days."

Lillie was grateful that she couldn't see his face.

THIS TIME LILLIE WAS SMARTER. SHE STOOD AS CLOSE to the door handle of the Social Services building as possible, blocking anyone from getting ahead of her. When it swung open, she asked the woman behind the window for a financial assistance application. Then she sat in one of the waiting room chairs with a magazine on her lap, tucked her hair behind her ears, and began filling it out. The young woman behind her got up and handed hers to the receptionist. Lillie wiped the sweat from her forehead with the tissue in her pocket and took a deep breath. Another woman crossed the room with her application. Lillie's hands began to shake. *Don't worry. Take your time.* She tried hard not to think about what anyone else in the room was doing. When she finished, she was fifth in line.

An hour and forty-five minutes after she arrived, Lillie sat across the desk from a social worker. Her hands were still shaking. "Mrs. Bradfurd, your solution is simple." The woman leaned back in her chair and smiled broadly. "Just take out a mortgage on your house."

Lillie smiled without intending it. The joy she felt when she had written the last check for her mortgage came to her mind. "No, no. I mean, no, ma'am. I can't do that. It took me a long time to pay it off."

The slim, well-groomed woman was gentle and reassuring. "Yes, it must have. And it's good you did that, so now, you have this resource."

Lillie felt heat rising to her face. She wondered how long the young woman had been a social worker and whether she truly understood her situation. "Ma'am, if I can't pay my light bill, how can I pay a mortgage?"

"You'll use the money you borrow to pay the mortgage *and* your bills."

Lillie thought that was a ridiculous idea—borrowing money to pay for something she already owned—and she couldn't bear to start over with such a large debt. She tried to sound appreciative and polite. "What will I do when the money runs out?"

"You'll cross that bridge when you come to it. Maybe your circumstances will change."

Although Lillie smiled and chuckled to soften the edge in her voice, she stopped pretending. "Ma'am, my house is sixty-eight years old. It has five little rooms. The roof leaks in three places. The kitchen and bathroom need to be replaced. It needs paint, inside and out, and doesn't have a lick of insulation. The yard's a patch of weeds. How much money you think the bank would give me on that?

"If I got a mortgage, the money would be gone in no time, and I'd be right back where I started, except I might lose my house. Then I'd have to move and pay rent. But if I couldn't pay, what would I do? Come here?"

The look on the social worker's face alarmed Lillie. She told herself to calm down and grasped one hand with the other to stop trembling. She considered apologizing for her rudeness, but realized it wouldn't make any difference so she decided to finish. "Ma'am, have you ever worried about not having a place to live?" Lillie slapped her chest. "I have. I know what it's like, and I'll tell you something. I'd rather starve *inside* a house than *outside*." She shook her head. "No, ma'am, I'm not going to risk losing my house."

LILLIE MOVED THE DRIVER'S SEAT OF THE IMPALA AS FAR back as it would go and stretched her legs. *Lord, help me with that temper. What will I tell Matt?* She heard herself say, "Hurry. You've got to get back," but made no effort to start the car. Instead, she covered her face with her hands. *I could cry a hundred years. Don't.* She wiped her eyes with the sleeve of her baggy brown sweater. *He'll be upset. It's easier on him when I'm mad.*

She yelled, "But what about me?" Barely able to see over the steering wheel, Lillie felt like a girl. "Foot!" She dried her cheeks with the sleeve. "Who makes things easy on me? If Matt wants to take care of me like he says, why can't he stop whining and feeling sorry for himself? Can't he act *happy* once in a while and ask how *I* feel?"

Lillie's gaze had settled on a magnolia tree beside the parking lot. She wished her father was here. People had told her how much he loved and spoiled her. They said her twenty-three year-old mother had blamed herself when he was killed in the car wreck and was overcome with grief. She had pulled out her hair, curled up, and stopped eating. Within two years, she was sent to the State Insane Asylum, dying the next winter from pneumonia.

At least, that's what people had said. The only part of it Lillie remembered was her grandmother— her father's mother. She had moved in with five-year-old Lillie and saved her life. When Lillie didn't want to start first grade, it was Grandma who sat beside her desk until the fear left. It was she who left work early, waiting outside the classroom for the bell to ring. It was Grandma's hand ready to clasp hers, whenever she needed it, day or night.

Lillie and her grandmother moved six months after her mother died. The mortgage hadn't been paid since the car wreck, and the bank took her father's house.

The first rental lasted a year. The owner needed to sell and asked Grandma if she would like to buy it. That was the time in Lillie's life when she began to hold on to experiences as memories, and the only time she saw her grandmother cry. Her sobs were as fresh and real to Lillie as they had been thirty-one years before.

Searching for the sun, Lillie rolled down the car window and leaned her head out. It was nearly straight up. *Got to get home.* A familiar discomfort arose around her eyes that prevented her from starting the car. *Seizure? Be quiet.* She touched her forehead lightly with her fingers and brought them across her face to the back of her neck. The feeling passed. *Stress.*

Seizures had been part of Lillie's life since she was nine. The only thing she remembered about the first one was waking up in a dark room saying, "I feel funny."

Her grandmother turned on the light. "Sick on your stomach?"

Lillie shook her head and went back to sleep.

After supper on a Monday in October, it had happened again. Lillie had a queasy feeling in her stomach. She was dizzy and felt a strange sensation around her eyes. Her left hand jerked and her eyelids fluttered. Grandma said her mouth moved as if she was chewing and her eyes were open, but she acted like a person who had passed out. Said it lasted about three minutes.

The next morning, her grandmother took her to a doctor who sent her to another. That one performed an EEG test on her brain and described the problem. "This little lady is having *petit mal* seizures. Good news is they're not *grand mal*—the big kind. We don't know what's causing them, and there's no cure. They can be managed with medication, which she'll take all her life. She needs blood drawn twice a year to make sure she's getting the right amount. The pills will affect her body in other ways, so we'll have to watch her."

"Watch her," were words Grandma had taken to heart. The two of them moved in with Lillie's mother's parents, so they could all watch her.

It was getting hot in the car. As Lillie took off her sweater, she wondered why she hadn't gone home. Myra was waiting. But she ignored the push to go, continuing her journey to the past. Thinking about the two years she had lived with three grandparents, she exhaled loudly. *Talk about stifling.*

The next house her grandmother found had a bedroom for each of them—but was more than she could afford. Lillie mumbled, "God was watching out for us." The owner had been a friend of Grandma's deceased husband when he was young and felt he owed him a debt. He said he had saved him from going in a direction that would have ruined his life and wanted to repay him by cutting their rent in half. And said they could live there as long as they wanted.

It was the most beautiful place Lillie had lived in. A brick fireplace in the living room stood across from an arched opening that led to the dining room. The side porch door, with its small glass squares, laid colored lights on the floor in winter. The porch was shaded by a plum tree and screened on three sides, allowing breezes to cross it freely.

After they moved into the house, their lives changed. They laughed every day. Her grandmother's face smoothed out. People came to visit. They had peaches, plums, and figs from their own trees. They planted a garden and canned vegetables. They felt safe.

When the man who owned the house died, he willed that it be sold to them for nine thousand dollars. Grandma had quit the embroidery factory but earned money by keeping children. Because Lillie was twenty-one and worked at the gas company, she was able to get a mortgage. When she and Matt married, he moved in with them and that's where they were still.

Lillie shoved the car seat forward and sat up straight. She turned toward the social worker's office. Tears rose and her voice cracked. "So, hear me good! I'll scrape together money for my property taxes before anything else, and you'll never take my house."

20

BETH AWOKE, FEELING CONFUSED AND GROGGY. SHE glanced at the clock. *Four in the afternoon?* She threw back the quilt and looked for the American History book she had been studying when she dozed off. It lay on the floor beside her bed. She picked it up, tucked the blanket around her, and propped the book on her abdomen to resume her search for the dates of America's wars. Her exam was scheduled for nine the next morning, and she still didn't know when World War II and the Korean War had started. Remembering the dates of the Revolution, Mexican, Civil, Spanish-American, and World War I was easy because her dad had repeated Grandad's stories so often.

She flipped pages, but her attention was lost. *House is too quiet.* Throwing the book aside, she slipped off the bed, tiptoed across the room, and touched her ear to the door. *Wonder how Daddy's feeling?* When her mother and father argued about their worries—they called it *discussing*—Beth felt relieved, because she discovered what was on their minds. But silence made it hard so hard to keep her mind on something like historythat she had made a C minus on the last exam. Silence pushed her imagination toward dread.

Beth shivered in her sweatshirt and underwear. Since the furnace was a wall unit in the living room and only put out heat there, her room was cold when the door was closed. Forcing herself to turn back so she could study, she paused to look out the window at the dark clouds. She smelled rain coming. *I wonder if—stop! Study!* Throwing herself on the bed, she picked up the history book and her nail file. *But what's going on? Why don't I hear Mama?*

Promising herself she'd be gone just a few minutes, she pulled on her blue sweatpants and opened the bedroom door. When she stepped into the hallway, she felt a rush of warm air. It reminded her of the day her mother had returned from a cousin's house with money to pay the light bill. Watching her mother sob with gratitude had made Beth and her father cry, too.

She crept around the corner to the living room. Her father was lying in his La-Z-Boy with his eyes closed. She looked toward the bedroom and saw her mother on the bed. Turning back to her father, Beth leaned over and listened to his breathing. It seemed too shallow for him to be asleep.

Noticing how pale his face was, Beth laid her hand on his arm and whispered, "Hey, Daddy. How you feel?"

Matt's eyes remained closed. "Okay."

Determined to get more than that, Beth patted his shoulder and made her voice cheerful. "Today's Sunday, you know. Had your tea yet?"

"Don't think I'll have any today."

She shook his arm. "Oh, come on. I'll make it for you. What about tradition? And Great-grandmother?"

Moving his arm away from her hand, her father sounded irritated. "Not in the mood. Let it go."

Squatting beside his chair, Beth realized there was another meaning to the term passing away—something besides the heart stopping and the brain dying. People passed from one way of being to another, like her father had. The man she had counted on to guide her was disappearing. He was moving to a world of pain and hopelessness where she didn't matter. And she demanded to know, right then, whether he would return.

She tapped him on the shoulder as she stood. "Now, listen. You're always picking on me because I don't drink tea with you. If you'll have some today, I will, too." She leaned over and kissed him on the nose. "*And,* I'll prove I know the story."

Her father raised his eyebrows and almost smiled. "You've got a deal."

Beth found the jar with the blue-gray leaves in the back of the pantry. She had watched her mother carefully pick the sage leaves and lay them on a towel to dry before storing them in old jelly jar. She made a face. The taste and smell of sage, whether in turkey dressing or tea, made her want to gag. She took out three leaves, crushed them with her fingers and dropped them into the mugs. As she poured the hot water over them, the steam that reached her nose forced her to turn away and talk to her stomach. *Behave. Don't get sick on me.*

After pouring half her tea into the sink, Beth carried the mugs to the living room. When she noticed how tired her father looked, she felt guilty for having disturbed him. "Want me to tell the story before I drink it?"

Matt sat up and sipped the hot liquid. "Sure you know it?"

Standing in front of him, Beth felt as nervous as when she had to answer in class. "*You'll* see. Now, don't help me. It was 1774, and the King of England put an extra tax on tea. People said my *sixth* great-grandmother Bradfurd loved tea just a shade less than she loved her children. Some suspected she loved it more. But she *hated* being taken advantage of. When Grandmother heard about the boycott they started in Charlotte, she convinced her friends to join in. They stopped drinking imported tea cold turkey and made their own from berries and sage. She said as long as she could give up what she wanted, she'd be free from any kind of tyranny."

Beth raised her cup. "Here, Daddy. To freedom." Trying not to smell the greenish liquid, she gulped the half cup, and then laid her hand on her father's head and fluffed his hair. "I'm going to drink it every Sunday, the way you do."

Matt smiled halfheartedly. "Good girl."

Beth knew he was trying hard to be involved with her playfulness but was probably wishing she would leave him alone. She sat down in her mother's rocking chair. Her father closed his eyes. Her long hair swung back and forth as she pushed hard with her heels to make the rocker go fast on the shaggy gold carpet. Although expressing herself was not usually a problem, she struggled to find the words she wanted.

She stopped the rocker and nervously twisted her hair as if trying to pin it on top her head. "Daddy?" Her throat felt tight. "Daddy, I need to know. Will you teach the stories to *my* children?" Pressing her lips together, she tried to prevent a cry from escaping. Then she blurted out, "Are you going to be all right?"

Her father blinked and leaned forward. He paused to clear his throat before answering with a strong voice. "Don't worry, honey. I'll be here."

Beth started the rocker moving, again, but slower this time. She sniffed and released words that surprised her. "Daddy, I want to go to college." Then she gazed at her father a moment before crying the way she had as a girl—before his surgery.

"Why you crying?" Matt pushed hard on the footrest of his chair. "*What* did you say about college?"

She pulled the rocker close to his chair. "I might not be smart enough. What do *you* think?"

Matt grasped her hand. "You're the smartest girl in the world. And I can tell you this." Beth thought she saw a sparkle in his eyes. "You're a whole lot smarter than our governor!"

Beth's mouth dropped open. Her face lit up. She wanted to respond to his teasing, and then jump up and tell her mother what she had seen, but she didn't do either. It was important to hear the answer to her next question. "Will we have the money?"

Her father leaned back and looked up at the ceiling. "Umm. Yes." They sat in silence a few minutes. "I'll get it. Don't you worry, gal."

IT WAS WARMER MONDAY MORNING THAN IT SHOULD HAVE been in late fall. Lillie had opened the bedroom window in front of Matt's chair and the door behind him to create a cross-breeze. He sat with his eyes closed, as the little wind touched his foot, brushed his arm, and then his face. His mind rested on one question. Where would he get the money to send his daughter to college? He thought a scholarship was unlikely. He'd heard about grants and loans but couldn't imagine getting enough to pay for everything. And there was work; Beth wasn't afraid of it, but it was pretty clear to him she would need all her time to study.

Then Matt remembered his own attempt to go to the community college. His mother had died, so he had to pay rent and living expenses. The fantasy of becoming an architect had clouded his vision until the reality of eight hours stocking shelves in a grocery store, followed by a three-hour evening class, set in. Although he struggled to study when he got home from class, most nights he fell asleep on the couch. And that reminded him of something he had discovered in high school. Learning didn't come easy to him.

Matt wasn't aware of Lillie being in the room until she laid her hand on his shoulder and dropped an envelope on his lap. "Hope I didn't wake you. Just couldn't wait. It's from the insurance company."

After glancing at the return address, he smacked the envelope on his thigh a time or two before ripping it open. "All right. Here it is. Says eighteen months have passed. Our COBRA policy's over. We can get health insurance through a HIPPA law." He looked up at Lillie. "Whatever that is. But it'll cost more and won't cover my back for the first year. I knew this train was coming, Lillie, but what can you do when you're tied to the track? We can't pay more than we do now." He flipped the letter on the floor. "One more thing—gone."

Rubbing the back of his neck with one hand and his shoulder with the other, Lillie spoke softly. "We'll find a policy. How could it cost more than the $537 we're already paying? Don't start worrying about it."

As she bent down to pick up the letter, Matt smacked the arm of his chair and yelled, "I'm tired of hearing you say that!" Startled, Lillie nearly fell head-first to the floor before grabbing her rocker and steadying herself. When he said, "I'm sorry, forgive me for that, girl," he noticed that she looked away.

Perhaps to get his mind off feelings of guilt for his rudeness to Lillie and worries about college money, Matt decided to do something, immediately. "Myra's sister still sells insurance. I'm going to call her."

Sounding confident, the woman told him not to worry. His coverage extended two more weeks, and that would be plenty of time to find a new policy. Ten days later, she called back. The cheapest policy cost $768 a month and wouldn't cover his back, leg, or foot for a year. Matt found himself trying to make her feel better. "Don't apologize. You did the best you could. We'll be all right."

As Matt walked slowly from Nell's house through the red and brown leaves in his yard, the toe of his right shoe was caught by an exposed tree root. Pain exploded in his back, causing him to cry out and throw himself against the plum tree. Panting, he wrapped both arms around it, laid his face against the rough bark, and wondered, *Will my touch cause you to die?*

When he reached the bottom of the front steps, Matt took out his handkerchief, blew his nose, and wished he could pick up his foot and beat himself to death with it. That would be easier than telling Lillie he had failed again.

As he opened the door to the living room, he said, "Well, looks like Santa brought an early Christmas present—a lump of coal."

Lillie was helping Bella put a dress on a doll. Patting her on the back, she said, "Just a minute, honey." Her brow furrowing, she grunted and pushed up from the sofa. "Well, don't...oh, I mean, we'll manage."

Matt was surprised at the effort it took for her to get up. Hearing the words and looking down at the sweetness on her raised face, he realized how brave she was. She was forty-four years old, seriously overweight, and had just been told she couldn't have medical care if she got sick. Her response was the same as always: trust God and take it one day at a time.

And there was her loyalty. Although her husband provided no financial security, she would never criticize or turn her back on him. Sometimes, like this moment, Matt wished she would. *Go on! Get mad. Yell at me. Make me feel better.*

Speaking words he hadn't planned with an intensity that sounded like he was angry at her, Matt asked, "We will? Manage with what? I keep taking things from you. Don't you know that? Now, my daughter needs money for college, and I can't give it to her!"

Feeling ashamed and imagining that even the little girl could see he was a failure, Matt turned away. His voice lost its strength. "I'm dragging you both down."

When Lillie hugged him around his waist and laid her head on his back, her large breasts and soft belly felt warm and comforting.

"Don't say that. Beth loves you. I love you. My heart would be empty if you didn't fill it every morning with your love." Letting go of his waist, Lillie stepped in front of him. "Now, stop!" The green in her eyes had intensified. Her cheeks were flushed. She rushed toward the kitchen, the girls laughing and following in her footsteps. Within seconds, she returned holding a pen and a sheet of notebook paper.

Her speech and movements reminded Matt of a scene from an old *I Love Lucy* television show. Gusts of wind pushed her one way, then another.

"I have a great idea." Lillie handed him the pen and paper. "Make a list of our medicines and add them up. Tegratol, eighty-five. Blood pressure, diabetes, anti-inflammatories, pain pills. What is it?" She looked over his shoulder as he listed them.

"Okay. $365.20 a month. That's not as much as we pay for insurance. See? Here's what we'll do. We'll use the insurance money to buy medicine. If we need a doctor, we'll ask to pay on time. If they say, no, so be it." She shrugged. "We just won't go."

Matt wanted to grab his wife's arm, slow her down, and ask, "What will happen if one of us ends up in the hospital? Could we pay *that* on time? How many years do you think it would take?" But he didn't want to embarrass her, so he nodded and said, "That might work."

Standing in the middle of the living room with a little girl holding each hand and twirling like tiny ballerinas, Lillie continued. "And let's look at Christmas different this year. Why buy stuff we don't need? Why not be thankful for what we have? How can we show God we're grateful? I know! Let's do something for other people.

"Remember you used to visit Little Red and take him food? He must wonder where you are. And that elderly couple—you mowed their yard. You're good for people. Go talk to them. Come home and tell me about them."

The girls had stopped dancing and gone back to their dolls. Lillie sat on the arm of Matt's chair and pointed a finger. "Right now, I want you to call Dr. Latham and tell him you have to drive. Tell him you won't take no for an answer."

Matt reached around his wife and pulled her toward him. His lower lids cradled tears. "What have I done to deserve a woman like you?"

ONCE LILLIE HAD MENTIONED LITTLE RED'S NAME, MATT couldn't get him off his mind. She was right. He should visit again. And he wouldn't tell Dr. Latham about driving.

Matt ate his black-eyed peas and cornbread quickly that night. Knowing Lillie would be in the kitchen a while longer cleaning up, he said, "Think I'll go lie down."

He paused as he left the kitchen to make sure she wasn't following, and then closed the bedroom door. Opening the top drawer of the chest without making noise was difficult because it didn't fit its frame. Matt steadied himself to make sure he didn't fall—that would bring Lillie in a hurry—and jerked the drawer.

His wallet lay on top of his clothes. Slipping two fingers under his driver's license, Matt grasped the thin paper. When he looked at the small picture, his face relaxed. He remembered the day he had put it there—exactly two weeks after his wedding day. He had torn the picture from the newspaper and carefully trimmed the ragged edges with Lillie's sewing scissors. Below the picture, he had marked out the name, Johnny Cash, and had written Matt Bradfurd, before slipping it in his wallet. When Beth was born, he had put her picture on top of it.

Several weeks later, he had seen Johnny on television and felt an intense longing to buy a guitar and stick out his thumb in front of any truck heading to Nashville. He had an urge to zoom down the highway like a rocket, like a man shooting for the moon. He wanted to become the most famous country-western singer in the world. He would dress like Johnny—long-sleeved black shirt, black jeans, black belt with a round silver buckle, black boots, and a big white cowboy hat.

Matt hadn't gone anywhere and had kept his desires a secret from Lillie. And he hadn't told her about buying the black shirt the day he helped a friend move to Winston. When they had finished with the furniture, Matt said he wanted to find a store where they sold black shirts and cowboy belts.

He scoured the city until he found what he wanted. The belt looked like it belonged on him, so he took his old one home in a bag. At home, Matt slipped in without Lillie seeing him and hung the shirt under another on his side of the closet.

When Lillie saw the belt, she laughed. "Well, Lord have mercy. Look at my cowboy! You gonna buy a horse next?"

Until the day of his surgery, the belt had left his waist only when he went to church and to bed.

Matt held the picture up close to his face. The paper was so thin the man's features were fuzzy, but there was no mistaking the resemblance. Johnny Cash looked enough like him to be his brother. It was the shape of the face, the way the jaw was set, and that easy smile. He wondered if Johnny loved to sing as much as he did.

This might be the right time. Slipping the picture back into his wallet, Matt shook his head. No, he didn't want to go to Nashville but would like to learn to play an instrument. He could get a job with a local group and sing a few hours a week. He wouldn't have to stand, and the money should be good. He would choose the mandolin, because not many people could play it.

Lillie's idea to visit Little Red—the best mandolin player in the county—had come from nowhere. *Could somebody be guiding me toward this after all these years?*

21

WITH THEIR KNEES BENT AND THEIR FEET MAKING CIRCLES in the air, Rachel and Bella lay on pallets in the living room watching the Little Bear video that one of their mothers had brought that morning. During a quiet scene, Lillie heard a scratching sound at the front door. *A cat?* She hoped it would go away before the girls heard it. They would beg to bring it in, but she would have to say, "No, we can't trust stray animals." The scratching continued. *Maybe they won't notice if I raise the window and shoo you away.*

Feeling the cold air pushing to enter, Lillie struggled to get the window high enough to stick her head out. It had been painted shut so many times she was surprised it would move at all. Finally able to press her forehead against the screen, she saw the tightly curled figure of a small boy lying on the porch. He had taken off his shoe and was scraping it against the door. Shocked, she called out, "John. Lord have mercy!"

Wishing she could kneel and lift him up, Lillie was afraid her weight might cause her to fall, so she leaned over, took his small hands in hers, and pulled him to his feet. "Child, what are you doing in short sleeves? Your arms are cold." As she led him to the sofa, the girls ran to him. They patted his back and looked up at Lillie. "Go back and watch Little Bear. I have to talk to John a few minutes."

While studying his face, Lillie felt a catch in her throat. A feeling of sadness settled over her and made her want to cry. Then, still without saying a word, he laid his head on her lap so lightly that she felt no weight at all. She ran her fingers through his thin, brown hair in an attempt to soothe him, still not knowing why.

John lived with his mother three houses down the road from Lillie. He looked like he was about four. Lillie knew him because he often appeared at the fence when she had the girls in the back yard. He didn't say much but was gentle with the children, so she didn't mind having him there. For a reason she had never understood, Lillie felt sorry for him. And it puzzled her that a child so young would be allowed to wander down the road alone. She had seen his mother just once, when she came looking for him. She had introduced herself as Judy politely enough but jerked John's arm hard as she fussed at him for leaving the yard.

Lillie gathered John onto her lap. Without thinking, she sniffed and pulled back—he needed a bath. "Is something wrong, sweetheart? Where's your mama?"

Closing his eyes, John nestled deeply into her bosom.

Stroking his forehead, Lillie asked, "What's your name, honey?"

The child burrowed further into Lillie's folds. When she arched her back, pushing him up toward her face, he answered, "John."

"Your last name? It's John *what*?"

Shaking his head, he held on tighter.

"Does your mama know where you are?" He didn't answer. "Honey, shouldn't you go home, so she won't worry about you?" His head moved from side to side. Lillie continued searching for answers. "Do you need something?"

He looked directly at Lillie for the first time, since entering the house. "I'm hungry."

Lillie placed him on his feet, and then struggled to rise from the couch. "My goodness, that's easy. Let's go to the kitchen."

About to hand him the turkey and cheese sandwich she had made, Lillie thought of his thinness, added an extra piece of cheese, and gave him a cup of milk.

As she watched him eat, Lillie realized she had to find out what was going on. Although she dreaded waking Matt, since he hadn't slept the previous night, she would have to ask him to walk down to Judy's.

WHEN HE RETURNED FROM JUDY'S, MATT STRUGGLED TO get his breath and talk at the same time. "This beats all." Limping to his chair, he groaned and eased down. "A car's there, so I knocked and knocked, but nobody came. Then, I walked around the house, called her name and looked in the windows, but didn't see a soul." His breath returned and his voice rose. Even tried to open the doors, but they were locked! Now, tell me this. How could a little boy get out and lock the doors behind him? And why would he be dressed in a short-sleeved T shirt and pants that don't even reach his ankles?" He shook his head. "We better do something!"

"And in a hurry. She might be sick, even hurt. Wish I knew some of her people. Guess we have to call the sheriff."

A woman at the sheriff's office said she would send someone out, but since it didn't sound like an emergency, it might be a while. She said they should keep John, and the deputy would pick him up after he saw what was what.

Matt massaged his leg until the cramping eased, and then said, "I'm going back to Judy's. Need to leave a note telling her where he is in case she wakes up and tries to find him."

Matt returned shortly and then lay on the bed to watch the road. About an hour later, a sheriff's car passed. It was moving slowly. He called out to Lillie, "Finally here." In another half an hour, dust rose from the sides of the road as an ambulance sped past.

All afternoon, Lillie kept her eyes on John. *Bless his heart. He's too quiet for a child.* By the time the deputy arrived at her house, the children's parents had picked them up, and she had fed John supper. Not once had he asked to go home.

The deputy said he had broken down Judy's door and found her lying on the floor beside her bed. Said it looked like she was a regular drug user and over-did it. She would probably be all right, but they had taken her to the emergency room to be safe. In a day or two, she would go to court. Meantime, Child Protective Services had found a temporary foster home for John.

Matt and Lillie offered to keep John until Judy returned home, but the deputy said it was against the law, since they weren't kin.

THREE DAYS LATER, THERE WAS A PIECE OF NOTEBOOK paper in Matt and Lillie's mailbox. "I'll pay you back BITCH" was written on it.

After supper that evening, they walked down to Judy's house. The car was gone and nobody answered their knock. The lady next door said Judy had left with a pile of clothes in her car that morning, but she hadn't seen John in a few days. Said she had seen a man come and go but didn't know who he was. That over the last few months, she'd seen a lot of men come and go and didn't believe they were up to any good. Matt and Lillie walked home in a chilly drizzle. Neither talked.

They never saw John again, though a vision of his frail body and his face drained of life remained with Lillie. When she felt powerless, it was his image that appeared. Later on, she paired his image with a fear that something bad was going to happen.

THE NEXT MORNING, A SOCIAL WORKER FROM CHILD Protective Services knocked on the door. Someone had accused Lillie of abusing the children she kept. The caller had said Lillie didn't feed them, left them crying for hours in a room with the door closed, and didn't change their diapers so their bottoms were sore.

Lillie felt like someone had slapped her. Stepping back, she shouted, "Not me!" Then she collected herself and smiled. "You must be at the wrong house."

The social worker opened a folder and showed Lillie a form with her name on it. "If your name is Lillie Bradfurd, I have the right person." Her voice was calm and assertive. "May I come in?"

Blocking the door with the width of her body, Lillie felt her grandfather's temper rising within her. She was tempted to say, no, hell no. Anybody who says those things about me can't come in this house. Instead, she said, "Yes, you're welcome here, but I've kept children twenty-two years and have never had a *single* complaint." She stepped aside to let the woman pass. "Come in and look around all you want."

The young social worker was dressed in jeans, a long-sleeved orange T shirt, and a denim jacket. She sat down on the living room floor, called the girls to her, and turned them around. Lillie hadn't noticed until the woman placed her hands on Bella's waist and shoulders that she was dressed so casually. Then it scared her to realize she hadn't asked for identification. The world of drugs and abused children was foreign to her. Could this woman be part of that?

Lillie reached for the girls' hands. "I'm sorry, but I should have asked for proof that you're who you say you are."

The woman took a badge from her purse and clipped it to the collar of her jacket, while the girls brought treasures to show and pattered her with questions. Lillie relaxed a bit and chuckled. *Careful, lady. They'll talk you to death if you sit there long enough.*

Trying to hold her attention, the girls followed at the woman's heels. Lillie stayed close behind, her arms crossed, cautioning the anger that wanted to take over. *She's only doing her job, exactly what I would do in her situation. But how could this happen to me?*

Lillie watched the social worker take diapers off the sleeping babies, look through each room, and open the refrigerator. She went outside to the fenced-in yard and saw shovels, buckets, and riding toys lined up beside the house. Rachel reached in a bucket and brought out a dead moth to show her.

The social worker sat down at the kitchen table and wrote a half page before turning to Lillie. "Well, things look all right, but I still have to investigate you. I have to make sure you don't have a criminal record and call the parents of these children."

Lillie alternated between feelings of relief, embarrassment, and anger.

The next afternoon, an older woman—dressed professionally, Lillie thought, in a nice suit and white blouse—arrived from the local office of the State Department of Social Services. She informed Lillie that she was keeping more children than allowed without a state daycare license: the law permitted two children, not four.

Lillie tried hard to remain polite but heard an ugliness that she was ashamed of in her voice. "Well, I used to have five. It was *your* office that told me I could keep *four* without a license. I applied for one but couldn't get it, because the changes I needed to make to the house would have cost too much money." Lillie choked, afraid she might cry. "My husband's been disabled two years, and this money's all we have to live on." Lillie continued in a shrill voice. "And these children won't understand what's happening if you take them away. Where will they go?"

The social worker was nearly as wide and at least half a foot taller than Lillie's five-foot-two inches. Her face was passive, showing no feelings that Lillie could identify. Her voice was untainted by emotion. "Those can't be my concerns. I'm here to make sure the law is obeyed and the children are protected."

Lillie's body felt like it was on fire. Her grandfather's temper longed to explode. And she was confused. This woman *was* just doing her job. "But, but. Shouldn't the law *help* people instead of hurting them?"

As the woman turned her back and opened the front door, she said, "It does look like the complaint against you was a hoax. The children's parents insist it isn't true, and there's no person with the name and address of the caller in this state." For a moment, she sounded kinder, and she turned back to face Lillie, placing her hand on Lillie's shoulder. "I am sorry this happened to you. But I must follow the law. I'll be back Monday and if more than two children are here, I'll have you taken to jail."

When the woman closed the door, Lillie sat down and cried. The babies heard her and *they* cried. The girls got on her lap, snuggled up, and laid their heads on her breasts. Matt came in from the bedroom, put his hand on her head, and whispered, "Don't worry. It'll be all right."

The four parents had similar reactions—tears and anger—when they picked up their children that

Wednesday evening. They promised to call every place they could think of to complain and pledged to sign a statement saying they knew the law but wanted Lillie to keep their children in spite of it. They were determined to tell everyone she was the best caretaker they had ever known. No, they said, she was more than a caretaker; she was a second mother to their children.

When the last parent left, Lillie followed him outside and sat down on the top step of the front porch. She pulled at her thin sweater, trying to make it come together across her chest.

Worn out and emotionally exhausted, she needed a few minutes alone. Across from her, she heard the caw, caw of a crow. "What!" she shouted. "You here to raid my nest, too?"

It took six or seven calls—Lillie lost track—on Thursday to the State Social Services office in Winston before she reached the department related to her problem. That woman was nice, but said she had no authority to change decisions already made and gave Lillie the name of her supervisor. Lillie left two messages with the supervisor that were never returned.

It was the babies Lillie gave up, believing the girls knew her better and would miss her more.

After calling the parents, she turned to Matt with a trembling voice. "I've decided to find a job."

He looked as if someone had struck him. "You can't do that! You love the children."

Knowing her words would hurt, Lillie dreaded having to speak them. "We can't live on five hundred dollars a month."

ANGER AT JUDY HAD GOTTEN LILLIE FIRED UP, CREATING a feeling that she could be successful at anything she tried. But it had taken ten days to arrange for Myra to stay with the girls so she could go to the employment office, and, during that time, her thoughts had shifted from Judy to John. Imagining the life ahead of him, Lillie's confidence had slipped away, leaving her with an ache in her chest.

THE MORNING OF HER APPOINTMENT, LILLIE HELD TWO freshly pressed skirts and blouses in front of the bedroom mirror. A smile lightly touched her face. They weren't as bad as she had thought. Either the greenish-brown that she saved for company or the dark blue one would work for the interview. But there *were* only two, and she had to work at least five days a week. *Maybe get a job with uniforms.*

Spreading the clothes on her bed, Lillie turned back to the mirror to face the curlers covering her head. She held her breath and released one of the giant rollers. A long strand of brown and gray-streaked hair fell limp and straight beside her face.

The rest did the same. Lillie laughed. Her neck was stiff from struggling all night to keep her head balanced on large rounds of plastic, only to produce what she started with—straight hair.

Lillie glanced at the picture of herself on top the dresser. The five-year-old wore an Easter bonnet and a frilly yellow dress. Under the bonnet was a head of curly hair. She chuckled. *Mama would be surprised to see me now.*

Sitting across from the woman at the employment office, Lillie decided the room was either exceptionally warm or she was having one of those hot flashes women talked about. Her face felt like it was a balloon filled with hot air and sweat trickled down the left side of her neck. According to the woman, they were making progress. Although no jobs with uniforms were available, there was an opening at the office of a hardware store. Lillie tried to be enthusiastic about it. The woman seemed to want her to. She smiled and said, "That's wonderful, just wonderful," but doubt made her voice sound like an irritating squeak.

When the woman offered to call the store and make an appointment for an interview, Lillie didn't refuse. The manager there said she could see her immediately. Since the store was only three blocks away, Lillie decided to walk. It would give her time to think.

Lillie stepped out the door of the employment office, and a cool strong gust of wind gave her a shove and flipped up her A-line skirt. As she walked toward the hardware store, she struggled to hold it down. Then another gust slung her hair across her face, so she didn't see the raised portion of the sidewalk when she tripped. Landing on her hands and knees, Lillie was startled but not concerned with the pain—she just hoped no one had seen her. *I must look like a pig.* As quickly as she could, she rolled over on her bottom and covered her knees with her skirt.

A man passing by insisted on helping Lillie up and was nearly pulled over in the process. To recover her breath and her pride, she sat down on the low wall in front of the post office and turned to face the wind, hoping it would soothe her. Her skinned knees—circles of blood on them the size of quarters—made her think of a seven-year-old and that was what she felt like at the moment—a child.

Embarrassing memories of her previous office job twenty-two years earlier flooded her. She had wanted to run away from that failure, too. Her boss and co-workers had been kind and tried to help. And the work was fine, as long as she was allowed to go at her own pace. It was when the boss said, "Oh, by the way, I'd like you to," that set up a reaction she couldn't control. Instead of concentrating on what she was doing, she thought of the next task and the next, and worried—would she be able to do it well and finish it quickly?

Within fifteen minutes of the boss's remark, her hands started shaking. After that, her lips quivered so much she couldn't speak. Although she talked to herself continually about relaxing, once the anxiety had taken over, the only way to stop it was to go home. When Lillie left to open a daycare business, she imagined everyone there sighing with relief.

The hardware store manager greeted her with a smile and a flick of the eyes that caused Lillie to think, uh-oh. As the woman scanned the form from the employment office, Lillie knew the interview might as well be over. Mrs. McCarn didn't like what she saw or read. She wouldn't even get a chance to speak. But when Mrs. McCarn thanked her for coming and said she would "let her know," Lillie remained seated.

The many things that had just *happened* to Lillie—all those times of having no say over her *own* life—surrounded her. They were numerous enough to fill the room and spill out the windows and door, smothering her and preventing her from living the way she wanted. She realized just how much she needed to understand why these things were happening. At that moment, something within *insisted* she ask a total stranger, "What am I doing wrong?" But Lillie didn't do that. Instead, she asked, "You're not going to hire me, are you?"

Mrs. McCarn looked startled. Moving her lips, as if she were about to answer, she stared at her desk, while Lillie watched and waited. Finally, she spoke. "I don't believe this job will fit you, Mrs. Bradfurd."

Lillie felt a surge of strength. "But why? I *really* need a job. Is it my weight? Because I'm fat?"

The woman fixed her gaze on something above Lillie's head. "No. That wouldn't matter here."

Lillie moved forward in her chair. "Well, please, tell me what it is. I need to know."

Mrs. McCarn looked directly into Lillie's eyes. "You haven't done office work in twenty-two years. Even then, it was just a short period of time."

Moving back, Lillie wiped her forehead and nodded. "That's true. But I can learn. It won't take long." She presented her warmest smile and was tempted to extend her hand. "You can trust me to work hard."

Mrs. McCarn didn't return Lillie's smile but spoke gently. "I don't think that would do it."

"What, then? I'm not smart enough?" Lillie hesitated before continuing. "Oh, maybe, my seizures. Is that the reason? I'm normal as long as I take Tegratol. Like you or anybody else. I don't have them."

The woman stood. "Mrs. Bradfurd, you *do* seem like a nice woman. But if you were in my position, would you take a chance on those things?" She shrugged and shook her head.

Lillie had to agree with Mrs. McCarn and respected her honesty. She lowered her head in a nod that was so low, it almost became a bow. "Thank you for telling me the truth."

22

GEORGE RUSSELL'S OFFICE DOOR SWUNG OPEN AND banged against the wall. Emily stood in the doorway with fists on her hips and feet planted firmly apart. Her words carried the force of a hurricane. "And the last thing your wife said was, 'You whore. If you're in that office tomorrow morning, I'll come and gouge your eyes out.' Then she hung up." She slammed the door shut and—arms swinging—swiftly crossed the room. "What's going on? Did you tell her?"

George was holding his breath and grasping the edge of his desk with both hands. As he exhaled, he shook his head. "She called you *here*?" He jabbed the air with a finger. "At *this* office?"

Emily smacked the desk. "I just said that! She told me to end our affair and get the hell out. And then she called me—"

"I heard you." George slumped down in his chair. "But how did she find out?" He hesitated. "Have you told anyone?"

As she walked around the desk, Emily raised her arm slightly, tucking the pearl and diamond bracelet under the sleeve of her blouse.

"You were going to tell people the bracelet was costume. Did you?"

She didn't answer. When Emily touched her lips to his ear, he shoved his chair back, causing her to stumble and cry out.

George grasped her hand. "I'm sorry." His voice softened. "I *am*, Emily, but we can't do that right now. There's too much else going on." Turning away from her, and then back, he said, "We need to take a break here. Don't come in tomorrow. I have to talk to Mrs. Barbee and get a temp. And I have to get home."

GEORGE'S STOMACH FELT QUEASY AND HIS ARMS trembled, as he gripped the steering wheel. The Mercedes moved him home as if on autopilot; it rolled through stop signs, red lights, and the iron-scrolled gates. When it deposited him in front of his garage, his eyes and thoughts focused.

He looked up at the side windows of the three-story colonial house and realized he had nothing to be ashamed of. *There, Rosalyn. I kept my end of the bargain. That's what you wanted—your house in Clear Creek filled with French Provincial antiques and clothes and jewels enough to compete with a movie star.* He slammed the steering wheel with his fist. *You can't criticize me!*

When he opened the door to the back hall, George remembered their plans for the evening and almost felt like himself. *This shouldn't take long. We have to be at the Harrells' at seven.*

The house was quiet. No music or evening news to greet him, no chatter from Rosalyn about her day, and no reminders to hurry. George started to call out to his wife but stopped, suddenly feeling as awkward and restricted as he would in a museum. Warily, he looked at the beauty and representations of life around him and felt a need to tread softly, not touch, so as to leave nothing of himself behind. He crept from room to room.

He found his wife in the last place he looked—the living room. She was sitting on an antique sofa that was never used for that purpose because it was uncomfortable. The clasp had been pulled from her ponytail, leaving blond hair hanging about her face. Her eyes were red and puffy. She shivered in the short sleeves and short skirt of her pink and yellow tennis clothes.

George didn't want to give the impression that what had happened was significant. He wanted to sound concerned but casual. "Hey. Still in your tennis clothes? Want me to turn up the heat?"

Rosalyn's face was colorless. Barely moving her mouth, she answered, "No."

He sat down on the edge of an equally uncomfortable chair across from her and leaned close enough to touch her knee but kept his hands back. An unpleasant body odor made him rub his nose and cough. "You want to discuss today?

We can talk while you're getting dressed for the Harrells.'"

Rosalyn slammed the hard sofa with her hand and screamed, "Good god! I'm not going anywhere tonight!"

Irritated that he had to endure such an outburst, George said, "All right, *what?* Tell me."

His wife jumped up and leaned toward George, causing him to pull back and cross his legs. He thought she was going to hit him. Instead, she lowered her face to his and yelled, "No. You tell me. And make it the truth for a change. I don't want your white-washed image, mister holier-than-thou. I want the *real* goddamn truth. How long have you been fucking her?"

George had never heard Rosalyn use those words or that tone with anyone. "How dare you? You sound like white trash!"

She staggered back a few steps and laughed. "Oh, pardon me. So, it's words that make you trash, not behavior?—like committing adultery?"

George shuddered. "Roz, stop. It was nothing— just physical. It's not the end of the world. Nothing's changed between us." Feeling like a child begging for something, he held out his arms. "And I swear— I've never done anything like this before."

The large window behind Rosalyn was filled with a diffused golden light signaling the end of the day. Standing in the center of the well-manicured lawn was a hundred fifty-year-old magnolia. Its creamy white blossoms, in the summer as big as Rosalyn's head, had turned brown and drooped. She pressed her forehead against the glass.

Alert, George watched her every move, feeling fear and uncertainty in her presence for the first time.

When she turned back to face him, a single tear crept slowly down her cheek. She wiped it with the collar of her blouse. "You see, that's exactly the problem. Like a fool, I would have believed anything you said yesterday." Her voice cracked. "But what's worse than not being able to believe you, is that, now, I can't trust my own judgment. If I can't tell when the man I've lived with for thirty-four years is lying, how can I assess anybody or anything well enough to take care of myself?"

Feeling an invisible blow to his abdomen, George remained seated, unable to move or speak, as darkness entered the house.

After a long stretch of silence, Rosalyn rose from the sofa and turned on a lamp. "By the way, aren't you curious? Don't you want to know how I found out?"

She sounded like she was having fun and that made George mad. "Oh, I don't know that it matters."

"Really? Don't want to know who betrayed you? Too bad. There was an anonymous call. 'You might want to ask Mr. Russell about his relationship with Emily.' From a woman. Probably disguising her voice."

Rosalyn continued taunting him. "Well, Georgie, wonder who else knows? People at work? Our minister? Hmm, wonder what he thinks about you fucking a twenty-five-year-old employee? A girl younger than your own daughters? The boys at the Club may *really* be impressed." Then she frowned. "But I'll bet their wives won't."

With that, Rosalyn lifted her husband's chin with her fingers, smiled at him, and walked out.

GEORGE WAS PROPPED ON THREE PILLOWS IN THE guest room bed with a ham sandwich and a bottle of 1997 Caymus Select Cabernet Sauvignon. He turned on the television to a wrestling match. When the platinum blond female wrestler stood over her opponent's prone body, taunting, it reminded him of the scene in his living room. He had been there with a wife he didn't recognize; a woman thirty pounds overweight and preoccupied with house, tennis, parties, and friends. A woman who mocked him.

And George wondered, where was the cute coed with the blond ponytail that swung from side to side when she walked? The girlfriend who smiled when she saw him and extended her arm to link with his? The wife who laughed at his jokes and whose voice reflected pride when introducing him to her friends? Where had *his* Rosalyn gone?

A female announcer clad in a low-cut silver leotard and tights entered the ring. She reminded him of Emily. He poured another glass of cabernet. *There* was a woman who admired him, was willing to accommodate him, and was interested in what he had to say. *There* was a woman who desired him.

George wished he could reveal his thoughts to his wife: Emily makes me feel important. She knows how hard I work and wants me for who I am, not for what I provide. It's always the right time for her. No excuses, no backaches. He wished he could say, "The truth is, Rosalyn, I thought you were relieved you didn't have to bother with it anymore."

When he picked up the wine bottle and found it empty, George swung it across the room and watched as red drops made a path on the pale blue carpet to the wing chair. Turning in the direction of the master bedroom, he yelled to a wife too far away to hear. "*You* pushed me into this with your self-centeredness."

ROSALYN SAT AT THE PEACH GRANITE COUNTER DRINKING coffee when George entered the kitchen. Her face was swollen and blotchy, and her hair a tangled mess.

In as normal a voice as he could manage, George said, "Good morning. How did you sleep?"

He poured himself a cup of coffee. In response to his wife's silence, he asked, "Oh, for Pete's sake, can't we put this behind us? It's over. She's gone now—thanks to you."

Rosalyn lifted her brows and grinned. Her voice was heavy with sarcasm. "Really? So, she won't service you at the office anymore?"

George stood beside his wife at the counter. "Well, since you want to discuss her, we will. Don't you think that phone call was inappropriate? Poor girl didn't deserve that. She's a nice person. You'd like her if you knew her."

Rosalyn leap from her stool and threw her cup in the direction of the sink. When a broken fragment hit his arm, George yelled, "Are you crazy?"

She stood with hands on her hips and glared at him a few seconds. "Am *I* crazy?" Her voice rose with each question. "What planet do you live on? You think I'd *like* her? All I have to do is get to know her, and I'll feel better? Why don't you think about what your words really say, Georgie boy?"

NOTICING A SLIGHT TREMOR IN HIS JAW AS HE COASTED into his parking space, George decided to spend a few minutes in front of his hills before meeting the new receptionist.

After hanging his suit jacket, he swiveled the desk chair around to face the floor-to-ceiling window, and then settled into the calfskin. The sky was an intense blue. Without the usual haze that lingered on the mountains, he could see the paths leading upward. Feeling a surge of confidence, he believed that within minutes, he would find his own way back to normal life.

The first thing George needed to determine was how to handle Rosalyn. Some distress at finding out about Emily had been understandable, but he believed she had reacted in a dangerously emotional way. Threatening to tell the minister was completely unacceptable and divorce would be out of the question. He would never let that happen.

His former friend, Otis Brewer, came to mind. When Otis divorced his wife and married his girlfriend, the women at the Club had started a quiet campaign encouraging him to resign his membership. Eventually, he did, and George hadn't seen him since, either there or at church. Even his children had stood beside their mother and rejected him. Shaking his head, George mumbled, "Poor bastard." *All that for a woman. Never, never. Generations of Russells would turn over in their graves!*

George's family was a prominent one, known across North Carolina, and had lived in this area for a hundred thirty-five years. His great-grandfather had left Winston in 1899 and settled in Cross Hill as minister of the First Presbyterian Church, the same church George attended. George's grandfather had become vice president of the bank and helped develop downtown. Then George's own father had entered the ministry and led the same church.

As he thought of his ancestors, George's head cleared. Proud of them and himself, he believed he had been a good steward of the family name and an instrument for God in the world, serving others with little regard for his own needs. He shifted in his chair and sighed. What he had inherited and earned was the core of his being, and he would not allow anyone to taint it. Rosalyn must understand that.

The circling of a turkey buzzard caught George's attention. Marveling that distance could make such an ugly bird look beautiful, he watched a few minutes, lulled by the graceful movement of its six-foot wingspan. Unexpectedly, the buzzard changed direction, using the wind currents to lift it to the top of the mountain.

He clapped his hands. "That's my answer! Get Roz out of here. Go on a trip, immediately!" He would offer Paris and a suite at The Bristol Hotel. That would get her away from the minister and her friends until she calmed down. *I'll tell her we need to be alone so I can earn her forgiveness.*

As George's thoughts returned to his wife's hysterical behavior, something occurred to him. *Didn't she go through menopause a year or so ago? That makes women more volatile. I'll ask her to see a doctor—maybe get a prescription for hormones.*

Feelings of excitement and pleasure returned. That was what George liked. In two years, after he retired, he would concentrate exclusively on play and allow nothing to interfere. He swiveled around to his desk and tapped it. *First trips will be to the wine regions of South Africa, Chile, and Australia. Yes! With Rosalyn.*

A note from Mrs. Barbee lay in the middle of his desk. "Dr. Latham called for the third time. Wonders if you found anything for his patient." *I can't even remember the man's name!* George flipped the note aside. *Why can't people take care of their own problems? I've got my hands full!*

But Ed Latham's name reminded George of something else. He shifted in his chair and tugged at his pants. For the past three weeks, he had felt a slight discomfort in his groin. The week before that, a small red spot had appeared on his penis. Although he had forgotten to schedule his yearly physical, he had intended to call for an appointment with Latham this week. Now, he wasn't sure he could face him.

Startled by the ringing of his cell phone, George lurched toward his jacket. Emily's home number was on the display. Reluctantly, he answered. Her sobbing made it difficult to understand her words. "George, I need you. Why haven't you called?"

23

MATT FOCUSED ON THE BLACKTOP BECAUSE HE HAD heard there was ice on the road. Although the air was crisp, it didn't feel that cold. He, Beth and Lillie were on their way to Bobby and Myra's for Christmas dinner. Since it was a special day, Matt had vowed not to make any comments about Lillie's driving.

Myra had insisted they not bring anything, but Lillie refused to go empty-handed. The sweet potato casserole Matt held on his lap was covered with a torn brown paper grocery bag she had taped to the sides of the glass dish. She had said she would kill him if he crushed the toasted marshmallows on top, and he took her warning seriously. Her care in whipping the potatoes to just the right degree of fluffiness and lining up the marshmallows evenly reminded him of the pride she had taken in her cooking before his surgery.

Lillie and Beth looked at each other and called, "That smells *good!*" when they opened their cousins' back door. The mingling of intense aromas made Matt's stomach feel queasy for a minute. He wondered whether a chronically hungry person felt that when passing a fast-food restaurant.

Everybody said dinner was Myra's best ever. The turkey and the cornbread dressing were moist and the giblet gravy thick. The green beans, mashed potatoes, rolls, all were perfect. While eating the coconut cake, all Matt could do was shake his head and moan.

Bobby pulled his overstuffed chair to the fireplace and told Matt to sit down and put his feet up. While the women were cleaning the kitchen and Bobby was bringing in more wood for the fire, Matt massaged his hip. He was relieved to be able to deal with his pain without having to describe it to everyone.

Arms loaded with wood up to his chin, Bobby returned to the living room. Using his cousin's distraction to his advantage, Matt said, "I told you not to vote for Randolph for the Senate. Look at the awful job he's done." Bobby dumped the wood on the hearth, not bothering to stack it, and jumped into the fray. For the next hour, the two men carried on like the old days, with Matt pretending his life hadn't fallen by the wayside.

Reality returned when Myra removed three gifts from a large pile under the seven-foot Christmas tree, handing one to Lillie, another to Beth, and one to him. Matt wished he could hide behind his chair. He knew store-bought presents added very little to a person's life. They were gone or worn out in no time. It was true what Lillie had said: only gifts of love and attention really mattered. And he acknowledged they had given plenty of that to Bobby and Myra. Still, he wished he had a gift to hand them. Having the ability to purchase something, even if he had decided not to because of his beliefs, made the difference. His embarrassment came from not having a choice.

THE DAY AFTER CHRISTMAS, MATT WAITED UNTIL LILLIE was halfway across the yard on her way to Nell's before calling out, "I'm going to see Little Red. Be home by supper." Afraid he could be discouraged, he didn't want to reveal what he was doing until he saw how it went.

Matt slipped his black shirt from the closet, folded it, and laid it in a plastic grocery bag. Then he took his belt with the silver buckle from the bottom drawer of his dresser and placed it on top of the shirt. He inched the picture of Johnny Cash out of his wallet and laid it beside the belt. *My last chance.*

When Matt was six, he met Little Red and his father at a bluegrass concert they were playing in at the high school auditorium. It was a fund raiser for the school band. Little Red was fourteen and attended that school.

Mr. Allen had thick, dark copper-red hair and was called Red. His son was named Joseph at birth but the name hadn't stuck. Although he had light-brown hair, he was too much like his father to be called anything but Little Red.

Red Allen worked in a sawmill during the day and played music with his son nearly every evening after supper. He was equally proficient on guitar, mandolin, banjo, and fiddle. His son knew the guitar and mandolin. Their instrumentals were considered the best country, bluegrass, and gospel in the central part of the state.

Watching them play that first night made Matt wonder where music came from. Grandad explained that the brain told the fingers what to do with the strings, and the vibration of the strings, along with the wood, produced the sound. But it seemed to young Matt that the Allens' bodies were already filled with music and the instruments just released it. At the end of the concert, Matt slipped up behind Little Red and pressed his palm against his elbow hoping the music would enter his own body.

After that night, Matt and his grandfather drove to the Allens' yard at least once a week to listen to them play after supper. Matt sat on the ground as close to Little Red's feet as he could and watched the movement of his fingers. After several months of this, Little Red began handing Matt his mandolin after the last song. Matt sat cradling it until Grandad coaxed him home.

Matt stopped the car about a mile from Little Red's trailer, pulled the black shirt over his T-shirt, and then threaded the belt through his pant loops. When a cramp in his left calf forced him to get out of the car, lean over the hood, and press on his toes to counteract it, he thought more about his friend's past.

Three days after Little Red turned eighteen, he received a draft notice for Vietnam. He was assigned to a sniper unit where he remained just short of two years. When released from duty, he moved in with his mother and father, went back to painting houses and pumping gas, but wouldn't touch his mandolin or guitar. And days went by without him speaking. Like his father, he had never talked a lot, so people didn't think much of his silence for the first two or three months. But as time passed, they became confused and irritated, and Little Red moved from one job to another. Eventually he stopped working altogether.

Little Red's parents took him to the Veteran's Administration Clinic in Winston but were told nothing could be done and that time would take care of it. A year and a half after his return from Vietnam, like a butterfly in reverse, he had completed the crawl back into his cocoon.

The cramp in Matt's lower leg traveled up to his thigh forcing him to bend lower to stretch it. In front of him was a freshly plowed field. After wondering why someone would plow in winter, the mounds beside the furrows carried him back twelve years to Red Allen's graveside service.

Mr. Allen's casket rested on straps above the rust-colored clay hole that would be his last home. Little Red and his mother sat on folding chairs in the front row, facing the casket. Beside them were his sister, her husband, and their three children. Chairs in the second and third rows held other Allens—some with that copper hair—who had come down from the mountains for the funeral.

Little Red's face had worried Matt: it looked too still. He wondered what was going on in his friend's mind. The man in the casket wasn't just a father to an adult son. After Vietnam, he had taken care of Little Red like he would a boy. And there was the music: the two men had taken separate strands of beauty and woven them together. If Little Red ever wanted to play again, could he do it alone? Then his name—"Little" Red without a Red? Maybe just Red? A fellow with brown hair? Joseph? Nobody would know "Joseph Allen." As the minister gave the blessing of peace, Matt had wondered—how can a man have peace with only half his soul present?

Little Red's mother died eight months after his father. His sister sold the family home and moved him into an Airstream trailer that she parked on the back edge of her fifty-six acres out in the country.

Matt started visiting him every other Sunday. He took a plate of food from lunch, watched him eat, and then drove him around for half an hour. Either Matt talked about things going on in his life and in the world or they rode in silence. Once in a while,

Little Red nodded hello or good-bye. Although not certain Little Red wanted him to visit, Matt went anyway, believing it was good for him.

Dreading what he might find but knowing he had to move along, Matt forced himself to start his car.

When he turned off the main road and saw the trailer in the distance, Matt chuckled. It reminded him of an eighteen-foot-long aluminum bug, or a cocoon itself.

Little Red stood in the doorway. Matt had forgotten how small his friend was. Although fifty-one years old, he looked much younger and weighed about a hundred-twenty pounds. His thin, limp hair flowed to his middle back. He leapt from the threshold—startling Matt with his quickness—and approached like a wary animal.

As Matt pulled on the car door to stand, he was afraid he had made a mistake. Shushing himself, he extended his hand, "Sure am glad to see you, boy," and then hesitated. "You remember me, don't you?"

Little Red nodded but didn't smile.

Matt leaned against the car door. "I'd like to talk to you but need to sit down first. Back's giving me some trouble."

The door to the trailer was two feet off the ground. There was a concrete block for a step but no railing. As Matt grasped the edges of the doorway and struggled to pull up, Little Red surprised him by slipping his hands under his arms and lifting him inside.

The trailer was about eight feet wide. It had a bathroom and a single bed at one end, with a small table and a straight wooden chair at the other. Placed between them were a couch and a television on a metal TV tray table.

Little Red wore a short-sleeved T shirt but Matt shivered. It was cold inside. "I feel real bad about not seeing you for two years," Matt said. He waited for some expression on Little Red's face but nothing emerged. "You remember I was going to have surgery? Well, it didn't work out. I've had an awful pain in my back and leg since then." He shook his head. "Sometimes I fall."

Matt felt awkward. Little Red's face remained blank. He tried to remember whether it had seemed that empty before. "Well." He rubbed his forehead. "You working?"

When Little Red shook his head, no, Matt thought he glimpsed some expression of emotion.

Still not knowing what to say, Matt hoped someone would guide him in the right direction. "I'd like to start coming again." His friend's eyelids flickered, but Matt didn't know what it meant. "If you want me to."

Little Red looked directly at Matt and said, "All right."

Astonished, Matt leaned forward. "Did you say something?"

His friend nodded and repeated his words. "All right."

Matt wanted to jump up and yell, *Hallelujah! You talked. Did you hear yourself? Does that mean you're better?* But thinking he should act like it was a normal thing to do, he continued with his own concerns. "That thing I needed to talk to you about?" He pushed his body deeper into the length of the couch.

Since Little Red was his friend, Matt wanted to be honest but was too ashamed to tell the *whole* truth. He didn't want anyone to know Dr. Latham had told him to go on the dole. Lillie was the only person who knew he was *that* worthless.

Matt cleared his throat and sat up straighter. "I've got to make some money and have tried just about everything I can think of, except one. If I could learn the mandolin, maybe that would bring in a little." As he revealed his dream to Little Red, his words begin the flow. "Figure I could work two or three hours at a time. It would be sitting, not standing, and since not many people play the mandolin, I'd have a better chance of getting work. Only catch is." Matt's excitement vanished. "You'd need to teach me. And. I wouldn't be able to pay you until I started making money." Matt stared at the green indoor-outdoor carpeting covering the floor and wished he could crawl under it. He lowered his voice. "I really hate to ask while you're having such a hard time. But just don't know anybody else who could help me."

The silence that filled the trailer was a familiar experience when Matt was with Little Red, but this time it felt uncomfortable. He spoke quickly. "If you don't want to, don't worry." He moved his right arm and hand as if trying to erase a chalk board. "Forget about it. You won't make me mad."

Little Red jumped up.

Sucking air in between his teeth, Matt swung his legs off the couch. "Want me to leave?"

Shaking his head, no, Little Red motioned for Matt to follow and got in the passenger seat of the Impala. Then he pointed down the driveway and said, "My sister's."

As Matt drove, it occurred to him that this sister was the only relative his friend had in Cross Hill. Since he didn't have a car, why would she have placed the trailer so far away from her house?

When Matt turned the car into the gravel driveway in third gear, it stalled. Little Red jumped out and disappeared into a pine grove. Since Matt knew Little Red's sister only well enough to say hello at church, he planned to wait in the car, hoping his friend would return.

The house was the traditional farmhouse—white planked siding, a deep porch extending across the front, and a second story in the middle. Although it was December and too cold to sit outside, four rocking chairs were lined up along the porch. Little Red's sister stood in the doorway, arms across her chest. She was dressed in a black velvet warm-up jacket and pants that made her look younger than fifty-seven. As she walked down the steps toward him,

Matt thought how funny it was that the daughter had hair the same color as her father, but only her brother had been called "Little Red."

She smiled warmly. "What a surprise! You looking for my brother?"

"I brought him here." Matt pointed to the left. "He jumped out and ran that way."

Flipping her hand in the same direction, she said, "Oh, that old shed. Everything he owns is in it. About a year ago, I noticed his mandolin was dusted off and pictures of Mama and Daddy were sitting out. I worry some about his gun, but it doesn't look like it's been touched." She rubbed her arms. "It's cold out here. Come have some tea."

Matt followed her into the kitchen and sat down at the round glass table. "I'm glad you've come. The only contact he has is with my family, and that's not much. He'll only eat with us every few months. Once a week I deliver his groceries and pick up his dirty clothes."

Saralynn took a pitcher of tea from the refrigerator and two tall glasses from the cabinet. Her voice rose as she poured the tea, splashing some on the table. "He worries me to death and makes me mad as fire. Why do I have to be his mother?" She slapped a dish towel on the table and sat down across from Matt. "Why won't he go on and talk?" She shook her head. "He's stubborn as a mule! And work? He never was lazy, but maybe that's it. Anyway." She patted Matt's arm. "I do appreciate you coming. You've been the best friend he's had."

While waiting for Little Red, they drank two glasses of tea, and she told him how upset people were at the preacher for the Christmas music he had chosen this year.

Matt hadn't heard the door open, so he gasped when he saw Little Red standing in the doorway pressing a mandolin against his chest.

Without acknowledging his sister, Little Red motioned for Matt to follow and turned toward the car.

When they reached the trailer, Little Red sat on the wooden chair, bent his body slightly to the left, and lowered his head over the mandolin. He plucked one string, then another, and stopped. Raising his head, he stared at Matt a few seconds before tucking his long hair behind his ears. Then he wiped his eyes with a sleeve and played.

During the next hour, Matt stretched out on the couch and remained as still as possible. Tears flowed down his cheeks, but he didn't wipe them, not wanting the slightest sound to interfere with the music. When pain absorbed all his other thoughts, he struggled to his feet. Mopping his face, his voice cracked, "Can I come back tomorrow?"

Little Red nodded.

24

JIM HARTMAN TOSSED HIS WINDBREAKER ACROSS AN office chair and slammed the door behind him. Lifting his desk pad, he grabbed the note, "get appt for DAD with Latham," that he had stuffed there three months before. Crushing it in his fist, he dropped it into the wastebasket. *Damn!*

His father had asked for the date of his appointment four times in the previous two weeks. Once, Jim had pretended not to hear, and the other times, he said he'd have to look it up. He hadn't made the appointment, because he couldn't imagine his parents actually moving to Cross Hill. Unfortunately for him, they were settled in a rental house and talked about how happy they were.

Jim buzzed his secretary. "Tibby, didn't you say you could get my father an appointment with Dr. Latham?"

"Good morning, Mr. Hartman. His nurse is my best friend's aunt. She'll do it if she can."

Jim sighed. "Go ahead and get it."

At ten past twelve, Jim received a call from Dr. Latham. He tried to sound jovial and casual. If the doctor had been present, he might have slapped him on the back. "'Appreciate your call! My father moved here from the University of Michigan. Retired professor. Has heart disease and—"

Dr. Latham interrupted. "My nurse tells me you own a company that manufactures shampoo."

"Organic Botanicals. I assume you've heard of it?"

"Matter of fact, I have," Dr. Latham replied. "Ordinarily, I don't accept new patients, but it sounds like this is important to you."

Jim's palms were damp. It occurred to him that he may have sounded *too* casual when he answered the phone. When talking to successful men, especially older ones, he liked to present himself as competent and sophisticated, wanting to make sure they knew he was their equal. He answered quickly. "I would consider it a *personal* favor," he said, making a high-pitched grating sound meant to be laughter. "And if I may, well, how about some shampoo? Let me send you a sample pack. With conditioners."

IT WAS 5:00. TIBBY WAS REMOVING HER PURSE FROM THE bottom desk drawer when the reception room door swung open and a tall, slim, gray-haired man entered. He smiled broadly and walked toward her desk.

"Good afternoon. I believe you're Mrs. Lanier? I'm Professor Hartman, Jim's father." He extended a hand. "It's a pleasure to be in my son's business world for the first time. My wife and I moved here after Christmas. Are you a native of this area?"

She nodded. "My family's lived here many generations."

He slapped his hands together. "Wonderful! May I talk to you sometime? And there is a genealogical society here?"

Tibby smiled warmly. "Genealogy's my hobby. I'd be happy to show you our library."

Professor Hartman's blue eyes sparkled. "Perfect! Thank you. People are helpful here. And the weather—what a delight! Did you see that clear sky and feel the warm sun today? Here in the dead of winter! It was ten degrees in Michigan yesterday."

"Aren't you a little chilly without a jacket?"

The professor laughed and held his arms out in front of him. The shirt sleeves ended two inches above his wrist. "Feel my hands. I'm warm. My wife said I couldn't go out wearing just a shirt and slacks in January, but it's like spring."

Tibby found it hard to concentrate on what the professor was saying. Bewildered by the differences in physical appearance and personality between this man and his son, she wondered, why at least some of the man's friendliness and enthusiasm hadn't rubbed off on his son?

The professor looked at his watch. "Pardon me. I've taken up enough of your time. I didn't even ask—is Jim in?"

WHAT NOW? HEARING HIS FATHER'S VOICE IN THE reception room, Jim slammed his fist on his desk. *No!* Realizing his office was no longer his sanctuary, he felt a pain deep in his chest.

His father entered the office with arms extended, as if intending to hug his son, but dropped them when Jim stayed seated. The professor cleared his throat and inhaled deeply. "What wonderful scents in this building, Jim. What *are* they?"

Looking down at his desk, Jim was determined to ignore the pain. "What brings you here, Dad?"

Professor Hartman sat down in a stiff plastic chair across from his son's desk. He shifted in his seat, as if trying to become comfortable, and then frowned and turned to look at the chair. "I came to see your factory and have a talk. Am I interrupting something that can't wait?"

Holding up the production report from the previous year for his father to see, Jim said, "Well, I *am working.*"

The professor slowly stood. His face looked tired— drained of the energy he'd shown seconds before. Then he sat. "No, I'm not leaving. There're some things I need to say privately. Important things."

Uncomfortable with the softness in his father's voice, Jim flushed and shifted his gaze toward the door. "Go ahead."

Not taking his eyes off his son, the professor said, "I want you to know I'm proud of you."

Elbows propped on the desk and chin in his hands, sweat trickled down Jim's sides. His head felt like a drum with his father's words bouncing around inside. He could see that his father was waiting for something but didn't know what it was.

"Given our past experiences, you may not know that."

Jim glanced at his father's face and sensed a look of caring. He started to say something—he was not sure what—but his thoughts retreated, moving him to the familiar and comfortable position of silence.

"What? Talk to me!" His father slapped the arm of the chair. "This is the problem. Sullen. Withdrawn. How can we ever have a relationship if we don't talk?"

The furnace came on, bringing the smell of dust into the room. Following it was the scent of grapefruit the chemist had added to a new shampoo.

Finally, the professor leaned forward, laying his hand on his son's desk. "I'm sorry. That's not what I came to say." He coughed. "When I met Melanie at your wedding, I realized that a kind, loving, intelligent woman had seen something in you I had missed. I'd like to find it."

You never wanted to before. Get out of my life. Go away! Jim felt like he was trying to escape from danger, but a spotlight was following him.

"Your mother and I moved here to enjoy your family. Whatever our struggles have been, I hope we can put them aside. Now. Or very soon." The professor's voice sounded more like it belonged to him. "I'll go. But next time, I want to see your factory and hear how you learned to make hair products."

After his father closed the office door, Jim curled forward in his chair, wrapped his arms around himself, and longed to light up a joint.

ED LATHAM WAS FOLDING THE LONG EKG PRINTOUT HE had just read, as Professor Hartman stepped into his office. Fastening it with a metal clip and laying it aside, he extended his arm toward the well-padded leather chair facing his desk. "Please, professor, make yourself comfortable."

Silas Hartman sat down in his typical fashion—quickly, while talking. "Thank you. I hope you have good news for me."

The man in front of Ed was a genuine, intelligent, and very likable human being. That presented a problem for him: he had accepted the professor as a patient with the hope that he could discover why his son had cheated Matt Bradfurd out of workers' comp. He had even toyed with the idea of socializing with the family. Now, he realized he couldn't be dishonest with the professor. And if the son was anything like his father, he must be mistaken about Jim Hartman.

Turning his thoughts to the exam, Ed said, "Excellent. There's no change in your condition since you saw your doctor in Michigan. And you have no weight to lose." He paused. "Unlike some of us."

With questions and answers completed, Ed moved the chart aside and asked his patient how he intended to spend retirement.

Silas Hartman leaned back and pressed his fingers together. "Twofold answer. I came here primarily to get to know my son's family." Frowning, he said, "It's difficult with him. Jim and I have always had some.... Well, my wife wants me to remedy that."

Instead of satisfying his own curiosity, Ed tried to comfort his patient. "It's hard with adult children—can't treat them like kids, but, in some ways, they still want us to act like parents." Ed shook his head. "It was easier when they were young."

"Umm, it's never been...Well, we'll see what happens." The professor uncrossed his legs and patted Ed's desk. "Here's the interesting part—family research! It's my new adventure."

"You'll do it online?"

Silas Hartman's face held the excitement of a person leaving on a long sought-after vacation. Shaking his head, he lifted a spiral pad and pen from his shirt pocket. "Oh, no. My great-grandfather moved to Winston in 1867. I want to see where he lived, worked, died—all of it." He clicked the ballpoint pen and flipped some pages. "You must know many people in the area. Interrupt me if you have any information that would help."

Ed looked at the clock on his desk. *Uh, oh. Louise'll kill me for holding people up.*

The professor continued. "My great-grandfather came to establish a school for freed slaves but was nearly murdered when he got off the train. Fascinating experience." Silas grinned. "By the way, I'm named for that courageous man. I'm planning to write a book about him. He was saved by a Cross Hill family. I want to find their descendants and see what information they have. And I want to explore what motivated them to help."

Ed glanced at the clock again. He knew he should finish with Professor Hartman, but he didn't want to. It wasn't often a person held his interest like this one. "Before you continue, tell me—how did you end up in the Midwest?"

The professor laid his pen aside. "My father left Winston and moved to Indiana in his twenties. Not certain why. You know, many questions are left unasked as we attend to our lives. After I left for college—I'm ashamed to say—I only saw him once a year and that was with other people around. It wasn't until he died, and my grandfather's journals were passed to me, that I cared about our family history.

"Great-grandfather Silas had a son and a daughter. She married and moved from Winston to Cross Hill. According to the journals, her husband didn't approve of the school. The race issue, you know? That old burden of fear. I have their surname and believe I've identified a cousin in town."

Ed was about to ask who, when Louise tapped on the door. "Dr. Latham, may I help you?"

"Hmm, sorry, Professor."

The professor slipped the pad and pen in his shirt pocket. "Please, call me Silas. Shall we continue our conversation outside the office?"

As Ed stood, a small groan escaped and he mumbled, "A little arthritis." He laid his hand on his patient's shoulder. "How about breakfast Saturday? By the way isn't the name of the family that rescued your great-grandfather in his journals?"

Opening the door, Silas Hartman almost shouted, "Incredibly, no! Only names of the two families he was meeting in Winston—a Methodist minister's and a Quaker's. Maybe church or their family records will give me a clue. In any case, I'm geared up for the hunt!"

25

BETH STRUGGLED TO FIT THE VACUUM CLEANER INTO the front closet. At home she would have crammed it behind the coats and closed the door fast, but this was her homeroom teacher's house, and she wanted to please her. Feeling cool air on her lower back as she bent over, she reached around to pull the navy sweatshirt down and the sweatpants up. The only time she wore them outside the house was when she was cleaning because they were too short and too tight.

Hearing a giggle and feeling a tickle on her back, Beth swung around, dropped to the floor, and pulled the six-year-old onto her lap just as Mrs. Long appeared. "Now, Maddie, don't bother Beth. You get to play with her after school. It's time to take her home."

The little girl continued to hold onto Beth, as she stood. After kissing her cheek, Beth lowered her to the floor.

Mrs. Long handed her twenty-eight dollars. "Here, honey. Wish I could pay you more than seven an hour."

Thanking her teacher and assuring her it was enough, Beth slowly folded the money and put it in the front zippered pocket of her backpack. She could barely respond to Maddie's chatter, as she thought about what to do with it. Her mother had insisted she use it for spending money and clothes. She had also encouraged her to go to the movies with Heather. But Beth had decided to stay away from her friend. She couldn't afford to share the cost of her pot and didn't really want to. Her parents were close enough to the edge already without having to deal with a pothead daughter. Beth leaned over and pulled her pant legs down. *Besides, I'll never be cool anyway.* And there was only one thing she actually longed for—a cell phone.

Each time Beth was paid for babysitting, cleaning, or working behind the drugstore cash register, a disturbing question flitted through her mind that pushed away all desires: what had happened to the money her parents had saved for their twentieth anniversary trip?

After checking the zipper to make sure it was completely closed, Beth swung the backpack over her arm and climbed into the passenger seat of Mrs. Long's minivan.

"Have the results from your last SATs come yet, honey?"

Shaking her head, Beth said, "No, ma'am. And I dread it. What if I do as bad as the first time? A college won't let me in, will it?"

"Well, it wouldn't be a problem with the community college. Your GPA wouldn't matter, either."

Turning away from the words, Beth chewed on a loose cuticle and wished she could ask her teacher to stop at the grocery store they were passing and buy food to take home. "I really wanted to go to a four-year college. Maybe I can get my GPA up."

Mrs. Long spoke softly. "Honey, a two-point-one would take a while to bring up. This is already the second half of your junior year."

When they reached the end of her driveway, Beth jumped out of the minivan and waved goodbye to Maddie. Glancing at the mailbox beside her, she wanted to dash to the house and ignore it but forced herself to open it and peer in.

With trembling hands, Beth ripped open the envelope. The list of SAT scores was nearly identical to that from the first test and all her scores were much lower than the national averages listed to their right.

Not caring whether she woke her father, Beth allowed the screen to slam behind her as she went in the back door and called, "Mama?"

Lillie rushed into the room. "Why are you yelling? You all right?"

Her mother wore pants and a blouse so faded Beth couldn't remember what color they had been. *And she wants me to buy new clothes.* Her flushed face and limp made Beth sorry she had alarmed her. Unzipping her pack, she thrust the twenty-eight dollars toward her mother. "Here. Take this. I'll talk to you later."

Leaving Lillie with a puzzled look, Beth ran through the children's playroom and into her bedroom, wishing there was a lock on her door. Tossing the backpack on the floor, she reached for the knob of a desk drawer and jerked. The entire front of the drawer came off in her hand. Startled, she stared at it for a moment before flinging it on the floor. Then she stuffed the test results into the opening of the drawer and threw herself on her bed.

She thought of how much money she had wasted taking those exams—money she had borrowed from Mrs. Long and paid back with hours of babysitting and cleaning. Then she wondered, *am I that dumb?*

Pulling a heavy burgundy sweater over her head, Beth opened her bedroom door slowly, trying to prevent it from creaking, and paused to determine the location of her parents. Water was running in the kitchen, so her mother must be there. Then she leaned forward, peering into her father's bedroom and saw him lying on the bed. Tiptoeing across the living room, she opened the front door just wide enough to slip out, and then closed it quietly behind her. Stopping a moment, she shivered.

Beth crunched along the side of the road until she reached the place where the road sloped downward. Then she stopped. The sky was a canvas of faint gray with wide streaks of blue traveling like a roller coaster across it. Before it stood great black trees, branches extended like the outstretched fingers of a giant, with evergreens nestled against the trees as if trying to keep them warm. The square house stood at the end of the road, the yard on each side strung with the spreading arms of clotheslines.

The front door was ajar. From the steps, Beth saw Mrs. Johnson and Miss Caroline leaning over their ironing boards. She crossed the porch and took a deep breath. "Umm, smells like Christmas dinner in there!"

Mother and daughter looked up and called out, "We're glad to see you!" Mrs. Johnson added, "A customer had an extra turkey and gave it to us. We thought January twenty-fifth was a good day to celebrate. Why don't you stay and eat with us?"

Beth stumbled as she stepped across the threshold. Her head felt light, spinning a little. The scent of roasting turkey combined with the easy sounds of laughter was overwhelming. Tears rushed forward. Blinking and pretending to cough, Beth covered her face with her hands and wiped away the tears.

Mrs. Johnson dropped the shirt she was holding and bent down to slip her shoulder under Beth's arm. Miss Caroline shouted, "Whoa, girl," and rushed to the other side.

Insisting she was all right, Beth shook off the women's hands and envisioned herself sitting between the mother and daughter—laying her head first on one shoulder, and then the other and crying like a baby. She heard herself begging them to make her daddy well. She described how she had tried to help—*I entertain the girls for Mama, clean the house, and watch Daddy every minute I can. He worries me, but makes me mad, too! He's either too quiet or too hateful! Mama wants me to show compassion, but I don't know how. And ordering me to be kind doesn't work—it just makes me madder! Tell me how to make them happy.*

Mrs. Johnson asked, "What happened, darling?"

Continuing her pretend cough, Beth's voice was hoarse. "I'm sorry. Maybe I ran here too fast. Cold air makes me cough."

Mrs. Johnson picked up the shirt and motioned toward the couch. "Sit down and talk to us a while." Then she asked, "How's your daddy?"

Beth slumped down on the sofa. "All right, I guess."

The cord from Mrs. Johnson's iron swirled about her like a lasso, stopping only when she propped the iron on its heel. As she picked up a hanger for the smooth, fresh shirt, she peered over her glasses at Beth. "That reminds me. I can't place your daddy's people. They from around here?"

"Yes, ma'am, they sure are." Feeling back to normal, Beth jumped up and stood at the end of the ironing boards. "That was one of great-Grandad's stories. The first Bradfurd—my *seventh* great-grandfather—came in 1750, and got a land grant of six hundred forty-three acres on Jack's Creek. Cost him ten shillings. I don't think he owned it, because he paid rent to an English lord until the Revolution. After that, it was his, free and clear."

Hearing her own excitement, Beth realized how much she loved Grandad's stories, though another burst of sadness caused her to stop talking. She wasn't ready to take her father's place.

Without looking up from the napkin she was ironing, Miss Caroline asked, "Then what?"

"Every time somebody died, the land was broken into smaller pieces and passed to their sons. My grandfather ended up with twelve acres, but it was sold to pay his hospital bill when he died. Daddy never got a single speck of that land." Beth hesitated, thinking about the way her father moved his hands as he finished the story. "But here's the funny part. That's when our name got the weird spelling, with a U. Daddy says that's how the clerk spelled it. All Bradfurds spelled with a U in this state—maybe the whole country—are kin to us."

The scent of roasting turkey made Beth want to take deep breaths and hold them, as she sprinkled and rolled a white blouse to ready it for ironing. She felt like someone had untied a cord from around her head. It was a relief to be in a house of ease and laughter. She hadn't planned her next statement. "I took a test—twice—and failed it."

For a moment, the ladies were silent. Then Mrs. Johnson asked, "Can you try again?"

Shaking her head, no, Beth saw tears dropping on the white blouse.

26

George Russell heard a bang against the outside of his office door. Seeing it was five o'clock, he wondered what it could be. Since Emily had been fired—transferred, he liked to think—no one came after his last consultation at four. Mrs. Barbee routinely buzzed at four fifty-five to ask if he needed anything before she left and—that reminded him—why hadn't she called? Believing it impolite to call out, "Come in," George had made a habit of opening the door for anyone entering. Emily had been the only exception to that, since she had just barged in.

Standing in the doorway, a stack of files in each arm, was the woman he referred to outside the office as "That fine, fine lady, Mrs. Barbee." George leaned forward, took those from her left arm, and asked, "Clients?"

She nodded, placing the others on his desk. "May I talk to you a few minutes?"

Ever the Southern gentleman, George held the large plaid wing chair across from his desk for his secretary, sat down in the one beside it, and asked how he could help. While Mrs. Barbee talked, he gradually shifted his gaze toward the window behind his desk. As he watched the winter sun disappear behind the mountains, his thoughts became murky.

Mrs. Barbee spoke harsh words with great gentleness. "Mr. Russell, all the files you see here are incomplete. For the past few months, clients have been complaining and asking for results. I've given you detailed notes describing each call." Mrs. Barbee paused. "Are you aware that the work is not getting done?"

George felt a sensation of warmth fill his chest and move up into his neck and face as his loyal employee of eighteen years, very politely and with great care, asked if something was wrong in his life.

Shocked to be so unaware of what was going on around him, George felt confused and fumbled with his words. "Yes, there is something. Rosalyn is going through a bad time." Looking down at his tie, he rolled the bottom around two fingers. "My mind's on her. I'm trying to help."

Letting go of the tie, George straightened in his chair and clasped his hands together. "Thank you for your concern. Let's meet every morning to plan my day until the work is caught up. I'll pass all my new clients on to the other accountants, but—," he looked away as he told her—"I will continue playing golf on Wednesday afternoons."

GEORGE'S MERCEDES RODE AS IF THE HARD, UNEVEN pavement never touched its tires. That was the way he wanted his life. His fifty-seventh birthday had reminded him life was getting short, and he needed to hurry and get all that he deserved.

While sitting before a red light in his black carriage, the thought that he may have been dishonest with Mrs. Barbee crossed his mind. "No!" he insisted. "Roz *is* my problem!"

After Rosalyn had found out about George's first relationship with Emily, he had soothed her with the trip to Paris and with his assurance that it would never happen again, she had gradually settled back into her old routine. He had ended the relationship with Emily and had gotten her a job in an insurance agency owned by a client who owed him a favor.

During the weeks that followed, he had felt relieved. Every day when returning from work, George had kissed his wife and asked about her day. Although they were usually rushing off to a social engagement, he made a point of putting his arm around her on the way to the car. Proud of himself, he had stayed on the wagon ten weeks. Even after he and Emily renewed their relationship, life had gone smoothly until the past two or three weeks, when Rosalyn had, inexplicably, struck out at him.

George flushed and turned up the air conditioner when the driver behind him beeped. As the car surged forward, he was reminded of his excitement the day Emily had called. She asked to meet him for lunch. He had resisted, telling her he couldn't do that anymore. But all she wanted, she said, was to discuss some problems at work. And she wanted to make sure he was well.

Every word, scent, and movement from that meeting still clung to George. He had arrived early at the restaurant in Clement to order a bottle of pinot noir and give it time to breathe before drinking it. While he waited for Emily, he smoothed his pink shirt and hoped she'd be pleased. It was the color she liked best on him. He had adjusted his tie, straightened his jacket, and wondered why he felt so impatient.

As George looked around the restaurant the third time, several heads turned toward the door. Emily wore a leather skirt that showed the definition of the firm muscles in her thighs and a wraparound sweater that dipped into her cleavage. The scent of her perfume spread across the room as she moved.

Emily leaned forward, greeting George with a kiss on the cheek and a peek at the rose tattoo on her breast. "How have you been, Georgie? I've been so worried. Has she been mean to you?"

George reached for her hand and sighed. She was more beautiful than ever.

"Oh, Georgie, I've missed you." Emily's eyes watered and her voice cracked. "Everything—the sunrise and the sunset—reminds me of you."

AFTER GEORGE CLOSED THE MOTEL ROOM DOOR, EMILY slowly untied her sweater, and then paused, before unbuckling his belt.

With her head on his shoulder and their damp naked bodies pressed together, Emily talked. The problem with her job was the low pay. She wished George would find her one that paid more—perhaps with a law firm. And she wasn't sure she could live without his emotional support. She begged to see him just one afternoon a week, certain she could arrange to have the time off.

Feeling a surge of anger when the Mercedes deposited him in his garage, George slammed the door with all his strength. *No. I don't feel guilty!*

He found his wife in the sunroom sitting in the white wicker rocker that faced the window overlooking the golf course. The glass in her hand contained a small amount of clear liquid and a wedge of lime. Her smooth blonde hair brushed her shoulders, and she wore a long-sleeved St. John Dress. An overhead fan stirred the air.

Hesitating at the door, George admired a scene that could have come from those in the magazines on the wicker table beside her, and he smiled at the comparison.

"Great! You look ready, Roz. Where're we going tonight?"

When Rosalyn answered, she sounded like she was talking to herself. She didn't turn around. "Nowhere. I went back to my psychiatrist."

George stepped closer to her chair. "Why? Well, okay. What did he say?"

"Same thing as before—we need marriage counseling." Then she faced him. "You need to go with me. I told you months ago."

Slumping down in the chair to her left, George watched a squirrel scamper down a longleaf pine beside the fairway. He had once considered going to counseling with her but had concluded it was unnecessary. He didn't think the man had done his wife any good and wondered why she wouldn't try hormones. As far as George was concerned, they just needed to go back to their normal routine.

And now that he had renewed his relationship with Emily, he couldn't risk that he might slip and reveal it, so counseling was not even a consideration. If Rosalyn found out, she'd leave him and tell the whole town why.

George tried not to show his frustration over her lack of cooperation. "Hmm. We've talked about this many times. What if somebody saw me there? I can't let people think I have problems. By the way, that taupe color suits you."

As Rosalyn jumped out of her chair, she struck the table with her hip and her glass landed on the gold and blue Persian rug. The scent of gin reached George.

Stepping close enough to bump his knees, Rosalyn yelled, "Damn you, you hypocrite. You *do* have problems. When's the last time you had sex with your wife?"

Turning his head to the side and raising his arms as if deflecting a blow, George felt confused and angry. Who was this crazy woman, and why had his life gone in this direction? He pointed to the rug. "Look what you did! You know what that cost?" He stood and spread his arms. "Who do you think buys all this for you? What more do you want from me?"

Standing on one high heel and one bare foot, Rosalyn leaned over to pick up her glass but lost her balance, falling to her knees. Reacting so quickly that he nearly fell, too, George reached his wife and lifted her to the loveseat, where he pushed two pillows aside to make room. He turned on the lamp, sat down beside her, and laid his hand on her knee.

"Come on, Roz. Get yourself together." As he looked at his wife's face, George was certain that he loved her and felt a longing for their good times together. He spoke tenderly. "Let's go back to normal—entertaining, the Club. Look at your closet—shoes like Imelda Marcos. That's good. It's us. Let's take a trip."

George swung his arm around his wife's shoulders and pulled her closer. "Don't you miss it?"

Rosalyn eased out from under his arm and shook her head. "Something's wrong. We need help."

Picking up a pillow from the loveseat, George threw it against the dining room door, as he crossed the sunroom. "No! I told you. No counseling. If you've got a problem, fix it. I'm fine."

THE NEXT MORNING, GEORGE FOUND FOUR MESSAGES on his office desk: the third one on the list was from Professor Silas Hartman. "My grandfather had a sister here who married a Russell. You're her grandson. May I invite you to lunch?"

27

SATURDAY MORNING, THE DRIZZLE ENDED. GRAY AND white clouds sailed across a faint sun, creating patches of shadow and light in Lillie's living room. As she pushed the vacuum cleaner on the faded gold carpet, sunlight revealed a misshapen and frayed couch, yellowed lampshades, and dingy walls. She shook her head. *Better not to see what's around me.*

Suddenly feeling exhausted, Lillie leaned the vacuum against the arm of the sofa and sank down beside it. *Tired. Of watching my daughter work so hard she has no energy for school. Of unpaid bills. Of carrying a pencil and paper in my hand to the grocery store to add up what I have before getting to the cash register.* She sat up straight. Anger joined her discouragement. *And sick to death of Matt's pain and depression.* "No!" she called out and clapped her hands as she sometimes did to get the girls' attention. Guilt replaced the anger. *Ah, my husband. God forgive me.*

Leaning forward, she pushed up. *Get going. Be a good girl.* Tightness spread along her forehead. She slumped back, pressing the back of her cool hand against it, and then massaging her temples. Feeling confused, she wondered, *But what does that mean now?*

Since Lillie had been a young girl, she had tried to please people: she was careful to use "sir" and "ma'am," to never interrupt or ask for anything, and to be ready to do whatever they wanted. She had believed that her parents had left because she wasn't good enough. And she cautioned herself that others—Grandma or a favorite teacher—might do the same if she wasn't careful.

But as Lillie had matured, adult reason insisted that her parents hadn't wanted to leave. Reasoning told her she should behave in a kind and considerate way toward others but that standing up for herself was important too. And sometimes that meant displeasing them. She could mostly put that into practice, except with Matt. His needs always came first. Her child's voice held on, whispering, "Careful, you'll end up alone."

As Lillie pushed and tugged at Matt's La-Z-Boy to vacuum behind it, she wondered whether or not the path she had chosen was still working. Nothing seemed to please her husband now.

When the handle of the vacuum crashed through one of her treasured beveled-glass panes in the side porch door, Lillie collapsed on the floor, picked up a shard, and cried. *It's all in pieces.*

Lillie heard Matt pulling himself up the front steps. Her face still wet and not wanting to tell him how she felt—or to worry him—she dabbed the tears with her sleeve and stood.

Matt tilted his head and briefly looked through narrowed eyes at the broken glass. "I'll nail some plywood over that."

Bracing himself with the back of his chair, the thrust a letter toward her. "This came yesterday." He raised a fist, "That damn light company! Oh!" before lifting his right foot. "Hurts." Keeping his weight on his heel, he hobbled around to the front of the chair and dropped down.

"I called and told a woman our situation. You know what she said?" He swung his head from side to side, mimicking her with his voice. "'We're real sorry, but as of Monday morning, your power will be off until you pay your bill.' Then she said, 'Now, you be *sure* to call, when you want it back on.'" He looked up. "When we want it back on? Can you believe that?"

Lillie tossed the letter on the couch and shrugged. "Oh, well. They can just keep their electricity. We're having a warm spring." She laid her hand on his shoulder. "We'll go to bed when it gets dark. Get more rest that way."

Matt unlaced his right sneaker and removed it. "You're in a mighty good mood about this. Have you thought about how you'll keep the food cold? Or cook?"

Lillie bent down, placing her face in front of his and spoke in a high-pitched voice. She felt ashamed of herself as she was doing it. "Do you know what we have in our refrigerator? Half gallon of milk, pack of bologna, jar of plum preserves, and a stick of margarine. We can put that in Nell's refrigerator. Sandwiches don't need cooking. It won't change much."

"I guess that's it in a nutshell." Matt took off his sock and turned up the sole of his right foot. The joint at the base of his big toe was red and swollen. He squeezed it gently. "Sure is sore. Must be a bunion."

As she swept the broken glass into the dust pan, Lillie noticed the letter from the electric company on the couch. Leaving the broom propped against the side porch door and the dust pan full of glass on the floor, she went to the bedroom, changed into the greenish-brown skirt and blouse that she saved for company, and told Matt she was going to the grocery store. He asked whether she had any money, and she answered, "$11.87."

When Lillie drove into the parking lot at the Cross Hill State Bank and turned off the engine, the Impala shuddered. She patted the dashboard. "Please, not you, too."

She removed the green savings passbook from her purse and pressed it against her chest. Then Lillie turned to the first page and read the words she had written nine years before. "Twentieth Anniversary Trip. First deposit, one hundred and three dollars." As she turned each page, a catch in her throat made it difficult to whisper the amount and date of each deposit. Turning to the last page, she saw the only withdrawal. It had been three months before. She and Matt had taken half of it to buy medicines and vowed not to touch it again. But if her plan worked, she could begin replacing it with her first paycheck.

Lillie threw open the car door and then jerked it closed. Was it wise to use the only money standing behind them? And how would Beth feel? She had looked forward to the trip as much as they had. Slapping the passbook on the steering wheel, she opened the door again and got out of the car. *I'll tell her we'll start over soon. And someday, we'll get to Mount Rushmore and the Grand Canyon.*

Lillie circled the K Mart parking lot three times before finding a spot two spaces from the front door. The arthritis in her right knee was giving her trouble because of the dampness, and she was determined not to limp. Peering in the car's rearview mirror, she put on light pink lipstick and fastened her hair into a ponytail at the nape of her neck. Hoping she looked professional, she smoothed the collar of her jacket, brushed the lint from its sleeves, and reviewed her plan. She would stand up very straight to make her weight less noticeable, and would try to avoid questions about health. If asked directly about medications, she hadn't yet decided how she would answer.

Allowing herself to limp on the way back to the car, Lillie was grateful the manager had told her right away he didn't need part-time people, so she hadn't had to lie.

Her next stop was McDonalds, though she had her doubts about applying for a job there. A fat woman behind the counter might send a bad message to customers. If only she could wear a sign explaining that she really didn't eat that much. And she'd like to say she had tried dieting more times than she could count. She had even borrowed a friend's Weight Watchers book and tried to follow it but found it too confusing.

Several people had suggested staying away from bread and potatoes and filling up on meat, but that was too expensive. Not frying food had helped—she lost ten pounds once from that—but she was left with another hundred-thirty-five to lose. Eventually, she had gone back to frying because it was more filling, and she hadn't had to eat so much to feel satisfied. Feelings of hunger scared her, making her worry that they'd trigger a seizure.

It was eleven-thirty by the time she arrived at McDonalds. The wind had died, allowing the day to warm up. Dampness around her collar made her want to remove her jacket, but she thought she looked slimmer with it on. While getting out of the car, she heard her stomach growl and vowed to buy a hamburger for Matt and her if she got the job.

The manager seemed interested when Lillie told him she could start at six in the evening and stay as late as he needed. When he asked her to walk over to a booth and sit down with him, in her excitement, she forgot about her knee and limped. Placing his hand on her shoulder, he thanked her for coming and said he would let her know soon.

Needing to trust his words, Lillie kept her jacket on until she closed the car door. Out of breath after her struggle to remove it in front of the steering wheel, she rested for a moment and allowed her eyes to stare unfocused across the parking lot. *Well, Lord. You must have something else in mind for me.* Her stomach still growling, she said aloud, "No more tears. Trust." Laying her forehead on the steering wheel, she wondered, *But what could it be?*

AN UNFAMILIAR FEELING OF PRIDE USHERED LILLIE INTO the Southern Electric office, where she handed $328.60 in cash to the woman behind the desk. Although she knew the answer, she wanted to hear it from someone else. "Now, you're sure my power won't be turned off?"

As she drove to the grocery store, Lillie turned on the radio and hummed with her favorite Lite Listening tunes. Surprised to see her fingers tapping on the seat, she realized the dread that weighed down her every step had disappeared.

Piggly Wiggly's sliding glass doors sparkled in the sun as they rushed open for Lillie. The aroma of warm cinnamon buns struck her. Other scents competed for attention while she pushed the cart down the brightly lit aisles and loaded it with flour, white and brown sugar, mustard, mayonnaise, corn meal, Crisco, packages of pinto beans, coffee, tea— even allowing herself two cans of Vienna sausages and a pint of pimiento cheese. It was half full when she turned a corner and faced a refrigerated case the length of the store.

Plastic-wrapped packages of meat, cut in ways she hadn't allowed herself to think of for the last two years, lay before Lillie. Leaning on the cart while pushing it slowly along the case, she silently read the names and prices of her favorites, until coming to an abrupt halt before a package holding three pieces of cube steak. *Anniversary supper tonight! Cube steak, mashed potatoes, gravy, green beans with fried onions on top, and nice rolls.*

Carefully laying the package on top the box of Cheerios, she snatched a pound of hamburger before heading for the dairy aisle and adding a half gallon of whole milk and two dozen eggs to her basket.

As she stood in the checkout line, Lillie's excitement turned to fear. Her hands began to tremble. She had forgotten to add up her items. One after another, the numbers flashed on the computer screen, while she clutched her purse and prayed. When the last one was dragged across the sensor, Lillie grinned and— hands still trembling—gave $114.03 to the clerk.

Moving her cart out of the way of the woman behind her, Lillie stopped inside the sliding doors

and counted the money remaining in the white envelope. Thirty-four dollars and nineteen cents. *Why
did I do that? What will he say?*

PRESSING A PLASTIC BAG FILLED WITH ICE CUBES AGAINST
his throbbing bunion, Matt remembered his reaction when Lillie had returned from the bank and
grocery store. At first, he was happy and wanted to
share her excitement about having a full kitchen.
He had watched her expressions of joy as she un-
loaded six bags of food and marveled about opening a refrigerator that held more than one thing on
a shelf. And how fresh the cloverleaf rolls looked!
Wasn't it a treat to have them again?

Taking their anniversary savings to pay the
light bill had been the right decision, but spending
most of the remainder on food was questionable,
in his opinion. At that moment, the furnace came
on, pushing warm air through the living room. *We
should have saved it so this furnace could come on
again next month!* Then the aroma of frying cube
steak reached him. He chuckled and headed for the
kitchen.

Matt sat with his right foot propped on a kitchen
chair and a pillow tucked behind his lower back,
watching his wife move smoothly from mashing potatoes to stirring gravy to checking the green beans.
She appeared to embrace the stove and everything

on it. Her face shone with what could only be described as the light from her soul. And her green eyes glistened like spring grass with a covering of dew.

They talked about ordinary things: he told her how well Myra's mother was doing after her knee replacement. She said she planned to bake a chess pie and take it to her the next day. Leaning forward, Matt patted his wife's bottom. "How about one for us, girl?"

The back door slammed and Beth ran into the kitchen. "Mama, what do I smell?"

"Just supper, darling. You're right on time. Go wash your hands." Lillie's eyes met Matt's and she whispered, "No serious talk. We're enjoying ourselves."

When Beth saw Matt's swollen toe, she teased him and asked if Grandad had a story about something like that.

Lillie offered to pay for Beth to go to the movies with Heather, but Beth shook her head. "Can't. Want to do homework."

Matt slapped the table and grinned. "I've never said that in my life!"

After he had wiped away the last pool of gravy with his roll, Matt grasped Lillie's hand and winked. "Happy anniversary, girl. You did good."

28

Matt was thinking that the smell of food cooking had made him feel so peaceful the last three days when he heard Lillie scream and rushed to the kitchen.

She was in front of the stove, bending at the waist, pulling her scoop-neck shirt away from her chest with two fingers. From just above her left collar bone to her breastbone was a bright red area the size of her palm.

Words mixed with tears said she didn't know how it happened. "Grease just flew up in the air!"

After quickly turning off the electric burners under the sizzling hamburgers and onions, Matt grasped her hands. "Hurry. Let's get to the emergency room."

Lillie's arms shook, but her voice was strong. "No, no." She jerked her hands away. "Get the margarine."

Barely able to look at the large blisters forming on his wife's chest, Matt shook his head, no. "This is bad. You've got to go."

Pointing to the refrigerator, she slumped down in a chair. "Grandma used it."

Familiar with his wife's stubbornness, Matt knew when he could talk her out of something and when he couldn't. Any reference to her grandmother meant she would hold her position. Whispering, "This is not right." he unwrapped a stick of margarine and thrust it toward her.

Her face glistening with sweat, Lillie bit her bottom lip and dug her fingers into the margarine, smearing it on the burn. As skin slid from her chest onto her shirt, she cried out.

Before he knew what he was doing, Matt leaned over the sink and gagged, grateful that his stomach was empty. He splashed water on his face, wiped it with the sleeve of his sweatshirt, and reached for Lillie. "Sorry. Let's get you to bed."

As slowly and gently as his back would allow, Matt eased his wife down on the bed and ripped off her baggy shirt. Then he placed a clean towel over each of her shoulders and breasts, careful not to touch the burn, and tucked the blanket around her waist. While wiping her pale face with a cool washcloth, he pleaded with her to go to the emergency room. She closed her eyes, shook her head, no, and asked him to put the hamburger and onions in the refrigerator.

Keeping his weight on his heel, Matt limped to the bathroom. The Tylenol bottle had five pills in it. When he dropped three in Lillie's hand, she picked one up and placed it on her tongue. He insisted, "*All of them and don't argue.*"

After putting the meat and onions away, he sat on the side of the bed and held Lillie's hand, asking every few minutes if he could get her anything. Finally, she insisted he go rest his feet, assuring him she would call if necessary.

Instead of going to his chair, Matt went to Nell's and called Rachel and Bella's parents, asking them to not bring the children the next day. On the way back, he noticed a single green leaf hanging vertically below a limb of the plum tree. Its stem was hooked to the silk of a spider web, causing it to spin, helplessly, like a top. Sadness enveloped him: he had a sudden urge to rescue the leaf.

Lillie refused to eat anything Matt offered, even a bowl of Cheerios—she just wanted to sleep. He lay beside her—his hand touching her upper arm—listening to her light snore when she drifted off and to her tears when she awoke. Determined to avoid his usual two or three-hour sleep, he pulled up on the side of the bed twice to shake himself awake. Her unspoken answer to why she refused to go to the emergency room hammered his mind. "Too expensive. Can't afford it." Then his own conclusion: "Not taking care of my wife."

First thing the next morning, Matt went to the drugstore. The pharmacist told him, "Using margarine was the wrong thing to do. Use an antibiotic cream and keep the burn clean."

Lillie was sitting at the kitchen table with the towels draped across her shoulders when Matt returned. Her unbrushed hair hung beside her face. She touched it. "Must look like a rat's nest." Matt shook his head, no, instead thinking how exhausted she looked.

Having intended to put the antibiotic on Lillie's burn as soon as he got home, Matt now found himself stalling. Each time he glanced at it, he felt queasy and turned his eyes away. When she grasped his arm and took the cream from his hand, he said, "Be right back. Have to make a call."

Feeling light-headed, Matt leaned on Nell's back door while waiting for her to open it. His first call was to the doctor who took care of Lillie's seizures. After describing the burn to the receptionist, he asked how much it would cost to treat it. She referred him to the business office. The woman there said a visit was ninety dollars, but additional charges were possible, depending on what the doctor ordered.

Hesitantly, he asked, "Do you ever give discounts?"

"Of course, we do," she answered. "Every insurance company receives a negotiated rate. Whether it's an HMO or a PPO, you get a discount. Which do you have?"

"Well, we don't have any." Glad he could hide his embarrassment behind a telephone, Matt asked, "But, you're saying we have to pay more than an insurance company?"

The woman answered in a matter-of-fact tone. "People who pay out of pocket pay our standard rate. Of course that's higher."

Matt's second call was to a nurse whose children Lillie had kept several years before. He asked if she would come by after work to look at the burn. Saying she would be there at lunch instead, she suggested he call the medical school in Winston and ask about their low-cost clinic.

Matt checked the time on the cuckoo clock hanging above Nell's TV. *Ten after ten. An hour to get there. Can be there by twelve.* Then the throbbing in his right foot reminded him he would be driving with his left.

The medical school operator described a clinic staffed by students, interns, and residents that charged on a sliding scale according to income and gave him that number. He waited while the woman in scheduling searched for the next available appointment. Although it was two weeks away, Matt eagerly gave her Lillie's name and address. "Oh, no," she said. "You live in Cross Hill! This clinic only serves residents of Forsyth County."

Noticing he was cradling Nell's phone book when he heard the cuckoo call out eleven, Matt knew he was frozen in more ways than one. Eight months before, Dr. Latham had told him he was disabled and should apply for benefits. But, no, he had been too—many words came to him—stupid, selfish, and hard-headed. "Irresponsible," he mumbled and slapped the book. *Pride!*

He opened the book and searched for two numbers: Dr. Latham's and Social Security.

While telling Dr. Latham's nurse he was thinking of applying for disability, she interrupted. "You haven't, yet? The doctor sent a letter months ago saying you hadn't been able to work since your surgery. Let's see, that's—"

"Two years, three months, and fifteen days."

Hearing that Dr. Latham had already told them he was disabled, Matt decided to go to the Social Security office instead of calling. The nearest one was in Clement. Nell told him to take his time; she had the whole day to spend with Lillie.

Traffic on the bypass was light, though Matt wished he could have taken a back road. Fifteen miles wasn't far, but he wasn't sure it was legal to drive with his left foot. In spite of his apprehension, he had a good feeling—like a man accomplishing something. It wasn't long before he heard himself whistling, "Old McDonald Had a Farm." Laughing, he thought of the many times he had wished Lillie would sing something besides that to the girls.

The dark bricks of the one-story building looked like they had absorbed a great deal of dirt and exhaust over the years, and Matt hoped, for the sake of the people working there, that the inside looked better. A glass partition separated the receptionist from the people in the room. A sliding window made her available, or not. Matt waited at the closed window, while she talked on the phone. When she finished, he waited a few more minutes before tapping on the glass.

After he explained the situation, the receptionist responded abruptly. "Mr. Moore can't talk today. Come back tomorrow after one."

Her tone caused Matt to step back. There were many things he would like to have said besides, "All right, ma'am, I'll be here," but he pushed them away by thinking of Lillie's burn.

As he pulled into the parking lot at the Social Security building the next day, Matt glanced at his gas gauge—an eighth of a tank. That reminded him of his mother's words: "Nobody drives on vapors as far as you do. You could probably make it to Kingdom Come." He peered in his wallet: four ones.

Matt reached the receptionist's window at exactly three minutes after one. He watched the clock on the wall until two-thirty, when she sent him into Mr. Moore's office. The man remained seated at his desk. He greeted Matt with a nod and half-hearted smile, like a man in pain, Matt thought, before saying, "I'm sorry to keep you waiting. We're busy here. But there's nothing for us to talk about anyway, until your referring doctor fills out these forms." Then he handed him two sheets of paper. "And this application's for you."

Matt tried to describe the letter that Dr. Latham had sent, but Mr. Moore waved his hand and stood. "Letters don't matter. This process cannot begin until I receive those completed forms. Have your physician send them directly to me."

MATT WAS PLEASED WHEN DR. LATHAM'S NURSE CALLED to say she had sent the forms to Social Security. He had mailed his own the day before, so hoped that everything would be in Mr. Moore's hands by Monday. Assuming he would hear from him by Wednesday, Thursday at the latest, he expected to have disability money in hand the week after that.

Although the nurse had come to the house three times to check Lillie's burn and said it looked fine, Matt still wanted a doctor to see it. He was certain she would agree to go once he got a commitment about the disability.

He waited until four-thirty on Wednesday to call Mr. Moore. The receptionist said she would leave a message. Matt continued, "Ma'am, I just need to make sure he got my application and the papers from Dr. Latham. Will you let me know?" She said she would.

Two days later, Matt still hadn't heard from Social Security. Although he felt guilty about using money for gas, he couldn't wait any longer. By the time he reached the car, he realized the pain in his foot was taking more of his energy than the pain in his back. As he held onto the door to steady himself and catch his breath, he noticed the white and purple buds of the bearded irises beside the driveway. They were about to burst. On the other side of the road, deep pink blossoms covered a redbud tree. When had spring come?

When Matt asked the receptionist at Social Security to see Mr. Moore, she continued typing as she answered. "He's busy and you don't have an appointment."

Leaning on the counter for support, Matt remembered Lillie's suggestion that he use a cane. "I'm sorry, but he didn't call me back, and I need to find out if he got my application."

The receptionist turned her head from the computer screen to Matt. Sounding frustrated, she replied, "You have to have an *appointment.*"

"He won't talk on the phone?"

The printer released six pages: she fastened them together with a paper clip and laid them on the left corner of her desk. "He's busy. Do you want an appointment?" Turning back to the computer, she said, "What about Thursday of next week?"

When Matt turned the key in the ignition and heard nothing but a grind, he chuckled. *This place has rubbed off on you!*

Finding a pay phone at the Shell station next door, Matt felt lucky that he had change in his pocket and that Nell answered on the first ring. She promised to tell Lillie what had happened and to ask Bobby to pick him up after work.

Matt left the car door open and stretched out on the back seat. His thoughts drifted: during mandolin lessons, he could mostly block out his pain. Learning to play was giving him the most pleasure he had had since his surgery, though the sounds he created were sometimes hard to bear. And it was taking longer to learn than he had thought it would. Little Red wanted to lend him his mandolin for practice, but Matt wouldn't take it. He believed it was good for his friend to keep it with him. It seemed to be the only connection to his past life that he had left.

He had seen changes in Little Red over the past few months. Occasionally, he greeted Matt with a smile, and he had begun talking about the notes and chords, as he demonstrated them. But some things remained the same. One day his friend had nearly scared him to death. Little Red was playing the mandolin when Matt arrived and may not have heard his car.

When Matt opened the door to the trailer, Little Red dropped to his knees and turned the mandolin around, holding it like a rifle. His face had the look of a wolf about to attack. Matt backed down the steps and fell to the ground. After Little Red helped him up, they both collapsed on the step until they stopped shaking.

When Matt sat up to look for Bobby's car, he noticed pink and red azalea shrubs tucked against the corner of the ugly, box-flat Social Security building.

Nearly four feet high, they had spread over each other. The sky was painted a deep rose and gold, making it look like the entire earth was on fire. Stirred by the beauty around him, Matt was, momentarily, removed from the pain that had spread down his legs. He marveled, "My, my," just as his cousin turned into the parking lot.

Bobby whistled and then called, "Let's go, you lazy bum. I'll bring somebody over to fix that rattle-trap tomorrow."

Determined that nothing would interfere with getting the disability money, Matt arrived fifty-five minutes early for his appointment with Mr. Moore. He remained cheerful when he asked the receptionist how she was and received no answer. He told her he was in no hurry and could wait as long as needed.

At the appointed hour, Mr. Moore called him into his office and stood inside the closed door. "Mr. Bradfurd. I don't think you understand what a complex process this is. I don't have the authority to just go by Dr. Latham's statement and grant you disability. Much more is involved. My next step is to get medical records from every doctor you've seen about your back. That takes time."

Mr. Moore's voice softened, as he turned toward his desk. "You don't need to call anymore. I'll let you know when I'm ready to discuss your case."

29

JIM FINALLY GAVE IN TO HIS FATHER'S CONTINUOUS
requests to see the research aspect of his business.
He waited outside the lab door while his father got
into the white coat required of everyone entering.
Allowing his father to go ahead, Jim bent slightly
at the waist and tried to burp. His chest felt like
someone was sitting on it. He was trying to ignore
it because his local internist had diagnosed it as
a kind of indigestion. He didn't want his father to
know about it, since it would add to the long list of
questions directed at him.

Jim wouldn't have told him the truth, anyway.
He had dodged his father's questions since he was
twelve and had gotten good at it until recently, when
he had begun to feel backed into a corner. The demands of living in the same town with a retired father who wanted to become a friend were constant
and nearly intolerable.

Professor Hartman shook the chemist's hand
vigorously and asked him to explain the process.
Then he made a loop around the room, his white

coat swinging, before spinning about and spreading his arms. "Jim, it's brilliant!" He raised his chin and wiggled his nose. "Is that grapefruit I smell?"

Jim shrugged. The pain in his chest was burrowing through to his back. "Have to get moving, Dad. Got a lot to do."

The six-foot-one-inch man leaned over his son. "You must be proud of yourself! Where did the idea come from? How'd you learn to do this?"

Jim stepped back and spoke firmly. "I have *work* to do."

As the professor removed his white coat in the space separating the lab from the packaging room, he bumped the back of his son's head with his elbow. When Jim whirled about with fists clenched, his father raised his eyebrows and stared at the angry set of his jaw. "I'm sorry. What *is wrong with...?*" He looked away. "Never mind."

In silence they stepped around boxes filled with shampoos and conditioners on their way to Jim's office. When they reached the closed door, the two men stopped. Professor Hartman's voice lacked enthusiasm. "Jim, I had some news to discuss. Maybe another time."

JERKING OPEN THE BOTTOM DRAWER OF HIS DESK, JIM lifted a Macanudo from its wooden case. He inhaled deeply and pounded his chest with his left fist as if trying to smash the pain. *Why won't he leave me alone?*

Stuffing the cigar in the ashtray, Jim slammed the office door behind him and said to his secretary, "Back in three-four hours. Or maybe not at all."

Jim revved the big engine of the M5 BMW before pulling out of the parking lot on his way to the medical school in Winston. He had seen a doctor there for a second opinion about his chest pain and was scheduled to hear the results of his tests this afternoon. Believing that doctors looked for something wrong to keep people coming so they could make more money, he was angry at himself for going in the first place. In spite of that, driving there and back would be fun. The pain in his chest subsided as he smoothly threaded in and out of lanes, passing all the cars in front of him.

His father had asked the same question that morning—"How did you learn to make shampoo?"—that he'd been asking for five months. Eventually, Jim would have to come up with something plausible. Certainly not the truth. That would never fly.

The blur of yellow and purple wildflowers beside the road created a vision of Starshine. Her face glowed with purity and simplicity, and she'd pinned a flower above her ear. Thinking of Starshine made Jim smile. She was the only authentic hippy he had ever known.

Jim and Starshine had met during his junior year at State. Although she wasn't a student, she lived with her boyfriend in the three-story house that four of Jim's friends rented near campus. He often crashed on their living room couch after parties.

The first time they were alone together was a Monday in February. That morning, too hung-over to go to class, Jim dragged himself to the kitchen hoping coffee would jolt him enough out of his stupor to attend afternoon classes. But the regular coffee pot had been broken the week before, and the four stove burners were covered with Starshine's pots.

Jim looked down at the stovetop, then at Starshine, and muttered, "What the fuck?" If her boyfriend hadn't been one of the renters, he would have taken one of her pots off a burner and made his coffee. Or if he had felt better, he would have walked the half-mile to the café. Instead, he slumped over the kitchen table and waited while she, ever cheerful, described what she was doing.

As Starshine moved from pots to ceramic bowls to the glass bottles she had lined up on the counter, at first Jim concentrated on the jiggle of her braless breasts. Then, for some reason that he would later attribute to genius, he began paying attention to her words: she was making her own shampoos and conditioners. Two of the pots were filled with boiling water that she was purifying. Another held large clumps of mint and the fourth long sprigs of rosemary she had grown at the window in her boyfriend's bedroom.

Starshine instructed Jim as if he was a valued pupil. "This bowl holds dried peony buds." She pointed to another. "And this one, lilac. They must be grown organically—no pesticides."

Jim stood beside her and began to nod.

"Steep them in purified water until their essence is removed, then add oil and vinegar." She looked around to make sure he was watching. "Only buy it at the health food store and mix it in glass. Plastic leaks toxins."

Then Starshine sat down in a kitchen chair and swung her thick, gleaming, honey-brown hair across her shoulder. "Close your eyes. Stroke it," she said. "There's no blockage of chi. You can feel it pulsing."

As they shared a joint—organically grown by her—Jim asked questions. Why two shampoos and conditioners? Since they had no preservatives, how long would they last?

Again, Jim noticed the blur of wildflowers beside the highway—reds and yellows this time. Squeezing the soft, black leather on his steering wheel, he laughed. *Poor dumb girl. So gullible.*

After that one morning with Starshine, it had taken Jim only two weeks to decide what his career would be. Since he was a business major, he would start a company around these hair products. To get the formulas in writing from Starshine, he told her his aunt's hair was growing back after chemo treatments for breast cancer, and he wanted to make a gift for her with his own hands. She told him how sorry she felt for his aunt and showed him, step by step, how to make all four products.

During his senior year, Jim cultivated a friendship with a fraternity brother, Raymond Preston Palmer III. That, too, was easy; Ray loved pot, and Jim had an unending supply. Ray's last name was connected to a large amount of money and the ability to open doors in New York. His father had made it clear that he could do anything he wanted as long as he had a job and stayed out of trouble. Ray became Jim's bank and the company sales representative.

As Jim turned the silver BMW into the med school parking garage, he noticed a slim young woman with long, straight hair approaching. His hard shove on the brake threw his body forward until it was caught by the seat belt. Looking alarmed, the woman rushed toward him. "You all right?" His hands shaking, Jim nodded and steered his car into an empty space. *So much like her.*

Since the day he had started the business, Jim lived with the fear that Starshine would discover his products and recognize the original four as her own. He had tried to eliminate them from the inventory, but couldn't because they were the most popular and carried the others financially.

Ducking, he slipped quickly from the car. *What if she does find out?* Stopping at the bottom of the stairs, he shrugged and stood up straight. *She wasn't forced to give me the formulas! So I used them. So what? She didn't have a patent!*

While waiting in the reception room for the chairman of the department of gastroenterology, Jim tried to guess what his bill would be. He had seen the chairman of cardiology and had an EKG, treadmill, and blood work before being sent to gastroenterology. There he was given a barium X Ray and upper endoscopy exam. "Thousands," he said aloud. *I've spent thousands. My chest still hurts and this damn jaw.* He paced around shaking his head, as if he could sling away the pain.

The doctor sat behind a square wooden desk so large it made Jim think he had to shout to be heard. The man was repeating what his internist in Cross Hill had told him and that made him mad. *Nobody has listened!*

Frowning, the doctor said, "Mr. Hartman, I can see you're unhappy with my diagnosis, but you *do* have gastro esophageal reflux disease—GERD. I'm sure you've seen the pharmaceutical ads on TV about it. It's very common."

Leaning forward, Jim lightly slapped the doctor's desk. It was hard to trust a man who spoke so slowly and sounded like a hick. "But I have *chest* pain."

A large, well-built man, the doctor began a slow rocking motion with his chair. "Yes, sir, you do. As I've explained, some people with this problem experience it. Some don't. Medication will relieve your symptoms, and it sure would help if you'd cut out that alcohol and those cigars."

His feet planted firmly on the floor in front of his chair, Jim wanted to spring across the cluttered desk and strangle the doctor. "It has to be something..." His sentence trailed off as he stood.

The physician eased out of his chair. His folksy manner had disappeared. "Mr. Hartman, you've had the best medical care available in this state. If I were you, I'd follow my advice. Maybe cutting down on that stress would be a good idea, too. That might help your jaw." When he extended his hand toward his patient, Jim turned and walked out of the office.

Stress, my ass! Jim slammed his car door. *Nothing a joint couldn't take care of.* He thought of his father. *Or getting out of this damn place.* That thought surprised him. Leaving would mean selling the company five years earlier than he had planned.

Sometimes Jim didn't acknowledge how profitable the business had been over the past eleven years, though he realized it when he was doing his taxes. Even after splitting it with Ray, his half would be enough to live on for the rest of his life. And, he knew that if he got bored with retirement, he could start another.

Selling the business and moving back to Ann Arbor could solve several problems. His father and mother would follow and would be distracted by his brother's family, taking the pressure off him. He could go ahead and build his houses, forcing his father to see what he had accomplished. Jim laughed. *And rubbing my brother's smug face in my money would relax me!* Taking his name out of the company would also eliminate the fear that Starshine might someday make a connection between her formulas and Organic Botanicals.

JIM WAS CONCENTRATING ON THE RAPPER'S LYRICS coming from the five speakers in his car, when he rounded the curve to his street and saw his father's Jetta parked in front of his house. He slammed on the brakes. *Damn! Go home! Why does Mel encourage this?* He sat by the side of the road a few minutes trying to decide what to do. He could leave and return after dinner, but his father and mother would probably still be there. He stroked the smooth leather of his steering wheel before grabbing it as if he were choking it. He released his grip when tears came to his eyes. *What the hell?* Sniffing, he pulled in the driveway and crept in the back door.

A blast of cold air struck him. The air-conditioning was always set higher when his father was there, and he hated that. The professor called out from the family room, "Wonderful! Come in. I'm having trouble waiting to share my news."

Melanie reached Jim while he was trying to decide whether to go in or to pretend he hadn't heard. Embracing him, she pressed her cheek against his and whispered, "Sorry, honey. Take a minute. I'll stall."

Jim sat down on a bench in the mud room before dragging himself to the family room and dropping onto the flowered sofa beside Melanie. His father started talking. "Now, then, here's the big news. First, your brother. He's moving to California."

Jim removed his arm from his wife's shoulders and met his father's eyes. "What the hell?"

The professor shook his head. "Well, I didn't put it that way, but it surprised me, too. *Until* I heard why: he was offered a full professorship at the University of California, Santa Barbara. They've built a dynamic, exciting physics department still new enough for him to make a mark. He'll work with Nobel laureates. It's an extraordinary opportunity."

"Yeah, right." Jim shrugged. "And there's probably some *extraordinary* trailer park he can live in. Can't afford anything else."

The professor sat forward in his chair, his eyes wide and face bright. "It's unbelievable! They have new subsidized housing for professors right beside the campus—white stucco, red tile roofs, Mediterranean. His family's getting a four-bedroom."

"How exciting," Melanie turned toward Jim. "I've always wanted to visit Santa Barbara."

"One more thing, and then I'll let someone else talk." Professor Hartman winked at his wife. "I've located descendants of the Methodist minister who brought my great-grandfather to Winston. They believe some of their relatives have his papers. They'll search them out and will try to find church records from that time." He crossed two fingers on each hand and held them up. "So, once we get the family's name we can trace their descendants."

Jim was tired of hearing his father talk about dead people. Although he had just put a large piece of cheddar in his mouth, he started telling him that. Since his words were garbled, he raised his voice. "I don't understand your preoccupation with this name," Jim said. "The people alive now had nothing to do with saving your grandfather's life. The ones who did are dead. But even if they were alive, so what? It was no skin off their backs to hide a man for a few weeks."

Jim saw his mother look down at her fingernails and his father close his eyes.

Melanie took a deep breath, exhaled, and broke the silence. "Well, honey, your father feels an obligation to—"

Jim jumped up from the sofa and rushed toward the kitchen. "I need a drink."

Once he got to the kitchen, Jim knew he had to disappear. But the only way for him to get to his bedroom without going through the family room was to go out the side door. As he placed his hand on the knob, he noticed the dinner table was set for six, and he smelled the chicken and broccoli casserole that Melanie knew he loved. So, he reached instead, for the bottle of Macallan scotch that he saved for special occasions, poured a double, took a gulp, and returned to the family room.

"When are you meeting with the people in Winston?" Melanie asked her father-in-law. She patted the cushion beside her, and Jim sat down, staring at the brown liquid in his glass.

"Tomorrow." The professor still sat forward in his chair, but his eyes had lost their sparkle and his voice its enthusiasm. "Jim, let me tell you what your great-great-grandfather wrote in his journal. 'When I left Boston, I believed I was going to a land of devils to rescue innocents. As men lifted me from the forest, I was certain they were taking me to the house of Satan. But I was wrong. God's people were waiting there to help.'"

The professor leaned back in his chair, propped his elbows on the arms, and laced his fingers together. His smile had not returned. He sounded like a teacher trying to discuss material his student hadn't bothered to read. "Jim, our ancestor was a threat to their culture and beliefs. How many people would defend a person like that? And during a military occupation? Do you know anybody that courageous?"

At that moment, Jim's two daughters ran into the room, waved at him, and threw themselves on their grandparents' laps.

The professor said, "Look! These girls exist today because of that courage. Six generations of Hartmans were saved! Think of what a simple action taken on behalf of a stranger can do." He hugged the granddaughter on his lap and reached toward the other with his long arms. "I want to stand before that family's descendants and express our gratitude. To, literally, show them what their grandfather did."

Jim finished his scotch and stood. "I need another."

Having a hard time concentrating, Jim decided to just ignore everyone at the dinner table. He felt guilty for not keeping up with what the girls were saying but vowed to listen carefully the next evening.

The news about his brother was bad. Now, there would be no incentive for his parents to return to Ann Arbor. And as long as they lived in Cross Hill, Melanie would refuse to leave. But Jim had to admit she probably wouldn't have left anyway. She had taken a new volunteer job with a program sponsored by the Women's Club to identify people in the community needing food and financial assistance.

After saying he had to go to the bathroom, Jim poured another scotch and went to bed.

30

IT HAD BEEN A HOT DRY SPRING. CLOUDS OF PINK DUST followed Matt down the hard-packed dirt driveway. When his car came to a stop at the trailer, Little Red appeared in the open doorway, his hand raised in a wave.

"Got this problem with my foot," Matt called out. "Can I lean on you to get up that step?"

Surprised to see three springs of crepe myrtle—two lavender and a white—in a water glass on the table, Matt tilted his head, wrinkled his brow, and settled his gaze on Little Red. His shoulder-length hair seemed thicker than usual; it had been washed. That reminded Matt of other things. During the past two months, he had seen his friend laugh a few times, and he hadn't worried so much about saying the wrong thing to him.

When Little Red thrust the mandolin toward him, Matt shifted and settled deeper in the couch. He heard the hum of bees through the open window behind him. "You mind if I don't take a lesson today? Need to do some talking. And there's a question I need a real straight answer for."

Little Red nodded.

"I'm sticking my nose in your business—I know that—and this probably sounds weird, but I don't feel right calling you 'Little' anymore." Matt shook his head. "Doesn't fit." Then he grinned and slapped his knee. "You may not be the biggest fellow I've ever seen, but, my god, boy, when you play that mandolin, you're twelve feet tall! Your music's fine enough to dance to in heaven!"

Hesitating, he glanced at his friend's face. It hadn't changed, so Matt continued. "And that war—man, you've been through hell carrying it for thirty years. You're tough! You deserve a name that shows you're a grown man."

Both men sat in silence. Matt turned his attention back to the hum of the bees. Thinking he saw a reaction on his friend's face, he waved his right arm. "Like I said, this is none of my business."

Little Red's voice was soft. "Call me Red."

Then Matt veered off the course he had set. Closing his eyes, he leaned his head against the back of the sofa and told Red things were bad for him and Lillie. Said he hadn't come more often because either he didn't have gas money or he hurt too much.

When he heard what was coming from his mouth, Matt felt embarrassed but couldn't change direction. "Red, I'm not getting well—I know it—and we're hungry, can't pay our bills. Dr. Ramsey thought I was lying about the pain or crazy, which amounts to the same thing as far as I'm concerned.

"But maybe I'm not thinking straight by now, who knows? And I'm ashamed to say I've applied for disability—it'll come any day now—but I have to have a way to take care of my family. And Beth works a minimum-wage job to help support us, instead of getting ready for college."

Matt felt his face flush. "My life is a rotten mess, Red, and I'm disappointed with myself. And I'm puzzled. Don't know why I didn't turn out tough and strong like Grandad." His voice softened. "What good am I to anybody in this world?"

Rubbing his forehead to hide his eyes, Matt sniffed and cleared his throat. "Sorry. I didn't come here to burden you. I just can't see any of this changing anytime soon—that's the worst part. I'm stuck!"

When his fingers brushed the silver buckle that he wore each time he played the mandolin, Matt thought about the sound he created with that instrument. He saw his stiff, slow fingers pressing its neck, as if trying to strangle it. Pointing toward it, he asked a question that was already answered in his mind. "Will I ever get good enough to earn money from playing that thing? Or am I spinning my wheels? Tell me the truth."

Red turned from Matt's flushed face toward the open window and coughed. "Well, it's mighty hard for a man to learn when he's older—especially when he don't have nothing to practice on"—but continued with words of encouragement that a parent would offer his child.

Matt had his answer but allowed Red to go on, finding pleasure in the man's expressions of caring. And he was amazed that he spoke so well. He watched as Red opened his eyes widely and made brushing movements with his right hand as he spoke, just as his late father had done.

"Appreciate your honesty." Matt's voice cracked. Grief unexpectedly slipped up on him, causing a stabbing pain in his shoulder; this last fantasy from his youth had been nothing but smoke.

Then he felt a sense of relief in being unhooked from another failure. Now he could just enjoy the music! As his mood lifted, he had an urge to talk about politics but had something more important to say. He shook his head.

"I still know this is none of my business, but I'd like to see you find a group to play with. *Anybody* would want you. I ran into your sister last week, and she agrees with me. She's real happy you're back with your music."

Feeling like he had said enough and knowing he had one more thing to do, Matt shifted his body and struggled to stand. His friend slipped quickly out of his chair and grasped him under both arms, smoothly lifting him to his feet.

Turning into his driveway faster than he meant to, Matt flattened the six iris plants on the corner.

When he hobbled past Lillie in the backyard, she asked how Little Red was. He answered, "Okay," but kept moving toward the bedroom.

Standing in front of his closet, he pushed the clothes aside and slipped his black shirt off the hanger. He pressed it against his chest, holding it the way he would a woman, before using one sleeve to wipe his eyes. Then he took the picture of Johnny Cash from his wallet, laid it on top the shirt, and rolled them up. He crept out the front door to avoid Lillie and rummaged through the shed, until he found the shovel. After laying the shirt and picture, gently, on the grass, he dug a hole in the soft dirt beside the fig tree and used the tip of the shovel to rake them in.

Mr. Moore called to tell Matt that he had made an appointment for him to see a psychologist in Clement. When Matt protested, asking why, he was told it was part of the evaluation process and the application couldn't be completed without it.

Matt's sore bunion had swollen so large that his right foot wouldn't fit in his dress shoes. Sitting in a kitchen chair, he lifted his foot while Lillie knelt on the floor and tied two shoelaces around the sole of an old sneaker she had cut up.

"Can you beat this, Lillie? They think I'm crazy!"

"No, no." Lillie's sounded like she was soothing a child. "They just have rules to follow."

"Ow!" Matt cried, as his foot dropped to the linoleum. "I want to tell them to watch a news program for an hour, and then tell me who's crazy! Bosses of big corporations change things on their books to grab more money than they can spend in a lifetime. Movie stars drive drunk and divorce one wife after another. Young people shoot each other at movies. Religious people hate each other." He shook his fist. "Those things are crazy! I don't act like that!"

Lillie had stood and was patting him on the shoulder. "Now, now."

"Don't shush me. I'm serious. *What does* crazy mean? Is it looking at a dog and thinking it's a horse? Or throwing your children off a bridge and claiming you didn't know what you were doing? Cutting yourself up, maybe? Why would they send *me*?"

CARS SPED BY MATT AS HE DROVE TO HIS PSYCHOLOGY appointment. Pressing the accelerator with his left foot caused his speed to be uneven. When a passing driver raised his middle finger and Matt yelled, "Asshole," he felt overwhelmed with sadness. *What have I done to you? What have I done wrong? Wrong?* He wiped his eyes with the back of his hand. *Let's see—decided to have surgery. Trusted my boss. Picked the wrong doctor. Acted like a baby. Everything!*

Then Matt added something else to his list. The day before he had been sitting in a backyard chair beside the kitchen window while Beth and Lillie were sitting in the kitchen.

"Will you be home for supper, darling?" Lillie asked.

Beth grunted. "Well, Mama. I wish I didn't have to be. Every time I speak, Daddy bites my head off."

"Oh, honey. He picks at me, too. He's just worn out and not able to control himself. He'll be back to his old self one day. Just you wait and see."

Beth's words had made Matt feel so ashamed that he looked around for a place to hide. Finally noticing a hole in the trunk of the hickory tree, he wished it was large enough for him to climb in. If only his body could turn inside out and vanish.

Another driver stared at Matt in his rearview mirror as he passed, but Matt's thoughts remained with Beth. His daughter was paying the highest price for his illness, losing her youth and her hopes for college. Guilt slashed at him. How he wanted to say, "Quit your job when school starts. Study hard. Go out with your friends. Play on the basketball team. Find a teacher who can help you get into college. Don't worry, we'll pay for everything."

Sweat ran down the middle of Matt's back, causing an itch that made him think of Lillie. If she was here, she'd scratch it for him. *Or would she?* Things were different between them: they hadn't had sex since the day before his surgery, because they were afraid it would injure his back. And more was gone—not love, they would never lose that. Fun and playfulness had disappeared.

Lillie *had* tried to smile and tease with him, but there was a strain on her face. He wanted to talk about it but was afraid she'd think he was blaming her. Although he found it hard to know what to do about it, something was sitting between them like the concrete barriers he was passing along the highway.

Matt's interview with the psychologist lasted forty-five minutes. He was dismissed with a "Thank you. I'll send my report to Mr. Moore."

When he reached the Impala, Matt banged on the top with his fist. He had done a good job keeping his anger at bay until the psychologist asked why he didn't want to work. The force in his answer shocked him. "You know the hell I've been through for two and a half years, because I *can't* work? My god, man! Why would I want to live like this? My life is gone—I might as well be dead—if I can't go back to work." But he didn't believe the man heard a word he said. He just seemed to react to the strong way Matt answered.

Before starting his car, Matt tried to calm himself. He looked up and saw large, thick white clouds tumbling freely across the Carolina-blue sky. Then

he noticed a small, gray, scraggly-looking one following behind them all. *That's what people think of
me. I'm the gray runt messing up the picture.*

Matt lowered all four windows and pushed hard
on the accelerator. Cars buzzed past, reminding
him of mosquitoes on the porch the night before.
Anger tried to boil over but he kept stopping it. He
didn't want to be mad when he got home. Leaning
his head out the window, he called to the wind.
"Come on, clear this crazy head of mine!"

THE AIR IN MATT'S BEDROOM WAS SO STILL THAT THE
window curtains looked painted on the wall. His
skin was sticky from the heat. He lay with his swollen right foot propped on a pillow and his head at
the foot of the bed watching for the mailman. For
twenty-nine mornings, he had lain in this same position until the mail truck turned the corner onto
his road. Then he struggled through the weeds and
long grass of his front lawn to the mailbox.

Fumbling with the glossy advertisements, Matt
glimpsed an envelope from Social Security. It was
tucked in front of a picture of a roaster that Piggly
Wiggly was selling for fifty-nine cents a pound.
Grinning, he ripped off the end of the envelope. *I'll
buy one of those. No, two!*

His hands shaking after reading the letter, Matt
stuffed the rest of the mail back into the box and

crossed the yard to call Dr. Latham.

The doctor asked three times *exactly* what the letter said. "But I'm telling you," Matt replied. "I'll read it."

Dear Mr. Bradfurd:

We have thoroughly evaluated your application to receive disability payments from Social Security Administration and are sorry to inform you that you do not qualify.

Social Security Administration

He listened to Dr. Latham say it was "an outrage," and he would "see about that." But Matt didn't feel the doctor's rage. He didn't feel anything at all.

It rained all weekend—a chilly, dreary rain that refused to let Matt see the sun. He punished the rain, the sun, and his own failure by staying in bed. A story Grandad had told him ran through his mind like a movie reel that no one could stop.

"Two brothers fought in the War Between the States. One moved to Iowa and joined the Union side. The other stayed with the Confederacy. They saw each other once on a battlefield. When the war was over, and the man from Iowa returned home, he found that his wife and son had died of typhoid. He blamed his brother for their deaths, saying if Southerners hadn't started the War, he could have kept his wife and son safe. He left Iowa, found his brother and killed him. After the Federals hanged him, the family buried the two brothers in the same plot. Sometimes nothing we do turns out right."

Monday morning, Matt moved from the bed to his chair. When Lillie reminded him of his blood sugar and offered him breakfast, he said he wasn't hungry. He just needed to be left alone to think. The sound of her voice and those of the children drifted about with his thoughts. Once, he opened his eyes and saw the girls sleeping on their pallets and heard Lillie snoring on the couch. Their skin had a sheen of sweat. He wished he hadn't made an agreement with the electric company not to use the air conditioner or television until the bill was paid in full.

After the girls' parents picked them up, Lillie set a plate of fried yellow squash, corn, sliced tomatoes, and biscuits on Matt's lap. Shaking his head, he handed it back. "Sorry, girl, thinking."

Still in his chair the next morning when gray light moved the darkness aside, Matt realized what he had to do. Hearing Lillie go to the bathroom, he pulled his aching back and numb legs out of the chair and, walking as straight as he could, went to the kitchen and sat down to wait for her.

Seeing the surprised look on his wife's face when she entered the room, Matt reached for her. As she laid her cheek on top his head and embraced him, he felt her body shake and knew she was crying. Gently pushing her back, he asked, "How about frying me an egg, darling?"

Husband and wife sat at the kitchen table drinking coffee and eating eggs and toast as if the morning had moved back in time.

"Beth'll be late for work," Matt said.

"No, she spent the night with Laura. She'll take her."

Matt shoved his plate aside. "She'll be here for supper, won't she? I want to talk to her."

Lillie had gotten up to put the dishes in the sink. "What about?"

Matt shrugged. "Just want to see her."

After breakfast, Matt sat in his chair and watched, with heightened awareness, every movement taking place around him. He listened to the stories Lillie read to Rachel and Bella and chuckled at their responses. Two or three times, Lillie patted him on the shoulder and, once, pinched his cheek.

When she took the girls outside to play, he went to the bedroom. Reaching in the far corner on the top shelf of the closet, he picked one bullet from its box and put it in the right pocket of his pants. He lifted his father's 30-30 rifle from the same shelf, slipped out the front door, and hid the gun behind the lawn mower in the shed. The scent of jasmine made him stop and turn around. The vine he loved so much had grown over the roof of the shed and tangled itself in the hinge of the door. Taking a deep breath, he squeezed a cluster of the white blossoms in his hand.

For the remainder of the afternoon, Matt talked to himself, oblivious to all around him. He was no longer useful to his wife and child and never would be again. He wasn't a man, but a log they were dragging as they searched for the best path to take. Holding them back made no sense. He needed to cut the rope and let them go on. He was proud that he had clarified the situation and certain of his decision.

He sat at the kitchen table, watching Lillie fry okra and boil corn, feeling comfortable and at ease. When she moved close enough, he took her hand and kissed it. Twice, he allowed his palm to drift, slowly, across her bottom. Hearing the back door slam, he wiped the sweat from his face and neck with a handkerchief, smoothed his hair back, and called to his daughter. "Hey! Sit down and talk to me!"

Matt ate little supper, wanting to save more for Beth and Lillie, and he told Grandad's favorite story, the one about trapping rabbits for food when he was a boy.

Satisfied with the memory they would have of their last day together, he went back to his chair. After Lillie and Beth fell asleep, he tucked the flashlight beside him. Pressing his fingers against the bullet in his pocket, he was certain there would be no paralyzed man to take care of.

Although the house held on to the day's heat, Matt shivered. He rubbed his arms and legs, pushed deeper in the chair, and reached for words of comfort. *The Lord is my Shepherd.* He repeated the words, reciting the Psalm over and over in its entirety until he fell asleep.

When he felt his body jerk Matt opened his eyes and looked into the darkness. He could see nothing. He pushed down his footrest and tried to stand but couldn't. *Wait! Where are you?* He felt his arms. They were warm. In the dream, there had been a great deal of light—similar to the soft, golden light of fall—allowing him to see everything in the living room. Heat radiating from the light entered his body, making him feel like he was expanding and becoming part of it. When he was no longer aware of his arms or legs, and entirely suffused by heat and light, the face of a man appeared. His features were familiar, though Matt couldn't place him.

The man asked, "Don't you know me?" This wasn't Grandad.

The man spoke a second time. "There is more to be done with your life. Don't be afraid. I am with you." Then the face and the light faded away.

Staring at nothing, Matt grasped his upper arms and made a rocking motion with his body. Then he took the bullet from his pocket and squeezed it tightly in his hand until streaks of rose graced the morning sky. As he left the house, he didn't close the front door for fear of waking Lillie.

Tears welling in Matt's eyes made it difficult to see the bottom step. He slipped, landing hard on his swollen foot. Grasping the iron railing, he leaned over and sobbed, realizing how happy he had been, believing it was his last day on earth.

When he opened the shed door, Matt felt dizzy. The fragrance of jasmine surrounded him. Pushing the lawn mower aside, he lifted a waded-up rain tarp from the corner and threw it over the rifle. Then he turned to the metal garbage can standing next to it, raised the lid, and listened to the soft ping as the bullet hit the bottom of the can.

31

THE RUSTY METAL CHAIR IN THE BACK YARD SQUEAKED as Matt shifted from side to side trying to identify the sounds coming from the birds in the oak and hickory trees. The high-pitched screech of a red-tailed hawk caused him to turn and watch it dive. He was greeting a new day and intended to use the same fierce determination as that hawk to solve his physical and financial problems. The words, "More to be done," demanded that he try again. Lillie had been right: he had to work with life as it was. He smacked a mosquito on his forearm as he struggled to remember the name Dr. Latham had given him more than a year before. Yes. George Russell. That was the man he would see for help.

Matt ate a scrambled egg with two pieces of toast. He asked Lillie to trim his hair and then he dressed in his best clothes. He regretted that he had to tie the rubber sole to his right foot and tried to make up for it by polishing and shining his left dress shoe with great care.

The ache in Matt's back and the throbbing in his foot nearly brought tears to his eyes, as he shifted his left foot from the accelerator to the brake. He tried to block the pain by whispering over and over, "I am with you." When the Impala stalled at a stop sign and the man in the car behind him beeped his horn, Matt smiled and waved.

Mr. Russell's office was located in an historical building on the main square that had been restored. The reception room was neither hot and muggy like the outside nor chilly like so many with air conditioning. The middle-aged woman behind the desk allowed her eyes to rest briefly on Matt's right foot but spoke politely. "I'm sorry, Mr. Bradfurd, but Mr. Russell's with a client. He sees people by appointment only."

The four wide leather chairs looked comfortable and there were two *Wall Street Journals* and a *Dispatch* on the table in front of them. Matt hadn't read a newspaper in months and had never seen a *Wall Street Journal*. He leaned forward and gently laid his hand on her desk. "I could wait." He noticed a water cooler in the corner. "Maybe he has a few minutes at lunch time. Or the end of the day. I'd appreciate it if you told him Dr. Latham sent me."

Surprised when the receptionist called him after fifteen minutes, Matt laid down the *Wall Street Journal,* knocked on Mr. Russell's door, and heard, "Come in."

Since the man didn't smile or offer to shake his hand, Matt thought he might be angry that he had waited so long to come. Mr. Russell pointed to one of the large wing chairs in front of his desk. "I've five minutes, Mr. Bradfurd. What can I do for you?"

Matt lowered himself to the seat as smoothly as he was able. "Well, sir, I apologize for not coming earlier. Since Dr. Latham already told you about my situation, I won't take up your time repeating it. He thought you might know people who could help with my bills. Utilities, medicines, groceries. Maybe, a group or club—something like that." When a cramp hit his back, Matt grinned to mask the look on his face and hoped the man hadn't noticed. "But to be honest, what I'd *really* like is a job."

Mr. Russell raised his eyebrows. "You have a college degree?"

Feeling his face flush, Matt shook his head. "High school." He wanted to run away from this man, but Matt was carried forward on the words from his dream. "Could you train me for something?"

Peering over his desk, Mr. Russell pointed to Matt's foot. "Looks like you have a problem. You couldn't work as a janitor."

"No, sir. I'd have to sit."

Mr. Russell looked at his watch. "I'll keep you in mind and ask around. Something might turn up."

The demons of discouragement slipped into the car with Matt and took hold of his mind. When he realized what was happening, he stopped at the next red light, opened his car door and said aloud to the demons, "Get out." Then he closed the door, said, "Sorry, Grandad," and turned on the radio to a country music station.

As he coasted around the corner onto his road, Matt saw Lillie sitting on the front steps beside the girls, reading them a book. *Why there?* When he pulled into the driveway, the girls jumped up and ran across the yard to the car. Struggling to rise, Lillie called, "Wait! Don't get out! You have to go to Dr. Latham's."

Rachel tapped on the car door and Bella reached for Lillie's hand. "Now, don't get mad. I called him about your foot. He said to come in the second you got home."

MATT LAY ON THE EXAM TABLE—THE RIGHT LEG OF HIS pants pushed up—watching the expressions on Dr. Latham's face change: first, from shock to confusion. Then he muttered, "How'd it go so fast? When did this start?" His face reddened, his brow wrinkled, and his gaze turned from Matt's foot to his face. "Why didn't you come in? What're you trying to do, kill yourself?"

"Well." Matt felt like a fool. He had watched the red streaks gradually make their way from his toes, across the top of his foot, and then up his lower leg. And he had sense enough to know something was wrong. But people had no real understanding—not even Dr. Latham—what life was like for him and Lillie. All he could do was pray day to day that God would strengthen his body to heal itself.

The doctor sounded kinder but spoke firmly. "I want to put you in the hospital, right now. I'll have a surgeon meet you there."

Matt struggled to pull himself up. "Thank you, sir. I appreciate that and everything else, but no."

Nearly crying out as he lowered the throbbing foot from the table, Matt looked toward the door and shook his head. "Can't afford a hospital. It would ruin us."

Dr. Latham pulled a chair close to Matt and sat down. He took his glasses off and rubbed his eyes and forehead. "I can't force you to do anything, but you've got to hear me. You're a diabetic. This is a serious infection that won't get better on its own. It *will* kill you or cause you to lose that foot."

"But what about the house? Can't the hospital make us sell it to pay the bill?" Matt asked. Although he was shaken by what the doctor had said, he couldn't allow it to matter. He had vowed to stop feeling sorry for himself and take charge of his life. "I won't have Lillie and Beth dumped in the street."

"Good god, boy!" Dr. Latham exhaled loudly and rose from his chair. He stood quietly and looked out the window a few minutes before turning back to Matt. "Let's make a deal. I'll have my receptionist ask the hospital what they do when people can't pay. Meantime, I'll drain that pus and give you antibiotics. If this thing doesn't look better by Wednesday, and I find out there's no risk to your house, you have to see a surgeon *in the hospital.*" The doctor extended his hand. "Agreed?"

A FAN ON TOP THE DRESSER SWEPT COOL AIR ACROSS his bed but sweat still soaked the sheet under Matt. The pain in his foot rivaled that of his back at its worst. When he saw a fly dive headlong into a window pane, his feelings detoured from the optimistic path he had taken, making him wish he could do the same thing.

At seven-thirty on Wednesday morning, Dr. Latham arrived at Matt's house and said the infection needed to be scraped off the bone by a surgeon. And the hospital billing office had assured him they had no authority to force the sale of a home to collect a debt. A payment schedule would be set up based on Matt and Lillie's income.

Matt lay on the operating room table shivering and whispering the Twenty-third Psalm, as the surgeon and the two nurses complained about the ninety-two degree heat outside. A nurse asked if he was cold, and he answered, "A little," though it wasn't true. The sound of metal scraping bones and the stench of decaying flesh were scaring him to death. When the doctor said, "Good news! Bone's not infected," he tried to calm himself by listening to the other nurse describe her weekend in the mountains.

"Stay off that foot and come here every day for two weeks to have it washed out," the surgeon said, as he pulled off his rubber gloves. "I couldn't sew it up because it has to heal from the inside out. And we still don't know for certain it will." He laid his hand on Matt's arm. "I'm afraid you're not out of the woods. Not by a long shot."

LILLIE LEANED OVER THE KITCHEN SINK AND WATCHED Matt cross the yard from Nell's, where he had gone to return Dr. Latham's call. If the doctor had wanted to know whether the hole in her husband's foot was still draining, the answer was yes, and that worried her. Although it had been four and a half weeks since the procedure, he still couldn't walk without crutches and the back spasms they caused had made him fall three times.

Matt sounded short of breath. "It wasn't about my foot. He wants me to hire a lawyer to get disability—like those ads on TV."

"Here. Sit down." She lifted his right foot and propped it on another chair. "But they turned you down."

"He says I can file an appeal." Matt shoved the crutches under the table. "Says I'm not able to work, and that's all there is to it."

Lillie was confused. "Why doesn't *he* tell them?"

Matt threw up his hands. "He *has,* Lillie, over and over. He wrote Moore a letter *and* he called him." Reaching across the table, Matt picked up the bills that he had insisted remain where he could see them. "Remember how much we owe?"

Lillie slumped down in a chair. "They're in my face all the time. How could I forget? Surgeon, $900. Hospital, $3,462."

Dropping the bills on the table and lowering his voice, Matt said, "You've got to help me decide."

She rose quickly from her chair. "Let's talk after we eat supper. I won't be so irritable."

As Lillie dried the dishes, she felt calmer, though they couldn't wait too long to have their talk. Her stomach didn't growl after black-eyed peas and cornbread, but her mind soon craved more.

Matt was snoring in his chair, when Lillie tiptoed into the living room. She crept toward him and sniffed. *Thank you, God.* Finally, the odor of infection had disappeared. Unwilling to wake him from a rare sound sleep, she turned toward her grandmother's rocker and collapsed into its familiar frame. The chair fit her body perfectly—there was no need to turn sideways or squeeze into it. And being all wood, it hadn't sagged or worn out like their softer, newer furniture.

Lillie liked the living room as it was at that moment—calm and hushed. It was the same feeling she had in an empty church. Light from the corner lamp wrapped her in its soft, yellow blanket and warm air from the furnace tucked her in. Tall, black windows stood as barriers to outside trouble. She touched the floor with her toes, beginning a peaceful rocking motion, until Matt awoke and brought the world back in. He raised his head and pushed himself upright.

"Dr. Latham's determined I get that lawyer." His voice rose. "But if something goes wrong, he's not the one who takes the hit."

Lillie pressed her foot flat on the floor to stop the rocker. "How do you mean?"

Anxiety squeezed Matt's voice. "If I make the Social Security people mad, they might try to get back at me. What if something *is* wrong with my head and they take me to court and tell everybody?"

"Hogwash!" Lillie was angry that Dr. Ramsey and Mr. Moore had tossed accusations of mental instability at her husband and left them as burdens for him to carry. That weight had pulled him down. "You're saner than half the people out there."

Matt leaned back in his chair and closed his eyes. "Just seems like we're too weak to take chances right now."

Lillie's gaze rested on her husband. Lately, she had tried not to look closely at him, because the physical changes upset her. He could be mistaken for a much older man: hair more gray than brown and the stubble on his face nearly white. Great dark circles surrounded dulled eyes, and his skin looked like canvas covering his body.

Pushing with her toes to start the rocker again, she looked around her living room. This time she saw other things: three brown circles drawn on the ceiling from the last rain. Plywood covering the missing window pane in the side porch door. Paint peeling from window frames that bordered walls dark with age. Perhaps, Matt was right and they were too weak to take chances. She stopped rocking.

But what about Beth? And Dr. Latham? They've worked hard to keep us going. Wouldn't giving up let them down?

Softly, she asked, "You awake?"

"Oh, yeah."

"You've got to try. We're not alone, you know."

32

MATT SAT BEFORE MR. GRIMES. HE WAS IMPRESSED BY the disability attorney's patience. Somehow his entire story had been revealed. "That's all I can think of."

The lawyer massaged his hands and glanced at his watch. "The Red Pig sure has good food. They may still be open for lunch. How about joining me?"

Surprised, Matt shook his head, no. "I better go on home. My wife'll wonder what happened to me. Well, what do you think?"

The lawyer held out the crutches to Matt. "You'd be doing me a favor. Eating with a man helps me decide whether we can work together."

Matt slipped his hand into his pocket and pulled out three quarters. "I'll have to pay you back when I can."

Mr. Grimes grinned like a boy who had gotten away with something. "No need. If I take your case, I'll make plenty off you."

Matt stopped inside the café, wishing he could stand there the rest of the day and breathe in its scents. He followed behind the lawyer to a table, his eyes darting from plate to plate. He read a description of every item on the menu, allowing his gaze to rest on the price before dropping to the next line. It was the country fried steak, mashed potatoes, gravy, two vegetables, and tea for six dollars and fifty cents that held his attention.

The moment the waitress set the plate before him, Matt lost awareness of his actions, until he was soaking up the last of the gravy with his third roll. Realizing he hadn't spoken, he said, "Guess I wasn't much company."

Bob Grimes set down his glass of iced tea. "Got all I needed. Let me tell you about Social Security. When somebody applies for disability, they string him along and try to confuse him, hoping he'll go away. If he doesn't, they reject the application and wait to see what he'll do." He grinned and banged his fist on the table. "Oh, we'll get 'em; don't you worry. Here's how my fee works—you pay it when you receive your first check." The lawyer pushed his chair back from the table. "By the way, you finally did get workers' comp payments, didn't you?"

33

E<small>D</small> L<small>ATHAM</small> <small>CLOSED HIS LAST PATIENT'S CHART AND SLID</small> it across his desk to the corner that signaled it was ready for his nurse. He groaned as he eased from his chair to stretch and look out the window.

The courthouse clock showed that he had ten minutes before Robert Grimes would knock on his door. The lawyer had asked to see him about Matt Bradfurd's disability. Ed was anxious to find out whether he had filed an appeal.

Damn that Moore! Remembering how confused and frustrated he was after the man suggested Matt was faking pain, Ed turned toward the fishing pole standing in the corner. That was about as logical as saying a bass had crawled out of High Rock Lake and into his bucket.

Sitting down at the desk, Ed picked up his wife's picture. "Darling, the world only seems rational when I talk to you and the fish. Nobody has common sense anymore. Or," he shrugged, "more likely, they just don't care about other people's problems. They give money to organizations, pat themselves

320

on the back, and think it's over. And an idiot like Moore will deny there's need at all."

Ed's nurse tapped twice on the door.

Robert Grimes approached with his hand extended. "'Appreciate you seeing me at the end of the day, doctor. You probably want to get on home to supper."

Having allowed the light in his office to dim as the sun retreated, Ed's first impression of the lawyer was that he was too young to be useful. But as the man moved closer, lines around his eyes signaled he was older than Ed had first thought. But the way he was dressed—sneakers, white socks, and a shirt that looked like he had been exercising—didn't fit Ed's idea of an attorney.

In spite of his misgivings, Ed felt an immediate liking for the man. Something about him was familiar. Opening a cabinet door to the right of his desk, he brought out a bottle of Jack Daniel's and two crystal glasses. "We ever met?"

Bob Grimes slumped down in the wide tan leather chair across from Ed. "No, sir. I worked in Atlanta quite a while after law school. Maybe, my father? You part of the Lathams near Deep River?"

Ed's face brightened. "That was my uncle's farm."

Bob Grimes leaned back, stretched his legs, and swirled the whiskey in its glass. "My grandparents lived around there when Dad was a boy."

Ed nodded and turned on the desk lamp. "Bet I knew him." Beginning a slow rocking motion with his chair, he took a sip of the warm whiskey. "Well, now, what can I do for you?"

"Matt Bradfurd's situation is stuck in my mind." The lawyer sat up straighter and his face brightened.

Ed stopped rocking and leaned forward. "Did you get the disability?"

Bob Grimes nodded. "Yes, sir. First check comes in four months. SSI until then." He frowned. "But some things I found out puzzle me—like this charge of mental instability. And why he didn't get workers' comp." He took a gulp of his whiskey and looked to the side. "I hate seeing people pushed around."

The attorney described what he had uncovered. His request for Matt's medical records revealed that Dr. Ramsey had left town. The doctor holding the records knew nothing about Matt's case so couldn't answer any questions. In his notes, Dr. Ramsey had written that Matt's employer—no name—had called to say he was a malingerer the last year or two before his surgery, and that he was considering firing him. He suggested Matt might fake pain to milk workers' comp. The employer called a second time to report that Matt had come to see him, and now he wondered about his mental stability.

Bob Grimes was drawing certain conclusions from these discoveries. Social Security had denied Matt based on suggestions of dishonesty and mental instability. He had a feeling they had been placed, deliberately, by an employer who didn't want to pay workers' comp or take Matt back into his company.

Setting his empty glass on the corner of Ed's desk, the lawyer continued. "I have a few questions you might clear up."

Ed reached for the bottle of Jack Daniel's. He found there was a brain beneath that head of poor-ly-cut hair. "Shoot."

"Is there *anything at all* in Matt's history that would lead you to believe these accusations? And. Did he have a back problem before beginning his job at Organic Botanicals?"

Swinging his head from side to side, Ed said, em-phatically, "No and no."

"Another thing. The orthopedist who gave a sec-ond opinion stated that Matt had a discitis. Doesn't that cause pain? Why wouldn't Ramsey deal with it?"

Ed rocked back in his chair and kicked the un-derside of his desk. "Ramsey's my fault. I didn't dis-cover what he was like until too late—incompetent, hardheaded, maybe too damn lazy to be a surgeon. You have to *work* with a body like Matt's. In the old days, we called it piss-poor protoplasm, but it was probably just the diabetes that gave him such a tough time. Where'd Ramsey go?"

"Las Vegas." Bob chuckled. "Poor bastards. Anyway, I sent the employer a letter with some questions. Want to shove him a little and see what happens." He stood. "I've bothered you long enough. Oh, yeah, one more thing. You know anybody with connections to Hartman's office?"

Ed almost answered no until he noticed the chart on the corner of his desk. "Ahh. I do. My nurse. Her niece is a good friend of his secretary."

"HE CAN'T THREATEN ME!" JIM HARTMAN FLIPPED THE letter from Robert Grimes to his right. He watched it flutter to the floor beside the waste can. *Good place for it. Trash!* Leaning over to retrieve it, he ripped it down the middle and laid the two halves in front of him.

While dialing his secretary to ask for Matthew Bradfurd's file, it occurred to Jim that she knew everything he had said or written about the man. Long ago, his wife had pointed out that each word he uttered could be heard in the reception room, so he had to assume that Tibby had heard his conversations with Ramsey and his promise to Matt that he could have his job back. She was aware that Matt hadn't received workers' comp and hadn't resigned. And she knew he had been a hard worker before surgery and was mentally stable.

Reminding himself to smile, Jim greeted Tibby at his office door and thanked her when she handed him the file. He placed it beside the torn letter from Robert Grimes and sat down to think.

If Grimes contacted his secretary, he needed to make sure she didn't answer his questions, but he had no idea how to influence her. He supposed he

could come right out and say, "Don't reveal anything you've heard in the office," and threaten to fire
her if she did. Although if Grimes hinted about taking legal action, she would probably give him what
he wanted. The only guide he could use was his
own set of beliefs about what motivated behavior:
he would give her a raise—a big one.

"Brilliant, man! Brilliant!" Jim leapt from his
chair, dumped the trash from the waste can on the
floor—leaving only the plastic liner—and set it on
his desk. Removing one page at a time from Matthew
Bradfurd's file—the summary of his five-and-a-half-
year history with Organic Botanicals—Jim tore each
page into eight pieces and dropped them in the can.
He laid the two halves of Robert Grimes's letter on
that and then stuffed the trash on top.

"Surprise, surprise?" Melanie called, pushing
Jim's office door open.

Giving the waste can a hard shove under his
desk with his foot, Jim asked, "What?"

His wife carried a medium-sized blue and white
cooler in her slender arms. Long smooth blond hair
hung about her face, glowing even in the artificial
light of his office. Sensuous lips pleaded with Jim.
"Heavy. Help."

Whenever Jim saw Melanie unexpectedly or
from a distance, he was stunned by her beauty.
The realization that she was *his* wife paralyzed him
momentarily.

"*Jim!*"

He rushed forward to take the cooler. "What's going on?"

She grinned. "Next Tuesday's your birthday. Don't you remember? Instead of just one day, we're celebrating our birthdays for a week, now! This is day one." She kissed her husband on the lips. "I ordered bratwurst and dills from Zingerman's!"

As Melanie laid a placemat on the desk in front of Jim and pulled a chair close to his, her joviality disappeared. "Something happened this morning. I promised myself I'd wait until tonight to talk about it, but I can't." She waved her hand back and forth, looked down at the floor, and shuddered. "Just give me a quick answer."

Melanie's previous volunteer job had been at the Senior Center. While talking with the elderly, she noticed that many needed additional food and financial assistance. And she wondered whether people in other age groups might also. She had convinced the Women's Club to create a volunteer position and allow her to investigate. Social Services had given her a list of families they suspected were falling through the cracks.

That morning, she had visited her fourth family. After she introduced herself, the man asked if she was Jim's wife. Surprised, she found that he had worked for Organic Botanicals until his back surgery, three years before. While exploring their financial situation, Melanie discovered that he had had no financial help since his last day at work. They lived on his wife's income from babysitting two children and his teen-age daughter's from her evening and weekend jobs.

Pushing her lunch aside, Melanie stared at her husband.

Jim usually felt like he was floating on a warm lake when she drew him into her wide blue gaze. This time, he shifted his eyes to the left.

She broke the silence. "Jim, could that be true? Is it possible for a man to injure his back at work and receive nothing *at all* from the company? His name's Matthew Bradfurd. Do you know him?"

Putting a finger to his lips, Jim pointed toward the closed door and whispered, "Shh. Remember, she can hear what we say."

Melanie sat back. The light in her face had been extinguished. With a trembling voice, she asked, "What about workers' compensation or something? Tell me, Jim."

A sharp pain hit Jim in the center of his chest and he roughly pushed his chair back and stood. He bent over and slammed his chest with his fist.

Melanie jumped up and grasped her husband's arm. "What is it?"

"You don't know anything about this," Jim said, jerking away. "Letting workers' comp get started in a small company would kill it!"

She put her arm around his shoulders. "Come on and eat," she said tenderly. "Sit down. We'll talk more tonight."

After Melanie left, Jim had an urge to talk to his partner. That was unusual because conversations with Ray were strained. He had a feeling Ray knew that the marketing end of the business was too relaxed to suit him.

When Ray answered his cell, Jim tried to sound casual. "Ray, my man! Where are you?"

His partner's voice was flat. "Here, working. Making contacts."

"Listen, I've been thinking. It's time to sell the business."

"What?" Ray cried out. "No way...why?"

Jim didn't know. It just seemed urgent that he do it. Beginning his answer by saying life was short and he wanted to spend more time with his family, Jim, suddenly, stopped. "Clairol would pay big bucks to scoop us up. Gives them a new niche. Now's the time."

Ray was silent. Jim asked whether he was still there. When Ray did start talking, Jim got his message quickly. He was satisfied with the way things were. Money was not an issue for him—his father was. If they sold, his father would insist that Ray do something else, and he had no desire to. Ray's voice took on a forcefulness unusual for him. Work allowed plenty of time to do things he enjoyed, and New York was far enough from Philadelphia to keep his family out of his hair. Then he reminded Jim that they both had to agree before either could transfer ownership of his half.

"But I do all the damn work!" Jim shouted.

Ray sounded like a man who had come into his own. "All you expected from me was my father's money to start this business. I think you're surprised at how well I've done. Now, back off, Big Jim. I used to call you that, didn't I? And no more comments about the amount of time I spend in this office."

Jim sat with the phone in his hand long after Ray had hung up. Instead of placing it on the receiver, he laid it on his desk and massaged his aching jaw. Later, he wandered over to the two-way mirror and looked down into the lab. Startled, he leaned forward, pressing his forehead against the glass. A young woman with straight honey-brown hair flowing over her lab coat stood at an angle, allowing him to see only part of her profile. *Starshine!*

Warm air rose from the furnace vent at Jim's feet. His face felt hot. Panic caused him to step back, and then rush forward. Misjudging the distance, he banged his nose hard against the glass. His lips trembled as he peered down at the lab again. The young woman had turned her face toward the mirror. She was the new girl the chemist had hired two weeks earlier.

Staggering backward, Jim dropped into his desk chair. A strange feeling of disappointment came over him. The one person—Starshine—who could truly appreciate what he had accomplished was also the person who could ruin him if she found out what he had done.

34

THE LID OF THE MAILBOX FELL OPEN WHEN MATT jerked it. A cool gust of November wind rushed up his sleeve as he raised the envelope and tilted the return address away from the shadow. He gasped. *Oh, Lord.* Starting at one end, he eased up the flap of the long envelope to make sure he didn't tear what was inside.

His shaking hands made it hard to read the letter.

Dear Mr. Bradfurd:

You will receive monthly cash benefits in the amount of nine hundred eighty dollars because of your physical disability, beginning April first of next year. Until that time, you may be eligible to receive monthly financial assistance from the Supplemental Security Income program. In addition, you may be eligible for Medicaid. Please call for information about the application process. Twenty-four months after your Social Security disability benefits begin, you will be eligible for Medicare.

Social Security Administration

He was panting by the time he reached the kitchen where Lillie was feeding the girls lunch. "Three weeks, Lillie. Look at the date on the letter." His voice rose. "All those months I waited—the trips I made—and it took the lawyer just three weeks."

Two days later, Matt pulled into the Social Security parking lot in Clement, grateful his appointment about applying for SSI was with a woman. He hoped he wouldn't see Mr. Moore, but if he did, he'd force himself to be polite. He wouldn't ask what had changed about his disability application after a lawyer got involved. He wouldn't say he felt sorry for Mr. Moore for being a person who ignored people in need. And he wouldn't tell him he was grateful not to have a job that required him to distrust people.

When the woman called Matt into her office, she shook his hand, and then placed hers under his elbow directing him to the small chair in front of her desk. Matt pulled the chair as close as possible, hoping the nearer he sat the better they would understand each other. She had a gentle look that made him hopeful. As she read his application aloud, his eyes searched her face and watched her every move. He told himself to breathe.

"You and your wife have a combined income of five hundred dollars a month." She paused and looked directly at Matt. "That's all?"

Sorry now that he was sitting so close, Matt feared she had read his mind. "There's something I wasn't sure about." He stared at his clasped hands. "My daughter. She's seventeen. She works at the drugstore three days a week after school and on Saturday or Sunday all day. She buys her own clothes and things for school." He met the woman's eyes. "But." He hesitated. "She does bring home a bag of groceries every week."

The woman waved her hand. "Forget that." She turned back to the application. "Your assets include a forty-thousand-dollar house, a six-year-old car, furniture, and two burial policies. Anything else? Stocks or bonds? Have an IRA or pension? Income from any other source?"

Matt was determined to answer her questions with as much care as a boy talking to his kindergarten teacher for the first time. "No, ma'am. Nothing, unless you want to know about our clothes."

She smiled warmly. "I see no reason why you wouldn't qualify. You'll also get Medicaid—just you, not your wife—though that'll take longer to process. I do have to come by your house tomorrow and make sure everything checks out." She reached over and placed her soft hand on Matt's. "Try not to worry. I don't foresee a problem. It's likely you'll have a check by December first."

December first was a Saturday. At eleven-fifteen sharp, Matt got in the driver's seat of the Impala and backed onto the brown grass to turn and face the mailbox. The mail should be delivered by eleven-thirty, and the bank would be open until one. Beside him lay a grocery list and a deposit slip for an empty bank account. He and Lillie had a plan: he would beep the horn twice if the check came, then leave for the bank, the grocery store, and the drugstore. She would call for a delivery of heating oil. Propping his watch on the dashboard in front of him, Matt's eyes darted from it to the road.

The mail carrier brought four pieces of junk mail and the light bill.

On Monday, December third, Matt followed the same plan. When he saw, "Pay to the order of Matthew Bradfurd, nine hundred eighty-seven dollars," he yelled, "Hallelujah," beat the horn with his fist without remembering to count, and swung the car out of the driveway.

Matt asked the pleasant young bank teller to deposit two hundred dollars and give him the rest in cash. She swiveled from her computer and nodded, handing him an envelope that meant medicine for his blood pressure and diabetes, food for his family, gas for his car, a warm house, and—proving he had a future—a deposit receipt.

THE SCENT OF BACON FRYING LED MATT TO THE KITCHEN. Lillie hummed as she stirred the bubbling grits and tended the spattering meat. Seeing her so close to the stove reminded him of the day she had been burned. "Stay back from that hot grease."

Lillie pulled aside her apron and the neck of her shirt and grinned. "Look at that! Completely healed. No tenderness at all."

Matt nodded and sat down at the table, keeping most of his thoughts to himself. *Yeah, but you've got a thick scar half the size of my palm.* "I'm going back to church this morning. What do you think of that?"

Lillie kissed him on the forehead. "Wonderful. Going to sing in the choir?"

He shook his head. "Wouldn't be able to stand. Not sure I'll even make it through the whole service. Will you go?"

"Not this time. I'll pray here."

Matt reached for her hand, stopping her movement about the kitchen and pulled her toward him. "It's your clothes, isn't it?" He pulled her closer. "Don't worry about that. When people look at you, they just see your beautiful face."

She put her arms around him. "You sure know the right thing to say."

Matt searched the bottom of the bedroom closet for the plastic bag holding his shoe polish. As he straightened, he noticed the rifle on the top shelf. That was the main reason he was going to church—the one he wouldn't tell Lillie. He was certain God had a hand in keeping him safe, and he needed to stand in His house and thank Him.

On the way to the car, Matt stopped at the pine tree to catch his breath. Rain from the night before had left drops of water hanging from the ends of the needles. Glistening in the morning sun, they could have been strands of pearls draped around the tree. Matt wished Lillie wouldn't worry about what she wore. *Nobody can match this, anyway.*

After Matt returned from church and they had eaten, he watched as Lillie placed half a chicken breast, mashed potatoes, and a roll on a plate. Pushing down the middle of the potatoes with a spoon, she poured in the last of the gravy. "Hurry on, Lillie. I want to get home from Red's before dark." But she wouldn't be rushed. She covered the plate with aluminum foil, carefully pressing its edges against the bottom. The precision and care she took in preparing the plate for his friend reminded Matt of the way she bathed a new baby.

They walked together to the car with Lillie carrying the plate. "Tell Red we'll send food regularly now. And don't forget to ask him to come Christmas Eve or Christmas day—or both."

Matt nodded. "Look." He pointed to the tiny buds perched on the tip of each naked limb of the fig tree. "It's getting ready for Christmas. Just needs lights and tinsel."

THE WOODS BESIDE THE ROAD TO RED'S TRAILER reminded Matt of hikes he had taken with Grandad when he was a child. They had walked for hours on thick fragrant cushions of leaves and pinestraw as his grandfather called out the names of the trees they passed. Occasionally, he stopped. "Shh. Listen to the whispering. The pines are welcoming us." Each time they left the woods, he said, "Trees give to the earth and reach for the sky at the same time, boy. Learn from that."

"Thank God," Matt said aloud. He was grateful that he could see the trees again. What he hadn't realized before his surgery was that a dark mind was worse than physical pain.

He turned off the engine and sat for a moment, expecting to see Red standing at the door or to hear the mandolin. *Glory be. He's gone somewhere.*

Matt knocked on the hollow metal door and called, "Boy, you there?" When he received no answer, he turned the knob and pushed. The door bumped against Red.

"Sorry. I didn't mean... You sick?"

Matt hadn't visited since his foot surgery three months before and he hardly recognized Red. He stepped aside to get a better look: Red's long hair was matted, the sallow skin on his face covered with a beard, and dirty clothes hung on his thin body. Matt leaned forward but resisted the urge to put his arm around his friend, afraid he might push him over. Instead, he pointed to the car. "There's food in..." He raised his voice and could hear the anger. "What's wrong with you?"

As if a light breeze had lifted him, Red drifted backward and settled into his straight wooden chair. "Not doing too good."

In the past, when Matt had asked Red how he was, he received an "All right," or a "Fine," as an answer. Astonished, he asked, "What did you say?"

"The dreams—they're bad."

Rising fear and trepidation were replacing Matt's initial shock at his friend's appearance. With a high-pitched voice, he asked, "What dreams?"

Meeting Matt's eyes, Red pointed down the driveway. "The ones from there—watching me."

Matt mumbled, "I better sit down." As he grasped the arm of the couch, he thought of Lillie's plate. He knew it would spoil if he left it in the car too long but was afraid of interrupting whatever was taking place. "I don't know what you mean. Tell me." Matt extended his hand. "And if you need something..."

Red began to talk as he turned toward the open door. He put words together in ways that didn't make sense. He clasped his thin arms and cried and that made Matt want to cry. Periods of silence stretched out.

When the small electric heater groaned louder and louder in its attempt to cancel out the cold, Matt leaned over and closed the door. His throat felt tight and his chest heavy. His head was shut down—closed to any connections he could make of what Red was saying. *Too many logs in the river at one time. Too big to make sense of.* Reaching for something he could understand, Matt asked, "Are you playing your music?"

Red nodded. "Only thing that stops the counting."

Counting? Matt was afraid to ask what he meant. He felt overwhelmed—numb in mind and body—and had to leave. He struggled to stand. "I'm going home. Be back in the morning—early."

When out of sight of Red's trailer, Matt stopped and shook the plate, dumping chicken, potatoes, and roll in a ditch. Not wanting Lillie to know he had let the chicken spoil, he gathered a handful of soft brown leaves and wiped it as clean as he could.

Before getting back in the car, he looked around. Stripes of deep orange, gold, and pink swung across a sky filled with enormous purple lilacs. Matt sighed and shook his head. If only he could disappear into that instead of returning to Red's the next morning. As loudly as he could, he called out. "You've got to hear me. I can't do this by myself. Sometimes, living is just too hard, Grandad."

As Matt drove home, he understood more of what he had heard. Red had been a sniper in Vietnam for two years. He dreamed of eyes—eyes that rose from each person he had killed. They followed him, sometimes watching from a distance and sometimes stopping right in front of his own. There could be one pair or a hundred, moving and blinking, belonging to men and women—he prayed not to children.

"At first, I thought they wanted me to count 'em, but when I tried, they left me. Thought that meant counting wasn't what they wanted, so I tried to figure out what it could be. I been trying to remember each one I killed in order. Well, it was really murder 'cause when you shoot somebody with a M-21 and scope at seven hundred fifty years it's not self-defense."

Morning arrived too early for Matt. As he turned into Red's driveway, a feeling of dread filled him. When he stopped the car, he rolled down the window, hoping to hear the mandolin but could only hear the sound of a mockingbird.

He opened the trailer door without knocking. Red was in the straight chair where he had left him the evening before. "Man you still sitting there?" Matt's voice rose. He felt an urgency to do something: pick him up, hold him in his arms, feed him, anything. "Did you go to bed? Eat breakfast? What about your supper?"

Red lifted his head, revealing tired dull eyes. "I'm all right."

"Let me fix you something to eat."

Red shook his head. "Guess I ought to talk a little more."

Matt was scared—uncertain what talking about the past would do to this frail man, and whether they could handle the result. "Boy, you sure? I don't want you to get hurt here. I could go for your sister, drive you to a doctor—anything you want."

Red almost smiled. His voice was firm. "You'll do."

Matt rubbed his forehead, lowered himself onto the couch and held his arms straight as he could to stop them from trembling.

Red's thoughts seemed more organized than the day before. Although his words made more sense, his voice was still flat, and his face showed no emotion. "I tried to talk about it when I got home, but it didn't work. Bothered people too much. They told me to forget it, but I couldn't. Those things crowded my mind, and I didn't have room for what was going on around me here. When I was with Daddy, words wanted to come, but I was afraid they'd make him ashamed of me. Or break Mama's heart. What could they understand, anyway?"

Suddenly, Red leapt from his chair and shouted. "You know what my sister did?" He spun around to face Matt.

Matt pressed his back against the sofa—alarmed at the anger on his friend's face.

Red's voice was a growl. "One day, I was in the kitchen by myself. She came in and slammed her pocketbook down on the table. Then she grabbed me by the shoulders, shook me as hard as she could, and said, 'Get on with life, you selfish baby. You're worrying Mama and Daddy to death. Stop feeling sorry for yourself. You came back alive. A lot of people didn't.' Then she stepped back, got that nasty look on her face, and pointed at me. 'You need to get *married!*'"

Tears filled Red's eyes, spilled over, and followed the creases down his face. "Shit!" He slumped down in the wooden chair, resting his head in his hands. "I've been with a woman three times in my life. All in Vietnam. And paid every one of them."

During the next hours, through Red's sobs, Matt heard about dead friends—how they were killed, what they said before they died, and whether they were surprised or afraid. He heard about letters Red wrote to parents for boys who didn't know how to write, about letters he wrote only in his head to his own parents, and about stories he hadn't told.

Searching for air, Matt tried taking deep breaths, but his chest felt frozen. He had to get out of there. Pushing up from the couch, he said, "I'll be back tomorrow."

Red nodded.

As Matt lowered himself from the step, his leg gave way, causing him to land on his left side in the rough dirt. Too worn out to get up, he rolled onto his back and looked up into a bare dogwood tree. Flitting about its branches was a bright red cardinal—a male. A female sat, quietly, on a high limb. When the male darted around his partner, as if teasing her, Matt could have sworn he saw her smile. Red's sister had been right. Red needed a Lillie. *And maybe, a Grandad.*

Turning back to the harshness of the dirt and gravel, Matt rolled over and crawled to the car on his hands and knees, and then pulled himself up with the door handle. He thought of the message in his dream: *you have more to do.* At that moment, unable to imagine what it could be, he was certain of only one thing: he was the luckiest man in the world.

35

GEORGE RUSSELL LEANED OVER THE FILE IN FRONT OF him, pretending to read. The client sitting in the wing chair across from his desk had just asked the same question twice. "I'm thinking," George answered. *But not about that. I can't remember your name.* He could have found it by flipping back a few pages but didn't want to. He wanted the sharp, quick recall he used to have.

The scent of the man's Polo aftershave was the other thing irritating George. He tapped the pen hard on his desk. One day the client had asked what kind he used and then started wearing the same. In the past, George would have been flattered by the imitation, but, now, he wanted to say, *Get your own life and leave mine alone.*

After the client left, George was finishing his notes when the phone rang. His wife's voice made him want to sling the phone across the room. *What now?* He sighed loudly and rolled his eyes. Rosalyn had been on a waiting list to see a pulmonologist about her cough. She said the doctor's office had just called to offer her the three o'clock cancellation that afternoon.

Several weeks before, Rosalyn had developed a fear of going out alone everywhere except to her psychiatrist's office and had insisted George accompany her. After taking her to the grocery store, and then canceling a Saturday golf game to take her to the hairdresser, he had said, "No more," and told her to hire a driver.

A week later, George received a call from the psychiatrist. Rosalyn had asked him to talk to George about her agoraphobia. Since she felt unsafe with anyone but George, and her recovery depended on her continuing to go out, he strongly advised George to go with her. At that point, George's resistance had collapsed, and he was at her beck and call.

For the past two Wednesdays, he had taken her to doctors' appointments. When he complained that Wednesdays weren't convenient, one of her infrequent smiles had appeared. "But Mrs. Barbee told me you take that afternoon off. Aren't you free?"

George's attention strayed to a brown spot on his hand. Laying the phone down on the desk beside his wife's picture, he licked the spot and rubbed it hard on his pants. It didn't come off. *No! One of those liver spots you see on old people.*

Hearing Rosalyn shouting his name, George picked up the phone, groaned, "Again," and protested that he, too, had an appointment that afternoon.

Heat rose to his face as a low chuckle came from his wife. "Un-huh. No doubt you do. See you two-thirty at the latest."

Now, what? He was supposed to meet Emily at the restaurant in Clement at noon. This would be his third consecutive cancellation.

Swiveling his chair to the window behind him, George was greeted with a rare surprise. Snowflakes filled the entire space. He felt a lump in his throat. *It's December. I should be in New York.* As he watched them fall, a particularly well-formed one began a slow ascent. He followed it with his gaze, until it was slapped sideways by an air current. Grasping the arms of his chair and shouting, "Leave it alone," George realized he was as out of control as the snowflake. Since Rosalyn had returned to her psychiatrist, she was an unpredictable wind, and he was caught in her draft.

Pushing hard against the wooden floor with his foot, George caused the chair to swing around so fast that he bumped his ankle against a corner of his desk. The pain reminded him to call Emily. Their relationship had lasted nearly three years, on and off, and he missed her after a few weeks. She was fun—playful and upbeat—like Rosalyn used to be. And she had been his only sex partner for many months.

But he dreaded calling Emily. She had begun to have expectations of him and to make demands. That aspect of her personality also reminded him of Rosalyn. When she didn't get what she wanted, her sweet, girlish manner became rough-edged. He wondered if that was part of the natural evolution of relationships or whether he just didn't understand women.

George looked at his watch—ten o'clock. After his next client left, he called. "Emily, can you talk? You alone?"

"Hi Georgie. Can't wait to see you."

Another thing George didn't like to think about was her discretion—or lack of it. Was it likely no one was *ever* in the reception room where she worked when he called?

After he told her that he couldn't see her that afternoon, George flinched when she moaned, "That's not fair." Both remained silent a few minutes. "My finances are in a mess. I need a loan."

He clenched his teeth. That was another problem. Every month or so, he had begun subsidizing Emily with loans that she didn't pay back. "How could that be? What did you do with the money from the last one?"

Her voice was firm, less pleading. "It costs a lot to live, George."

He sighed. "I've told you I'll help you set up a budget. You have to come to grips with your spending."

Her voice remained strong. "I'd be okay if I earned as much as when I worked for you. You were going to find me a job with better pay, but you haven't."

George gently laid the phone back on its cradle and turned toward the window. The delicate snowflakes had disappeared, leaving nothing but a flat gray sky. A question that occasionally flitted through his mind returned. *Would she blackmail me?*

He had forgotten all he wanted to say about his last client, but George finished his notes, anyway, and shoved the file to the left side of his desk. When he did, a note that must have been under the file was pushed to the floor. He picked it up and saw in Mrs. Barbee's handwriting, the name, Professor Hartman. "Oh, no." *What?* Clenching his fists in anger, George had an urge to lay his arm across his desk and rake all its contents to the floor. *Why can't people leave me alone?*

George crossed his office and dropped down on the long black leather sofa. The couch reminded him of good times with Emily, making him smile, and then chuckle. *Great in bed but not worth a damn as a receptionist.* He stretched his back and groaned. *She never followed up on the information I needed for Bradfurd. Caused me to lose a doctor I'd had for eighteen years.* Thinking of Dr. Latham reminded him of something else—another sore had appeared on his groin.

George's anger returned as he eased off the couch. *Latham. If he wanted something done, why didn't he do it himself?* "I work hard and don't ask for help," he said aloud. "For generations, my family has given, given, given, and I'm sick of it. Brother's keeper—forget it!"

Alarmed at his outburst, George returned to his desk chair and told himself to calm down. He swiveled around to face the window. Patches of blue had pushed aside some of the gray, allowing an outline of his hills to emerge. He talked to them. *Okay, here are the problems. Need solutions.* "Have to find a doctor." His head bobbed as he thought. Simple: the boys at the Club could recommend one. And issues needed to be resolved with three people: Roz, Emily, and Professor Hartman.

During the past few months, Rosalyn had refused to go to the Club or to entertain at home. Three weeks before, she had stopped going to church. For thirty-seven years he had been a good husband and expected her to be a good wife. This afternoon he would confront her unacceptable behavior and demand that she return to normal. George slapped the arm of his chair. *Excellent!*

Dealing with Emily wouldn't be easy because George felt something like love for her, though aspects of her behavior required change: no more loans and no more pressure to meet regularly. When he could arrange it, he would. If something came up that prevented it, she would have to accept it without complaining.

Then there was Professor Hartman. His messages had said he had a story to tell George about his family in the post-slavery period. George shook his head. He wasn't interested in a story, didn't need a cousin, and, most of all, didn't want to encourage a relationship with a dull history professor by meeting with him socially. He slapped his knee. *That's it!* He would invite the man to give a talk at a Rotary dinner meeting. He would sit with him, allow him to ask questions, and tell as many stories as he wanted. That would get him off his back once and for all.

The sky in front of George had cleared except for a strip of smoky blue haze across the base of the mountains, making them appear suspended in air. George took that as a message that he should clear his mind of others and sit above the cares of the world. After all the years of work for family and community, it was what he deserved.

IN SPITE OF HAVING TO CANCEL THE AFTERNOON WITH Emily, George was relieved to know life would be returning to normal. He sat up straight and gave a sharp salute while passing through the iron-scrolled gates of Clear Creek. Surprised that there was no response, he slammed on his brakes and backed up. "Where's Henry?"

"Quit," answered the stranger in the guard uniform.

"But he's been here since this place was built."

The new guard shrugged.

George almost felt like crying. *Why can't things stay the same?* By the time he pulled into the garage, he was furious with Rosalyn for spoiling his perfect life.

As he passed through the cluttered great room, George noticed two *Wine Enthusiasts* on the table beside his chair. He was surprised to see them there, since ordinarily he finished the magazine the day it was delivered. He picked them up to see if he had read them and found that he had not.

When George entered his bedroom a woman was standing on the other side of the bed with her back to him. Thinking she was a cleaning lady, he began introducing himself. His wife whirled around. "Roz? No. Roz, what happened to your hair?"

Rosalyn smirked as she patted the gray-blond hair that had been cut nearly as short as his. "Haven't you noticed? I'm letting it go gray. My hair-dresser came this morning and cut it. Easier that way."

Confused, George muttered, "But I loved..." He stared at her. The woman in front of him was a stranger.

Backing up, he slumped down on the green pais-ley loveseat in front of the window. "I can't believe this—your hair, the way you're dressed. Where's your makeup?"

She pulled a heavy brown sweater over her head. "Don't you understand, George? I don't need to look good anymore. Let's go. We'll be late for my appointment."

"Please, Rosalyn." His voice cracked. "I've worked hard. I want to enjoy this again." He swung his arms around and gestured, vaguely, toward the living room.

"Let's have some people over. I'll call the caterer. We could take a trip." He cried out. "Just anything!"

Picking up her purse and slinging it over her shoulder, his wife grunted. "No, thanks."

His face red with anger, George jumped up from the loveseat. "I'm tired of this," he shouted. "It's unacceptable."

Rosalyn had reached the door. Eyebrows lifted in surprise, she spun around to face him. "*You're* tired of it? Would it put things in perspective if I hired a private detective to follow you?" Stepping closer, she tapped his chest with her right index finger. "And don't get any ideas about leaving me, George. The whole world will learn about your little receptionist." She laughed. "Oh, that precious family name. Wouldn't you hate to see it dragged through the mud?"

THE NEXT MORNING, WHEN MRS. BARBEE CALLED TO say a client was waiting, George asked her to stall, saying he needed more time to finish the client's financial plan. Sitting before his office window, he stared at the mountains. His mind was blank. The harder he struggled for solutions to his problems with Rosalyn, the more exhausted he felt.

The ringing of his cell phone made him jump. Emily's voice was strong and clear. "I've thought of a way to fix your problem. I'm twenty-eight, and can't wait much longer to have a baby. Let's get married!"

36

MATT AND LILLIE HADN'T GIVEN THE PHONE CALL FROM the Social Security office much thought, except to express surprise that the woman was working on Christmas Eve. She had wanted to know whether they still owned the life insurance policies listed on their application for SSI, and whether they could be cashed in. Matt told her they did—they had bought them eight years before—but they were burial policies, not life insurance. And yes, he said, twenty thousand dollars was a large amount, but the insurance man had said funerals cost a lot these days. The cash value of each was a hundred eighty dollars. The woman had been friendly and seemed satisfied with his answers.

January sixth was one of the coldest days Matt could remember. From his bed where he lay watching for the mail truck, he saw patches of ice in irregular shapes on the brown grass. The SSI check that was supposed to arrive on the third had not, and a worry that wanted to grow, picked at his mind for fodder. He pushed it back by concentrating on the aroma of chicken and dumplings simmering on the stove and the rattle of the furnace as it blew warm air into the living room.

"This can't be real!" Matt shouted as he came in from the mailbox. Then with a soft, strained voice, he asked, "What kind of world is this?" and thrust a letter toward his wife. Lillie had been humming and wiping flour from the counter where she had rolled out the dumplings. She stopped to rinse her hands before taking the single piece of paper. The glow on her face faded. Flipping the letter from one side to the other, Lillie muttered, "Maybe there's something else." She stared at her husband's blank face, and then read softly, pausing twice to swallow.

Dear Mr. Bradfurd:

You are not eligible to receive SSI. The Supplemental Security Insurance program is intended for those with assets fewer than fifteen hundred dollars. You have two life insurance policies, each valued above that amount.

You are not eligible for Medicaid for the same reason. If your medical expenses reach forty-five hundred dollars in a calendar year, you will qualify.

You received a check from us that was cashed illegally. Unless we hear from you, and the money is returned immediately, you will be charged and prosecuted.

Social Security Administration

The letter slipped from Lillie's fingers onto the floor. She leaned back against the sink and shook her head. "We can't call. Today's Saturday. You think they'll send the sheriff tomorrow?"

Matt had no idea what they could or would do. Their world was too far from his to attempt a guess. But he answered, "No, they won't." Wrapping his arms around his wife, he held her tightly. When her tears soaked through his shirt, all he could think of was how warm they felt on his chest.

Jerking away, Lillie slumped down in a kitchen chair and covered her eyes with both hands. "We move up one step, and they kick us down three."

BETH LAY ON HER SIDE IN BED WITH ONE ELBOW PROPPED on two pillows and her head resting in her hand. She'd tucked two quilts around herself and was trying to hold *The Scarlet Letter* without exposing her hand and arm to the cool air. Her English teacher from last semester had given her an opportunity to submit another review of the book, allowing her to have whichever grade was better.

She had planned to write the paper over Christmas vacation but had found happiness as distracting as sadness. She and her parents had told stories and watched TV together. Her mother had taught her to make a caramel cake, and her father's friend Red had eaten Christmas dinner with them. The time had passed quickly.

Tomorrow she had to work at the drugstore, so this was her last opportunity to finish the paper before school on Monday. She glanced at the yellow pad on her desk and hoped something might just come to her if she started writing.

When she heard the back door slam and her father yell, Beth bolted upright, pushed the book aside, and untangled herself from the quilts. She opened her door and crawled back in bed to listen. After her mother read the letter, they each made a few comments, and there was a period of quiet before her father yelled, "We have to take care of ourselves!"

Then he told the story about Grandad's family raising everything they needed—milk from their cow, meat and lard from their hog, and vegetables from their garden. Sounding disgusted, he ended with, "What a pitiful creature I am to wait for the government to send me a dollar bill to live."

The words dollar bill reminded Beth of what her mother had done Christmas morning. "Here's a present for all of us," she had said as she kissed them on the cheek and dropped a dollar into the empty can they had used to save money for the anniversary trip. Beth jumped out of bed and opened the top drawer of her dresser. Reaching behind the pile of underwear, she pulled out a road map of the United States and Canada.

When she spread the map on the bed, it came apart at the middle crease. Pushing the two sides together, she leaned closer and placed her finger on the red line. Beginning at Cross Hill, she traced it northwest to Mount Rushmore, south to Grand Canyon, and back home again. She, her mother, and father had drawn that line many years before, when they had started saving for the trip.

Since that time, she had drawn another line with a yellow marker that her parents hadn't seen. It began at Mount Rushmore and ended at Fairbanks, Alaska. Beth had done it without telling them how much she longed to see the sun at midnight. Fearing they would give up their own desires for hers, she didn't want that. The grin on her face disappeared when she stood up to listen. Her parents had stopped talking.

Beth picked up the worn burgundy sweat pants and shirt from the floor, pulled them on, and shoved her feet in her sneakers. "Back in a few minutes," she called out before closing the front door behind her.

The front walk below the bottom step was covered with ice. Trying to avoid it, Beth landed in the slush of the yard. By the time she reached the road, each step made a squishing sound. She wanted to take the wet sneakers off but looked around and decided against it. If neighbors drove past and saw her without shoes or coat, they would stop and ask what was wrong. That would be difficult to answer.

Something had frightened her, though Beth didn't know what. It was the first time she had been scared in her home. Even when her father got angry at her, it never bothered her much. He would fuss and that would be the end of it. She sniffed. Hearing him express anger toward himself was harder, especially not knowing what he would do about it.

By the time she reached the Johnsons', Beth's arms shivered too much to knock, so she leaned against the front door and stammered, "Hey, there."

When Miss Caroline opened the door, she took Beth in both her arms and pulled her toward the black iron stove in the corner of the living room.

In her haste to reach them, Mrs. Johnson knocked over her iron. While picking it up, she exclaimed, "Dear Lord," and then, "Caroline, get a blanket."

Before Beth could protest, Mrs. Johnson had wrenched the soggy shoes off her feet, set them on a rack above the stove, and wrapped her feet in a blanket. Seconds later, Miss Caroline appeared with a quilt and draped it around her from her neck down.

Beth apologized for alarming the ladies. "I didn't realize how wet and cold it was when I ran out of the house."

Miss Caroline opened the glass door of the stove and shoved in two pieces of wood. Then she brought another chair from the kitchen. Mrs. Johnson sat down as close as she could and took Beth's cold hands in hers.

Beth was sorry for causing the women to stop their work and embarrassed for drawing so much attention to herself. She started talking as a distraction. In two days, she said, the last semester of her senior year would begin. Imagining herself as a high school graduate made her feel grown up. The women murmured praise and congratulations. She said the drugstore had offered her a full-time job with an increase in salary to seven-fifty an hour. That would give her a chance to get her mother and father out of their financial mess. After the first year, she'd get paid vacation, sick time, and could buy health insurance through the company.

"But you wanted to go to college," Mrs. Johnson said.

Beth's throat tightened and her smile disappeared. When Miss Caroline handed her a piece of apple pie, she touched the juice oozing from it and licked her finger. "Mmm."

Mrs. Johnson pointed out what Beth had tried to put out of her mind. During the last few months, when she had realized going to college was impossible, she had tried to convince herself that she'd be happier working at the drugstore because she was comfortable there. College wasn't for people in her world, anyway. Yes, her friend Heather was going, but her father was an insurance salesman, and her mother worked in a jewelry store. And it was possible—though she had never noticed it—that Heather was smarter than she was.

While eating the pie, Beth stared at the flames behind the stove's glass. She listened to the soft cracks of the burning wood and breathed in its comforting scent. Her attention shifted away from feelings of failure.

"That was good," she said to Miss Caroline, as she put down her fork. Then she turned to Mrs. Johnson. "I'm sorry I didn't pay attention. I guess I was hungry."

"But darling, what about your college plans?" Mrs. Johnson asked.

The tears flowing down her cheeks caused Beth to lift her eyebrows, and her voice cracked as she struggled to answer. "We don't have the money. My grades aren't good enough for a scholarship. SAT scores, either." She wiped her face with the sleeve of her sweatshirt. "I'm just not smart enough."

Miss Caroline leapt from her chair, grabbed an iron poker, and stabbed at the burning wood, causing smoke to spill into the room. "Yes, you are!"

Beth was startled. The voice that was normally an echo of Mrs. Johnson's held something unfamiliar.

"You worked all the time. When did you *ever* have a chance to study?" Miss Caroline continued as she snatched the empty plates from her mother and Beth. On her way to the kitchen she opened the front door to let smoke out of the room.

Mrs. Johnson wrinkled her brow and leaned so close to Beth that her gray-blond curls brushed her cheek. "Have you tried *everything?*"

Nodding and lowering her head, Beth felt like crying again but was determined not to let them feel sorry for her. If anyone deserved their pity it was her father and mother; they were the ones suffering. She threw back the quilt and tried to sound cheerful. "After I work a year and save some money, I'll take evening classes at the community college. One of these days, I'll be a kindergarten teacher."

For some reason, Beth felt better. "Another thing. I'm going to sell Avon. Or something like that. I'll get you anything wholesale." Then she wondered, had she ever seen the two of them in makeup? "You might not use much. But, hand cream. I'll get that for you."

Then Beth thought of something that allowed her to smile without forcing it. *I'll save that money and take Mama and Daddy on their trip.*

Beth pushed her feet into the tight sneakers. The ladies expressed regret that they had no car to drive her home but offered to call her father. Beth shook her head, no. She would run.

When she reached the edge of the Johnsons' yard, Beth felt dizzy, staggering a few feet before sitting down on the grass. Although the ground was still wet, the sun had come out and warmed the air. She lowered her head a few seconds, and then looked up at the house. It was a good place, made comfortable and warm by the happy women living there. If her life turned out like theirs, she would be lucky. They seemed to have everything they wanted.

But then she wondered: had they ever wanted to be teachers or to see the sun at midnight?

MONDAY MORNING, MATT STUDIED THE KITCHEN thermostat. *Fifty-four degrees. Chilly.* On the way to his chair, he picked up a folded yellow blanket that Lillie used for the girls' naps. Shivering, he sat down and wrapped it around him. *Brr. Lillie's plan.*

The day after the letter came from Social Security, Lillie had slipped into what Matt referred to as her whirling dervish mode. While dragging furniture to vacuum under it and picking up every toy in the playroom to dust, she talked about a plan. Each time she switched off the vacuum, she continued talking as loudly as if the machine was still on. "Think of something to say to the sheriff. How many helpings will two pounds of pintos give us?" Nothing Matt could say would convince her to stop. If he had been watching the scene on TV, he would have laughed, but seeing his wife in it made him sad.

Finally, she collapsed on the sofa. "I know how to make the flour and Crisco last until April. And the heating oil—we'll turn the furnace off when the girls leave and back on when they come in the morning."

Matt tried to convince her that the heating oil would last until spring even if they used the normal amount, but her response was, "What if they change their minds about disability, too? We may never get anything."

Matt noticed the overhead light in the bedroom flick on and off and listened to Lillie's movements as she dressed. When she tiptoed toward his chair, he pretended to be asleep to avoid an argument. She had insisted he call Social Security exactly at eight o'clock, but he wasn't willing to disturb Nell before nine. And she would want him to eat breakfast, though he wouldn't do that either. If the sheriff took him to jail, he could darn well feed him, too.

By the time the girls arrived at seven-thirty, the house was warm and Lillie was busy, so Matt opened his eyes. Lillie—wearing lipstick, but not her usual apron—told the girls they might be having company, so it was important to put books and toys away when they finished with them. Turning to Matt, she said, "If you-know-who comes, I'll take them to the kitchen and close the door."

At eight-thirty, a car pulled in the driveway. Matt was glad Beth was at school and wouldn't see him in handcuffs. His voice was urgent. "Lillie, there's a car."

Lillie and the girls were on the floor playing with a dollhouse. Looking frightened, she scooted over to a chair and pulled herself up. "Come, girls, we're—" she called. Then she said, "No," and went to the window and lifted a blind. A broad smile covered her face. As she swung the door open, her voice was playful. "Well, Lord have mercy. Look who's here."

The minister held a paper bag in one arm and hugged Lillie with the other. "My wife sent some ham biscuits from breakfast." Handing the bag to Lillie, he said, "She made me promise not to crush them."

Matt was so astonished that he didn't move. Instead, he laughed nervously, and said, "We won't tell if you did," while wondering what was coming next. Had the police gotten the minister involved in this? Would he have the embarrassment of explaining to this man why he had taken what amounted to welfare? When Matt realized he was still sitting, he pushed up from his chair and insisted the minister take it.

He and Lillie sat beside each other on the couch. Lillie was grinning and patting his knee, almost slapping it at times, while the minister talked about Red. Matt's face was feeling warm, and he wondered whether he was blushing. He felt like he had when he was a teenager and someone complimented him. He was glad Lillie was present because he wasn't sure he was understanding. She seemed clear. She kept making comments like, "Isn't that wonderful? Sure am proud of my husband."

After Christmas, Red had gone back to work painting houses and had put word out that he was available to play with a group. His sister believed his change was a result of what Matt had done. All the months and years he had visited, keeping him in the world, had finally paid off. Certain that Matt had saved her brother's life, she wanted the congregation to acknowledge it.

In response to her enthusiasm, the Church Board had appointed Matt chair of the Home Visitation Committee. They wanted him to recruit three other members and closely supervise them to make sure the sick and shut-in received all the help they needed. And they voted to provide him with a phone and to pay car and gas expenses for each visit.

When the preacher asked if he would take the job, Matt looked at Lillie. Pride had returned to her face, making him want to tip his hat and swagger with the confidence of John Wayne. He wished he could freeze her look and suspend them both forever in that moment. But he was near tears, unable to speak.

There was a puzzled look on her face, when she said, "You know you will." She turned to the minister. "Of course, he will."

Matt had never refused a minister's request but shook his head. "I'm sorry." His voice cracked. "I can't."

The foot surgeon had warned Matt that his left foot would likely become infected and need the same surgery. It had been throbbing for some time, but he was delaying the operation as long as possible, to avoid piling on another medical bill. He had vowed to keep it a secret from Lillie until the last minute.

The preacher leaned forward. "Do you understand?" He raised his voice. "This is a *gift* you have.

God means for you to share it with others. And it would be good for you."

Wishing he could explain the situation privately, Matt knew there was no point in asking Lillie to leave the room. She could hear him wherever she was in the house. He laid his hand on her arm and focused on the picture above her head to avoid her eyes. "My other foot's infected. We'll have to go through another surgery."

The girls were standing in front of Lillie dressing a doll on her lap. She reached over and hugged them.

The minister sat back. "Taking this job doesn't mean the rest of your life must stop." Matt noticed a change in the man's tone. He sounded like he had stepped behind his pulpit. "God will provide what you need to accomplish His mission. When you're unable to drive, you'll work by phone. The congregation will help this time."

Matt turned toward Lillie. She stared at him with glistening eyes. The pride in her face showed something else, too. Did she love him even when he was weak? She never demanded that he handle all things well. She reached for his hand.

"All right," he nodded. "Can't say no to that."

When the minister left, Matt ate a ham biscuit on his way across the soggy yard to Nell's.

He dialed the first three digits of the number for Social Security and then hung up. What good would it do to talk to them? He couldn't return the money;

it had been spent. And he didn't think the situation was his fault. Since they had made the mistake, why shouldn't they be the ones prosecuted?

Since the moment the letter arrived, Matt had wanted to call the lawyer. He had hesitated because he owed him money, not sure it was fair to ask for more until he paid his bill. He opened the phone book and closed it. Then he opened it and looked for Grimes. Fair or not, someone who understood the situation better than he should deal with it.

"Good god! Don't those people have anything better to do?" The lawyer spoke so loudly that Matt held the phone away and grinned. *Thank you for this man.* "Okay. Here's what'll happen. I'll call and raise hell. If they won't change their minds about SSI, you'll have to pay back what they sent when your disability checks start. I'll get them to spread it over eight to ten months. They'll make you pay a penalty the same way. Disability payments *will begin as scheduled,* April first. And don't worry about the damn sheriff coming. You will *not* be arrested."

Matt had been holding his breath. "You don't know what you've done for me."

"Forget it." Mr. Grimes continued. "Another thing. I'm working on something with your old boss. Pretty sure it'll turn out."

"A job?"

"No, some kind of money settlement. May take a while. Hang in there."

37

ED LATHAM WAITED ON THE SIDEWALK FOR LIGHTS TO come on inside the Red Pig Café. Several men drifted up. He nodded, saying, "Hey," or "'Morning," to each whether he knew him or not. The aroma of bacon frying was replacing the subtle one of forsythias blooming at the end of the block. Ed was getting hungry.

Hearing, "Good morning, my friend! Beautiful day, isn't it?" just as the waitress flung the door open, Ed grinned. Punctuality was one of the many things he liked about Silas Hartman.

Pointing to his short sleeves, Ed chuckled. "You look ready for spring."

The professor didn't miss a beat. "Go ahead, laugh, you wimp. If you had ever lived through a Michigan winter, you'd know what cold is."

Silas—Ed still called him Professor—and he had eaten breakfast together eleven times since Silas had become his patient in the past year. Although Ed enjoyed the man's company as much as that of his two oldest friends, he hadn't yet invited him to go fishing. Something had prevented him from being completely comfortable with him. He had a feeling it was the professor's son.

When Ed's suspicions about Jim Hartman had been confirmed by Robert Grimes, his anger had grown. He hadn't decided whether to let the lawyer pursue him or to do it himself. Somebody should take a stick to him, he thought.

The diner had nine yellowed Formica tables. A refrigerator, a pantry, and a grill spread across the rear wall. A bar with eight round stools attached to the floor faced the grill. A red ceramic pig, about a foot high, watched over Ed's favorite eating establishment from his shelf above the cook. Very little had changed since his father had first taken him there when he was twelve.

The two men headed for the row of booths along the wall to their right. Ed's favorite was the one nearest the front window. As they slid onto the faded blue vinyl, Silas reached for the single-page, plastic-covered menu. "I suppose you'll lecture me if I order ham and red-eye gravy."

"Remember that blood pressure, and," Ed patted the stomach that hung over his own belt. "You don't want one of these."

"Hmm, okay, oatmeal. Again." Silas leaned across the table, his enthusiasm showing no matter what the subject. "Getting old is fun, isn't it? Here I am answering my own rhetorical question, but, you know, *it is*. I'm enjoying life as much as when I was teaching. And *busy*."

When the waitress approached—coffee pot in hand—and the professor presented his wide grin, Ed shook his head. *How is it possible for a man to smile that broadly?* Patting her arm, Ed asked, "How are you, Judy?" She had been his sister's classmate in high school and his patient for eighteen years. When she turned away, her gray ponytail swinging, he noticed she had lost weight and fussed at himself for ordering pancakes.

"Reminds me." Silas's bright blue eyes widened. "My search is ending; I found the connection to Great-grandfather's Samaritans!"

Each time they met, Silas gave Ed an update on his search for the family that had rescued his great-grandfather. So far, Ed knew that the records of Winston Methodist Church had revealed the name of a minister who worked with the Quakers to establish a school for freed slaves. He also knew that Silas had found that minister's descendants and, with their help, had contacted five of them.

Silas retrieved the spiral pad from his shirt pocket and slapped it on the table. "One of those five had his journals. What a treasure! Since the Quaker community subsidized the school, the leader kept meticulous notes about the activities and the money that was spent. I suppose he recorded Joseph Bradfurd's name in only one place to protect his identity." The professor shook his head. "He was probably in danger from white supremacists, you know."

"Bradfurd?" Stunned for a moment, Ed regained his voice. "That's the name? You're sure?"

The professor set down his glass of orange juice and flipped a few pages of his pad. "Noted right here. I've spent the last two weeks in the genealogy library identifying Joseph's Bradfurd's descendants. What made it easy is this." Turning the pad so Ed could see, he pointed to the name. "*This* Bradfurd—he settled here in 1752—changed the spelling of his name from 'ord' to 'urd.' Subsequent generations continued it."

Ed nodded. "So they stick out like a sore thumb."

"Lucky for me. See here." Silas pointed to the last name on the list. "There's one male carrying the name in Cross Hill right now—a Matthew Bradfurd. There probably are other descendants here, but researching them through married names will take more time."

Ed turned his gaze from the professor toward the grill, watching the cook move smoothly and quickly from one end to the other. Happy that the professor had found what he was looking for, he was furious that a Bradfurd had risked his life for a Hartman after what Jim had done to Matt.

And he was sad for the father sitting across from him. He knew the responsibility a parent felt for his child's actions, even into adulthood. And the love. But also the sorrow when that child turned out to be a man he couldn't admire.

Silas folded his pad and put it back in his pocket. "Sorry, Ed. I get carried away. Lose myself in details when I'm excited. It's the history professor in me!"

At that moment, the waitress appeared with her coffee pot. Ed thanked her and asked how her son was doing. He wished she could stay. He needed time to think. "Tell me, what else is new?" he asked, turning back to the professor.

"Something odd. Remember I told you I had a cousin here?—his name's George Russell."

Pushing his plate aside, Ed leaned both arms on the table and muttered, "Good grief."

The professor continued. "I've received an invitation to speak at the Rotary Club dinner in April. The president asked me to talk about anything historical related to this area. Said it was Russell's idea and that we'll be seated at the same table."

"How's Russell kin to you?"

Opening his pad, the professor shook it and winked. "It's all right here. My great-grandfather, Silas Hartman, had two children—a son and a daughter. She married a Russell. George is her great-grandson." He slapped his pad closed. "Of course, he owes *his* life to the Bradfurd family, too."

"*Very, very* interesting."

Ed was angry at George Russell for ignoring his request to help Matt. Anger was a familiar feeling and not one he was proud of. His intolerance of people who didn't measure up to his beliefs and do what he wanted had been the motive for limiting his practice and withdrawing from the community. He had wondered whether that made him narrow-minded but didn't care. He had a strong desire for revenge against George Russell and Jim Hartman.

Ed leaned forward. "Here's a thought—what if you made your family story the topic of your speech?"

Silas nodded. "Not bad, not bad. Local interest. To broaden it, I could discuss the impact little people have on the course of history. Not just on individual families. Who knows whether the school would have survived if its first teacher had been killed? Would others have been willing to come? And." He tapped the table with his wedding band. "Might not the mob that attacked him have gained more power if citizens hadn't stood up to them? Where would that have led?"

Ed wanted to stay with his anger, to encourage his friend, to push him forward by saying, "Go get the bastards, Professor! Tell them they've done wrong." Then he reminded himself this was not 1867, and the current bad guys were this man's son and cousin. While still hoping George Russell and Jim Hartman would be humiliated for not helping a family that had done so much for them, Ed wasn't certain he could put his new friend in a situation that would cause him to do it. It was too close to betrayal.

Hearing the conversation behind him and remembering the interest people took in the business of others, Ed asked, "How about going for a walk?"

As the two men turned the corner toward Main Street, Ed listened to the professor extol the beauty of the late winter morning. His friend's comments about spring being near caused him to look around when they reached the square. Most daffodils had already turned brown, resting their heads on their stems, but a few lingered, cheerful and upright, among the purple hyacinths. The new leaves of the azalea shrubs were such an intense green that spring itself might have been waiting inside them.

The drifting scent of hyacinths soothed Ed's anger. Without determining the direction his words would take, he blurted out, "Just to show you what a small town this, Matt Bradfurd's my patient."

The professor swung around to face Ed, nearly shouting. "Perfect! You can introduce us."

Ed directed the professor to a recently painted green bench standing apart from the others. "Well, we'll see," he said. Then he described the events and circumstances of Matt's life over the past three and a half years, excluding only the part Jim Hartman had played.

"But he's not old." The professor slipped the pad from his pocket and searched until he found the right page. "Why these physical problems?"

"You never know for sure." Ed shrugged. "Probably a combination of things—a body predisposed to these illnesses and not suited for the kind of work he did, and a poorly performed surgical procedure. After surgery, not enough post-op care, poor nutrition, too much emotional stress. And all of it threw his diabetes out of whack."

The professor cocked his head. "I'm puzzled. Why didn't he get the care he needed after surgery?"

Ed averted his eyes. "Well, that's another story, but the simple answer is, no money. He was embarrassed to come to me because he couldn't make the co-payments. And he needed other things—physical therapy, blood tests, medications. Again, he couldn't pay, so his condition worsened."

The professor seemed agitated. "Forgive me for being obtuse, Ed, but something is missing here. Why no money—workers' comp or something?"

Ed was becoming more and more uncomfortable with the conversation. Thinking he had made a mistake by revealing anything, he wished for a moment he had never met either Matt or the professor. He couldn't save the world, even one person at a time, and nobody wanted to hear anything bad about their children. Should he tell the professor anything else? How might it affect what Grimes was doing? He needed more time to think.

Standing, Ed took off his jacket. "You were right. Going to be a warm day. Look at that blue sky." Hearing the courthouse clock chime, he said, "Nine o'clock. I bet I'm keeping you from something."

"No, sir." Silas Hartman patted the bench and looked up at Ed. "Please sit down. There's something you're not telling me, isn't there?"

After taking a deep breath and sighing, Ed finally said, "Well, yes, there is." He stared at the World Wars I and II granite monument in front of him as he told the professor everything he knew about the part Jim Hartman had played in exacerbating Matt's problems, and that a lawyer was investigating his son's actions.

Silas cried out, "Oh. Why am I not surprised!"

"I'm in deep—might as well add this." Ed looked up at the sky. "A couple of years ago, or more, I asked George Russell—wealthy, well placed—to help Matt, and the horse's ass ignored me."

"Oh?" Silas wrinkled his brow. "Why? Wouldn't it have been easy for him to make some calls?"

"George Russell is the most influential man in town. Many people owe him favors. He could have called one in and gotten anything for Matt. You're exactly right." Ed shook his head. "Why he didn't, I honestly don't know. It's foolish, maybe, but I thought he'd want to please me. I *was* his doctor."

Ed turned to face Silas. "I sincerely regret telling you any of this. When I suggested you reveal your family's connection to Matt at the Rotary dinner, I hoped Russell and your son would feel ashamed. Then I realized if the entire truth came out in bits and pieces that night, *you* would be the one embarrassed—or, at least, confused. That wouldn't be fair."

The professor closed his eyes, stretched his legs, and leaned back against the hard bench. He crossed his arms over his chest.

Ed longed to go home and hide from the world. Instead, trying to ignore the noise of cars and the smell of exhaust, he waited beside his friend.

When the clock struck ten, the professor sat up and laid his hand on Ed's arm. "I *sincerely* appreciate you telling me all this. I would never *ever* have gotten the truth from Jim. But you were wrong about one thing—he wouldn't be ashamed." He shook his head as if trying to fling something off. "Not a chance." Then he drew in a deep breath and blew it out. "God, Ed. What did I do wrong? Have you ever disliked one of your children?" He wiped his eyes. "The hardest part will be telling my wife."

Then the professor stood. "Okay. Just have to move forward. Here's my plan. I'll make sure, one way or another, this town knows what Jim and I owe the Bradfurd family. What we *all* owe people like that. And I'll think of a way to compensate Matt—maybe, the proceeds from my book. Something." He extended his hand to Ed. "My friend, I'm going ahead with that rotary talk. Will you come and bring the Bradfurds with you?"

Ed looked up, squinting from the bright sun. "Silas, would you like to learn to fish?"

Acknowledgements

IT IS TRUE, AS MATT BRADFURD DISCOVERS, THAT WE don't make it in this world on our own. I am indebted to my late teacher, Anne Lowenkopt, for her push to write this story and to do it with heart. Without my husband, family, and good friends in Santa Barbara and Chapel Hill, reading, rereading, and encouraging me every step of the way, I could not have done it. And more thanks to editors Dianne Comiskey, Nora Gaskin, and Linda Hobson who gave invaluable advice. Thanks, Nina and Kathy.

About the Author

LINDA HARDISTER RODRIGUEZ earned her living as a psychotherapist in Santa Barbara, CA. She grew up in rural North Carolina and currently lives with her husband and her dog, Buddy, near Chapel Hill.